PECKER'S REVENGE
AND OTHER STORIES
FROM THE FRONTIER'S EDGE

(

Pecker's Revenge

and Other Stories from the Frontier's Edge

Lori Van Pelt

University of New Mexico Press ★ Albuquerque

Printed in the United States of America

YEAR   PRINTING
10   09   08   07   06   05   1   2   3   4   5   6   7

LIBRARY OF CONGRESS CATALOGING-IN-PUBLICATION DATA

Van Pelt, Lori, 1961–
Pecker's revenge and other stories from the frontier's edge /
Lori Van Pelt.— 1st ed.
        p. cm.
ISBN 0-8263-3493-8 (PBK. : ALK. PAPER)
1. Western stories. I. Title.
PS3622.A5857P43 2005
813'.6—dc22

                        2005013477

❰

STORIES PREVIOUSLY PUBLISHED

"River Watch" appeared in *American West: Twenty New Stories from the Western Writers of America*, edited by Loren D. Estleman, Forge 2001. This story was also selected as part of "The Great Writers" series sponsored by The Met Theatre, Word Theatre, and the Autry Museum, and read by actress Wendie Malick at the Autry Museum in June 2004. A CD featuring some of the stories and performances of that series is being compiled now.

"The Diamond Ring Fling" appeared in *White Hats*, edited by Robert J. Randisi, Berkley 2002.

"Grave Dancer" appeared in *Black Hats*, edited by Robert J. Randisi, Berkley 2003.

"Natural Causes" appeared in *Hot Biscuits: Eighteen Stories by Women and Men of the Ranching West*, edited by Max Evans and Candy Moulton, University of New Mexico Press, 2002.

❰

Book design: Kathleen Sparkes
This book was typeset using Centaur 12/15; 25P6
The display type is Madrone and Playbill

☾

To the memory of my parents,

Carl W. "Bud" and

Irene L. Van Pelt

Contents

❨

Acknowledgments

The author appreciates the assistance and encouragement of
Kris Wendtland, Candy Moulton, Max Evans, Robert Randisi,
Loren D. Estleman, Dale Walker, Dan Slater, and most especially,
Eugene Walck, Jr. Bill Kratville at the Union Pacific Railroad and
Museum in Omaha, Nebraska, provided help with research,
as did Marilyn and E. W. Walck, Sr. I owe a special debt of
gratitude to Beverley Edens, who taught me to write and
gave me courage to try. I am grateful to Luther Wilson,
director of the University of New Mexico Press,
for publishing this collection.

☾

Introduction

IN 1999, LOREN D. ESTLEMAN ASKED MEMBERS OF WESTERN WRITERS of America to pen short stories for an anthology he was editing. He wanted the stories to blend the Old West with the new. Although I had been achieving some success in the nonfiction field, my true goal was to become a fiction writer, and so I jumped at the opportunity to work with Loren. He selected my submission, "River Watch," a ghost story set in Saratoga, Wyoming in 1895, as one of the twenty stories included in *American West* (Forge, 2001). He also encouraged me to write more fiction.

Soon after, Robert Randisi asked writers to send pieces for his anthologies, *White Hats* (Berkley 2002) and *Black Hats* (Berkley 2003), featuring real historical figures in fictional stories, and "The Diamond Ring Fling" and "Grave Dancer" found their way into publication. Candy Moulton and Max Evans also sought short stories, asking for writers who had lived on ranches or worked on ranches to write about their experiences. "Natural Causes" was chosen for their anthology, *Hot Biscuits*. These successes in short stories prompted me to consider Loren's original idea of blending the Old West with the new. I decided to write several short stories based on that theme, making my own collection. *Pecker's Revenge and Other Stories from the Frontier's Edge* is comprised of the fourteen stories that resulted.

Short stories focus on change, and the West provides an excellent setting for examining transformations. In the past century, the land itself has undergone tremendous changes as have the people who settled the land, built the industries, and created the cities and their descendants. Additionally, many of my stories depict characters on the edge, physically and emotionally, as well as at the edge of the frontier. Their explorations of new lands as well as new ideas and new hopes and dreams often don't turn out as they planned. Further, decisions made by our ancestors often affect our lives in ways we can't entirely comprehend. In keeping with the theme of blending old and new, I mixed the era of the 1880s with contemporary times. Stories passed down from my own family, from my husband's family, and from favorite legends of my childhood sparked some of these tales as did my research for my nonfiction books of the era.

I enjoyed writing these stories and am grateful to Loren Estleman for encouraging me to push against the edge of my own creative boundaries to find my way into fiction.

☾

Pecker's Revenge

MOVING FAST, I PLACED THE STILL-WARM PISTOL ON THE TABLE BY THE door inside my cabin. I ran to the woodshed and grabbed a shovel. I had to dig a grave for my friend, Pecker, and I had to be quick about it. In the short time it took me to ride from Pecker's cabin to my own, my skittish horse grew accustomed to the sour stench of death with Pecker's corpse draped across his back. Careful not to bump the body, I mounted and urged the horse on. "C'mon, Blue, a little way more to go, Blue, then we'll be done." The gelding nickered. We worked our way up the north hill, careful to take the back route. I didn't want to be seen, nor did I want to disturb the rocks and gravel on the more traveled road across the top.

In the cool evening twilight, I worked as rapidly as I could. The rocky soil made it difficult for me to dig. Sweat rolled from my forehead and dripped off my nose and soaked my back, giving me the shivers when I stopped to catch my breath. When I finally got a decent grave dug, I laid Pecker to rest, placed his faded red bandanna over his face, and began shoveling dirt over him. I scattered the rocks, trying to leave them as they had been before I came. The large scrub of sagebrush, irritated by my interference, released a pungent minty scent.

I buried Pecker in his favorite place. I'd seen him come to pray here sometimes early of a morning when the sun was just coming over the eastern mountains. He'd kneel down by this very clump of sage, take off his hat, and be still for several minutes. I envied him that peace. So, it was natural for me to bury him here. And the right thing, the decent thing for me to do, as I'd done the killing.

☾

Pecker Hughes's cabin stood on the eastern edge of the Sierra Madre mountains in southern Wyoming. His homestead wasn't his own. He squatted on my boss's land, that of Edgar Baker. Pecker's real name was John, but he got the nickname "Pecker" from an aunt who saw in her young nephew's behavior a peculiar knack for pecking away at his troubles until he found a way out of them. Some folks in these parts believed he got the nickname from his strange habits, and admittedly, Pecker's ability to stew over things could drive any sane person to distraction.

"I wonder if I wouldn't be better off in God's clear blue yonder than working myself to death up here," he said one night after we shared dinner. "But it's closer to God's heart here in these mountains than anywhere else I've lived."

This announcement seemed odd. Pecker hadn't complained a whit during the short time I'd known him. As I prided myself on my ability to judge character, practically from first impressions—a boon in my professional gambling career—I questioned my initial assessment. Pecker's circumstances likely would have set other folks to whining. Maybe he was the type who preferred complaining to doing after all.

"Isolation gettin' to you?" I asked, savoring a bite of a molasses cookie. Pecker baked them himself, he said, and he kept a good supply on hand. They were his favorite.

"Could be." He leaned back in his chair. "Sure does frustrate some folks. Never believed I'd be one of those kind." He scooted his chair from the table, making a rasping noise. "I'm mighty grateful you came along when you did, Adrian. Otherwise, I'd still be up there trying to fix that axle." He poured himself a cup of coffee and held the coffee pot in the air, tilting it toward me in offering.

"No thanks," I said, refusing a refill. "Glad to have been able to help." I had helped him repair the axle on his wagon earlier that day, thankful I'd apprenticed to a smith in my younger days and happy to share a meal with Pecker in return for my labors. I'd met Pecker on the Transfer Road, the bumpy, rock-strewn wagon track leading from the Sweetheart Silver Mine and the tiny town of Dyer Gulch to Saratoga, as I made my way into the mining district. Freighters ferried copper in wagons from the Rudefeha Mine higher up in the Sierra Madres on the Transfer Road down to Saratoga and from there to Walcott to meet the Union Pacific trains. The copper mine hummed with activity, and the money flowed like easy liquor. The silver mine had yet to produce enough of that precious metal to warrant wagonloads.

"Well, I can't pay you no more than this." As Pecker looked out of his tiny cabin window, a dreamlike trance came over him. "One of these days, that'll be different. I can feel it."

"This is more than enough. You're quite a good cook." Pecker was also a good housekeeper. His cabin was as neat as if a woman lived there with him and looked after things.

He laughed, a scratchy sound not unlike that of his chair scraping across the floor. "Learned to fend for myself a long time ago," he said. "And now, I'm too old to favor the company of any woman for long."

Old Pecker, I guessed, was well into his seventies. As he hadn't yet discovered his mother lode, he looked tired. His patched shirt and denim trousers bore a fine layer of dust from his mining labors. But his eyes told the real story. They were bright with anticipation, even with black circles digging sooty wells underneath them. "What about your-self, Adrian? Wherebouts're you from? What brings you to Wyoming?"

I swallowed the last of my coffee, considering my words carefully. "I've moved around a lot lately. I'm originally from Ohio," I said. No harm in telling him that much. I conveniently avoided mentioning my last place of residence, Santa Fe. I managed to turn the conversation back to him by saying, "I'd heard this was a pretty good mining area. I might take my chance if the opportunity comes up."

He narrowed his eyes, peering at me intently. "You're a smart man.

I believe there's gonna be plenty of opportunity and I'm not just whistling Dixie on that one."

"Good showing?"

He shook his head. "Not much showing yet. But I've staked a claim on a fine piece. I have reason to believe I'll strike a rich vein soon. And it's about time, too. I've been working at this too damn long."

Twenty years of hacking granite in the mountains in a place rugged and private, known generally by its record in the claim office, dwindled his scant resources. But Pecker was a dead shot, he said, so he often enjoyed venison or rabbit stew. I commenced wondering how much of this visit was conversational and how much was veiled warning. I felt my neck muscles tighten. I still felt on edge after leaving Santa Fe in a rush and found it difficult to trust others. But there was something different about this hermit miner. Despite my fidgeting insides, I tried to relax. After all, he knew me only as a helpful stranger. I liked the old goat. Pecker wasn't likely to know of my earlier indiscretions, just as he was unlikely to tell me more about the location of his prized claim.

Almost as if he read my thoughts, he said, "You oughta find yourself a claim, Adrian."

"Never fancied myself a miner."

"Well, come along on up to the Sweetheart one of these days and I'll introduce you to some of the other miners. They're working for pay at that mine. Boy," he chuckled, then said, "won't they be sorry. No one ever makes money working for wages. A living, I s'pose, but not true money." He shook a gnarled index finger at me. "To make that you have to take risk and you have to do it yourself. You can't get ahead working for somebody else."

"That's quite an idea coming from someone who lives on Edgar Baker's land and calls it his own."

He placed his elbows on the pine table and contemplated me for a moment. "Oh, Edgar. He'll get his share when I strike it. He's plumb content with our arrangement. You'll like him, I imagine. He's a pretty good feller to work for."

I nodded. Edgar and Mary Baker didn't pose much threat to me. An older couple, they needed a cowboy to tend their cattle and mend the fences. Edgar had recently suffered a bout of diphtheria and needed time to recover. I took a chance on them. They didn't often go into Saratoga, and it was unlikely that folks in Dyer Gulch—focused as they were on finding their own fortunes—would pay much attention to my presence.

Mary Baker had already told me what she knew about their squatter miner. She said he didn't often venture to town either so she saw to it that he had his fill of eggs and milk when she could manage that. She shared her homemade preserves with him, and sometimes the Bakers sold Pecker a steer. She added a tidbit that only a woman would have considered enticing, explaining that the widow Robertson at the Hotel Grandview in Dyer Gulch saved Pecker potatoes and vegetables from her garden. Rumor had it she'd once been sweet on Pecker but the romance died with the dusty dream of finding silver. Mrs. Robertson had not the patience to pursue a dream that would cost her the whole of her life. Mary had finished our conversation with, "That's one thing about Pecker, say what you will, he's stuck to his dream."

Pecker and I said our good nights, with him insisting that I come to see the mine in a couple of days after finishing my morning chores. I rode over the hill to the cabin the Bakers had allowed me as their hired hand, amazed at the day's turn of events and relieved to be hidden in the back country under the immense shadow of the Sierra Madres.

I treaded a fine line staying there. If I kept too much to myself, folks would get curious about me. I had to try to act like all was normal in my life, like the past had never happened. Other young cowboys spent time in Saratoga, seeking the twin treats of whiskey and women. I'd not sought the luxury of a woman since my fiasco in Santa Fe, but I reasoned denying myself such pleasures would only make me the target of idle talk. I didn't need that extra attention in my situation, and besides, the girls wouldn't take much notice of me if I were careful. Seeking the house of ill repute in the darkness gave me a chance of cover. One night, I visited Miss Lottie's on Garnet Road to enjoy some female companionship, surprised to discover the girls gossiping about some other residents of the community. They talked of the almost too-good-looking Wilson G. Tarrington, the new land office agent, and of his particular ways.

"Wants everything just so, that man does," said Lottie, fussing with the stray curl of blond hair that had fallen over her forehead as we dallied in the frumpy feather bed.

The image that came into my mind begged a question. "Did you?"

"No, no, no, my dear Adrian. Not *me*." She sounded startled that I'd asked the question. "The girls are always talking amongst themselves about some of the peculiarities of our guests. Mr. Tarrington, and his friend, that Dickens fellow, um, they like things a little on the wild side."

"They come here together?"

She nodded. "It's odd but then I've seen stranger things. That Dickens man, he keeps pretty much to himself. But I've seen them talking with each other outside after their visits."

"Not much time for talking in your place, is there, Lottie?" I asked.

"Depends on what you want, darlin'," she purred. "Talk will cost ya, same as anything else you'd like to try."

"I wonder what it is you'll be sayin' about me," I teased.

She looked thoughtful. "Depends on what you want, darlin'," she repeated.

At that, I tickled her bare waist and made her giggle. We didn't talk much after that.

☾

The next morning dawned clear. I made the rounds of the Bakers' ranch early. My duties consisted mostly of checking their fences, making certain they still held, and watching that the cattle herd remained intact. Satisfied that the fence line stood solid as it had the day before, I rode to the top of the hill between my cabin and Pecker's to check the herd, which hadn't scattered much. A few of the cattle lowed, but I recognized the muted sounds as calls to their calves rather than bellers of alarm signaling the presence of coyotes or other dangers. A sudden breeze tipped my hat. I slid it back into place and rode down to Pecker's cabin, anxious to see this fantastic silver mining country that promised quick riches in return for a throw of the dice in adventure. I still hungered for the thrill of the game.

By the time we reached the Sweetheart, the trees swayed and soil swirled about in dust devils.

"Nature's treating you to her usual show," Pecker said, smiling. "If you don't like it, wait a minute. The weather will change. Some folks can't stand day after day of blowin' winds. Makes 'em odd in the head." We tramped along a wagon track that served as a road of sorts. "Sometimes the wind brings rain. But not this year. Only dust on the wind this year." I heard the rushing waters of Coyote Creek nearby. Any other sounds of the mountains were stifled by the wind. At the mine, though, creaking wagons, the clopping of mule hooves, and occasional shouts by miners broke through the gale.

Pecker tugged on the windlass. "Let's go down and see her. They say the silver will be showin' soon down here."

"No, thanks. You go ahead. I'll wait here."

Pecker assumed my reluctance to accompany him on the windlass down into the shaft was due to fear of being underground. He wasn't far wrong. I didn't want to go below for fear that I'd be trapped with someone who would recognize me and reveal my secret. Pecker gave me a strong pat on the back and laughed that grating laugh of his. "Some folks ain't much for seein' six feet under 'til they got to," he remarked, and we passed on to tour the dining area, built especially for miners working in the Sweetheart. Numerous tents and shanties stood nearby.

He ushered me into the surprisingly spacious barroom of the Hotel Grandview, undoubtedly as dark as the mine itself after the bright sunlight outside burned our eyes. The hum of conversation made the place come to life. An oak bar stretched the length of the room. Several tables were crowded near the bar in the back of the room. Miners circled one, where a tiny, well-dressed man with a neatly trimmed beard sat, gesturing and pointing to a paper lying on the table.

Pecker ordered us whiskeys. We stood by the bar while the bartender poured the drinks. After taking a sip each, Pecker said, "Let's find out what's so interesting," and walked toward the back of the room. The motley group of miners parted, and the tiny man stood up.

"Gentlemen," he said, "today is your lucky day. I'm Jeb Dickens, here

to sell you a parcel in Dyer Gulch's newest mining enterprise." With a flourish of his hand, he indicated the map spread upon the table. "Have a seat
and I'll show you the properties of the Horseshoe Mining Consortium."

Pecker did not sit down. Instead, he scrutinized the map. He traced
a finger around what was drawn as the border of the Horseshoe. A deep
frown crossed his face. "All the way to Coyote Creek, hmm?" he asked.

"Yep." Jeb nodded.

"Pretty large claim, ain't it?"

"Has to be. The consortium will make money hand over fist, and so
will investors. That man who scraped the silver from a rock and held
enough in his hand to buy a decent living for the rest of his years? He
told me right where the lucky boulder sat, but then he told other people
different places. No one knows the exact location. We want to be certain we have the whole area claimed so we don't miss that piece for sure."
Jeb's golden pocket watch hung from a chain attached to his satin vest.
He rubbed it with his fingers, as if it were a good luck charm.

Pecker puckered his lips. "I'd say not," he said quietly. "I'll tell you
what I'm certain of, Jeb, you're a liar." The group of miners swilling beers
and other delights huffed in amazement. Pecker continued, undaunted.
"Mike Grant was my friend. He didn't tell you a dang thing about where
that placer deposit was, and I am for darn certain that he didn't tell
others. He kept to himself, Mike did. He wasn't about to go spilling his
story for the likes of you."

Jeb swallowed hard, narrowed his eyes. "So you say. If he told you
the right place, then why haven't you traipsed off to Californy with your
wallet heavy like he did?"

Pecker couldn't answer. He didn't want to disclose the location of
his claim to this man, I could see that. Besides, if Dickens had been
worth his salt, he'd have already found the claim listed in the land office.
"My friend Mike wasn't likely to have told anyone what he was
thinking."

"How do we know you're not spreading a big windy of your own?"
Jeb asked, scowling. The miners scattered a bit, preparing for the physical blows sure to follow this vocal disagreement.

"You don't, but I'm saying Mike for dang sure didn't go spreading around false locations to suit himself and stir everybody up. He believed everyone ought to have a fair chance at that fortune. He was an honorable man."

"Money does strange things to folks," Jeb said. "Doesn't change my mind. The Horseshoe is locating here, and selling off pieces to folks interested in claiming their right to the earth's wealth. Dyer Gulch will soon be known as one of the biggest mining regions in this here state. Folks who buy in now will be the better off for it. They'll get the biggest share of the earnings."

Pecker shook his head. "Well, you're right about one thing, Jeb. Money does make people strange."

"I'll thank you to leave and let me conduct my business, sir," Jeb said. The menace in his voice was unmistakable.

Pecker drew close and began to speak, but I caught his arm and held him back. I remembered Lottie's mentioning "that Dickens fellow" who frequented her establishment with the land agent. "Can't fault a man for loyalty to a friend," I said, smiling at Jeb. The miners, muttering amongst themselves, broke the ominous silence. "Good day to you," I said, pulling Pecker toward the door. He resisted just enough to show his anger and then left the premises with me.

Pecker avoided the fight, but I found out the fight hadn't left him. "That map he showed wasn't right, Adrian," he said. The Horseshoe claim had included his claim near Coyote Creek.

"I guessed something about it bothered you," I said. "Perhaps it's only a clerk's error." My words sounded false to my own ears. I kept my suspicions that Dickens was in cahoots with the land office agent, Tarrington, to myself. I had only the idle talk of soiled doves and a conclusion within my own mind after all. Still, the hairs on the back of my neck prickled.

Pecker scrunched his hat onto his head. "I'm going to the land office right now. You come along, Adrian. You can be my witness."

I balked. I didn't want any part of being seen in a federal office. Someone might notice me. Then, my chance at a new life would be over.

"You've filed on it and have been working your claim, anyone can see that. There shouldn't be any problem," I explained.

"Don't I know it," he replied. "I hate to see those big corporations come in and throw folks off course by claim jumping. I've seen it happen down there near Denver. Damn greedy bastards."

"I agree, Pecker, but you'd best go on your own. I don't know enough about mining claims to be of help."

He smiled and mounted his horse. "No, sir. You'll do fine. I've a sneaking hunch I need a witness for this. Something's not right, and it ain't only that Dickens fellow."

Reluctantly, I mounted my horse. I made a split-second decision. Once we'd settled Pecker's claim, I'd return to my cabin and pack up my things. I could head out at sunrise. No one would think I'd been anything more than a drifter, and there'd been plenty of their kind in these mountain towns lately. And the Bakers could manage on their own for a few days. Edgar had been getting stronger anyway.

Pecker interrupted my thoughts as we followed a wagon piled high with dark chunks of copper ore toward Saratoga. "I'll tell you what, Adrian. This just says to me that I'm gettin' closer to the lode. Otherwise those city folks would not be near as interested as they appear."

☾

Saratoga baked in the hot sunshine, with not so much as a breeze for comfort. The mix-up caused a stir in the claim office. The land agent, Wilson G. Tarrington, insisted his map agreed with that of Jeb Dickens. He knocked Pecker's actual claim off the map, stating that claim belonged to the Horseshoe Mining Consortium instead. Pecker's claim had been filed, all good and proper. But Tarrington would not recognize it. By doing so, he ensured my assumption had been right. Tarrington and Dickens were in cahoots with each other but I couldn't prove that. Pecker even offered to bring his location certificate—currently located in a lead-topped Mason jar nestled in a rock cairn at his mining claim as required by the more than twenty-year-old 1872 mining law—to the claim office in town. The haughty Tarrington would have none of that. He began harping about how he himself had certified this map and its claims and as a representative of the United States government, his word was law.

"Need I remind you, blood could be spilled on such questions, Mr. Hughes?" Tarrington intoned, a nasal twang accentuating his words. He peered down his beaked nose at Pecker as if he were little better than the soil and sweat that covered him.

Pecker said, "Blood often spills for less, Mr. Tarrington. You'd do well to remember that."

The wily agent peered over his reading glasses at Pecker. "I am certain you are not threatening me, Mr. Hughes," he said, pausing just long enough to let Pecker explain if he was or wasn't. On the cold silence that filled the pause, Tarrington continued, "Because threats are not taken kindly here. As I represent the wishes of our government, you would do best to comply."

Tarrington took a moment to look me over as well. I did not welcome his scrutiny and felt relief at Pecker's show of temper, releasing me as it did from Tarrington's intense inspection. I had my own reasons for not wanting to irritate the government man.

"You can't move a man's claim right under his nose. No man worth his salt would stand for it." Pecker fumed, his face reddening dangerously.

"I am bound by the law," Tarrington said. "The owners of the Horseshoe Mining Consortium found no evidence of claims being worked in this entire area. Claims are only valid if evidence of work can be seen. Therefore, the decision stands." He sat down at his desk and perused the papers laying atop it. The message was clear. Our conversation was over.

Once outside, Pecker seethed over Tarrington's arrogance and his insistence that his revised map be considered law. "Pickles to beans, Adrian, I staked the claim on the edge of Coyote Creek for a reason," he said as we left the claim office. "You've seen yourself I'd been diggin' thereabouts. Now the cotton-picking government moves it to suit themselves and some danged consortium. Hell, I've worked all over that country and I never saw no field prospecting or markers to support their claim." He believed his silver lay hidden from view in that area he'd claimed, though he was careful not to disclose exactly where he thought the vein ran. I'd have been willing to bet his friend, Mike Grant, had shared the location of his placer deposit with Pecker before he'd taken his fortune to find a new life elsewhere. "I'll be darned if I'm going to let the government take my claim on the word of a shiftless government man. This whole mess stinks to high heaven."

"What will you do then?" I asked, concerned about the redness puffing his wrinkled cheeks. I had to agree with his assessment that the whole thing looked like a paper sham.

He squinted his sprightly eyes at me. "I'll keep my claim, that's what."

And the matter was, for that day, at least, settled. I kept to my decision to ride away in the morning light. Pecker could fight his own battle for the silver claim. He had to protect his claim; I had to protect myself.

Part of what made him so angry, Pecker told me as we rode for home, was that his claim was staked so near to the place where his friend, Mike Grant, had found silver just laying in plain sight on the rocks. Mike had stopped for lunch, taking his sandwich from the Sweetheart Mine dining room out into the sunshine of a cool May afternoon. Sitting on a boulder, munching on his beef sandwich, he noticed something glinting in the light. He took out his pocketknife and scraped a sliver of pure silver off the top of the boulder where he'd perched. Unbelievable as that was, the metal netted him a fortune. He gave up his job and moved to California, settling into a comfortable life and revealing the boulder's location to no one. No one, that is, except Pecker, who swore that he knew where the rock had stood and thus had a pretty good inkling of where the silver vein was. However, people knew about the placer and the startling story about the silver being discovered so easily. Now the mountains were cram-full of people hoping to find their vein and strike it rich.

I felt sorry for myself. I'd have liked to have staked a claim myself but I couldn't do it now. Still, Pecker's story intrigued me. I liked the odds of the game.

☾

A woman's scream startled me from fitful sleep. Blinking my eyes, I dismissed it as yet another bad dream. Another figment of my imagination playing out that horrid morning when Caroline proved herself unfaithful and met me at the door in her nightgown, surprised to see me home a day earlier than expected from my business trip. Mistaking her amazement for happiness, I held her close and kissed her, discovering she felt anxious rather than amorous. When her paramour whimpered from inside his hiding place in the closet, my temper got the best of me.

Another scream, this time followed by a loud banging on the cabin door. The wailing I'd heard while dozing had nothing to do with my nightmares. I threw back the covers and raced to the door, grabbing my pistol and cocking it.

"Who's there?" I shouted.

"Adrian! Oh, thank the Lord. It's Mary! Mary Baker. Help me!"

I hurried to unbar and open the door. My boss's wife, flustered and teary-eyed, clad only in her nightdress, fell into my arms. "It's Edgar," she cried. "He's ill, Adrian. I can't help him. Oh, God! I can't help him."

I grabbed her arms roughly. She blinked and looked at me. "I'll fetch the doctor, Mary. Stay calm. He needs you."

She stood trembling in the doorway, wringing her hands, while I pulled on trousers and donned a shirt. I mounted my horse and pulled her up behind me. She'd not even taken time to put on shoes. "Stay calm, for Edgar," I told her as she dismounted at the door to her own cabin. "I'll be back as soon as I can."

The doctor from the Sweetheart had been the closest. Once awakened, he appeared as fresh as if he'd rested through the night instead of being disturbed at an odd hour of the morning.

His confident manner soothed Mary, who had managed to don a wrapper and shoes during my absence.

"I believe he's had a heart attack, Mary," he said. "Fighting the diphtheria may have weakened his heart. Bed rest and quiet. That's all we can do. I'll call again tomorrow." Seeing the fright fill her eyes, he gripped her hand. "Steady now. You get some rest yourself if you can manage it."

He looked at me. "Watch her," he commanded. I thanked him and sat with Mary through the night. I don't know why I stayed after daylight came—out of some perverse loyalty I suppose—a yearning for my younger days when the world was an easier place, where wives didn't cheat on their husbands and flaunt their lovers in plain sight, where anger didn't rise up through a man's body like a living thing. I pulled the trigger that day in Santa Fe and had no one to blame but myself for the scoundrel's death. I came here an outlaw. Yet my upbringing didn't leave me. I still was the man I'd been before but a tarnished version of my former self. Evil men with devilish intentions seldom get caught, but those of us who maintain that streak of goodness find ourselves in more dangerous straits. I couldn't have left the poor old soul in her distress, even if it had meant spending the rest of my life in prison. Only one more day here. Then I could leave without triggering suspicion.

By the morning, Edgar had improved somewhat. He felt well enough to speak to Mary. She insisted on making all of us an early breakfast, so I stayed and feasted on feathery biscuits, currant jelly, scrambled eggs, and bacon. I thanked Mary for the meal and embraced her before I left. "You're a good wife, Mary," I told her. "Edgar's a lucky man to have you."

Once outside, I saw my chances for escape dwindling further. Wilson G. Tarrington rode with determination toward Pecker's cabin. *What the devil did that scalawag have in mind?* I should have headed north right then. Instead, compelled by curiosity and a misguided notion of helping Pecker, I followed him.

They argued. I heard their raised voices through the door. Dismounting quietly, I slid my pistol into the back of my pants and threw my shirttail out to cover it. My decision to follow Tarrington had been a bad one. I knocked and entered. Tarrington, his back to the door, did not turn round, but looked sideways, eyeing me with obvious distrust.

"Brought you a jar of Mary Baker's currant jelly, Pecker." Thankful for Mary's generosity, which this morning provided me an excuse to interrupt, I sat the jar on the table. Pecker nodded, his eyes not leaving Tarrington.

Tarrington's gaze burned into me. "You are Adrian Hascall, aren't you? You're wanted for murder. I saw your picture on a wanted poster in Cheyenne. Knew it when you came into the office the other day."

Pecker was incredulous. "Adrian, he's come here telling me tales about you. He only wants to swindle me out of my silver. You're not a criminal."

"He has me confused with someone else," I agreed.

Tarrington was shaking his head. "No. I don't make mistakes with faces, Mr. Hascall. You're that gambling house owner who killed a man in Santa Fe. You'll be coming along with me to town. Mr. Hughes, you might as well join us. You've been harboring a fugitive from the law. You've dispensed with any rights to any claim you supposedly had."

"Pecker's claim is more valid than any of your half-baked schemes, Tarrington," I said.

He had none of it. He drew his pistol. "I'll thank you to stay quiet."

"Adrian?" Pecker asked, frowning.

I looked at Tarrington. "He's in cahoots with that Dickens man we met in Dyer Gulch the other day," I said, playing my hand. "They sell property to people at inflated prices and make a dirty profit for themselves. Especially when those mining claims start paying. Right, Tarrington?"

"I don't know what you're talking about," he answered peevishly. "But I do know you are a murderer, plain and simple. And, as I told Pecker here, I intend to claim the reward for your dastardly hide."

"That money means nothing, Tarrington."

"And what about your loving wife?" He sneered. "She deserves the peace of mind knowing you are jailed and will not kill again."

"Adrian?" Pecker spoke quietly. "What's all this about?"

I looked the old man in the face. He'd been too good to me to live in the shadow of a lie. "It's true. I shot and killed my wife's lover in Santa Fe."

A wry smile lit Tarrington's reptilian profile.

"Well, I'll be go to hell," Pecker said. "Been living right next to you all this time and didn't even know." Keeping watch on Tarrington, he chanced a sympathetic glance at me. "She cheated on you, huh? That's a crying shame."

"Enough of this talk," Tarrington said. "Let's go." He motioned towards the door, turning his full attention to me.

Pecker reached forward and pushed the table toward Tarrington. The kerosene lamp slid to the side and wobbled precariously, but the jam jar slipped and busted to bits on the floor. Shards of glass glinted against the oozing red jelly. Tarrington switched his attention to Pecker, aiming his gun at the old man. I shot first. The sound echoed in the tiny cabin like cannon fire. Tarrington, wounded in the head, clutched his side and fell, his shoulder slamming into a glob of jelly. He died before he hit the floor.

Silence came over us, Pecker and I.

"I never thought it of you, Adrian," he said, sadness evident in his rasping voice. We faced each other square, over Tarrington's body. I read his eyes. Pecker realized I'd saved his life but now my secret had been revealed, he knew as well as I did what I must do next.

"I never did, either, Pecker," I admitted. "You've been a good friend." My ivory-handled Colt Frontier felt slippery in my grasp.

If he noticed my anxiety, he didn't speak of it. He didn't whine that we could say I shot Tarrington in self-defense, which was true enough. He didn't offer to stand up for me in court. He didn't tremble in fear. He merely watched. For a moment longer, I admired his courage. Then I pulled the trigger.

Hurrying to cover my tracks, I dragged Pecker's body outside. Then I ran back inside, found a match, smashed the kerosene lamp and started the fire. On impulse, I threw my gun into the flames and grabbed Pecker's.

The flames—that's what drew folks. After burying Pecker and saying aloud a hasty prayer over his grave, I returned to the blazing cabin and swung my shirt against the ravenous flames a few times. When others began arriving, they applauded me for trying to save Pecker's home and Pecker, too.

The investigation didn't amount to much. People believed my tale that Tarrington and Pecker had had a falling out over a claim. I suspected Pecker's temper flared and he killed the land office agent and fled. I did not explain I'd let Pecker's horse run when the fire started, but curiously, no one paid attention to whether or not his horse remained. They questioned more the fact that he'd left his fancy-handled pistol behind. Why would a man running from a murder leave his pistol? He'd surely need it one day. I couldn't answer their questions, I said, as I'd been drawn by the fire. But I did figure out why no one seemed to take notice of me in particular despite the wanted posters Tarrington had seen in Cheyenne. Tarrington's greed kept him silent about my existence. He had planned to claim the large sum of reward money for my capture for himself alone. In a way, that greed sealed his fate and opened the way for my escape.

I regret having to kill my friend. I'll regret it to my dying day. But I saved him some trouble. I'll say right here and now that I didn't do it for the money. I left Pecker's claim alone. I killed him to keep my secret, but he died with the dignity of knowing he'd sacrificed all for his dream of silver. He wasn't going to make a cent off his claim, and he'd almost wasted his whole life trying. Why not let him see his reward early and enjoy that instead of wasting away with not a thing to show for it but a silly false hope?

Sometimes our fondest dreams become our undoing. I had no intention of becoming a murderer. My life just worked itself out that way. One killing led to another. And I left Dyer Gulch with regrets instead of redemption in my heart.

❰

Standing beside a substantial pile of rocks near the creek, Roger Carter, Saratoga's eldest and most prominent historian, addressed the group of people gathered around him. Sunshine glinted off the windshields of the assorted four-wheel drive vehicles they'd used to reach the spot. "This part of our trek is most interesting, I think," he said, motioning to the creek. "This used to be called Coyote Creek, but it's now known as Pecker's Creek. People started calling it that because a miner, John 'Pecker' Hughes, is said to have located a silver claim here." He told the group of hat-clad, sandal-footed tourists the oft-repeated tale. Pecker supposedly had a falling out with a land office agent named Wilson Tarrington over the location of his claim. "Though it's not known exactly what happened," Roger paused for effect, "most people believe Pecker killed Tarrington and left the area. Pecker's cabin burned down that very day. The only odd thing about the story is the fact that Pecker left his gun to burn in the fire. No one ever worked his claim, far as I know, and it's somewhere here near the creek. We haven't been able to find any markings as of yet. Of course, this is government property now. Belongs to the United States Forest Service currently."

"Was anyone else involved in the killing?" a woman asked.

"Not so far as we know," Roger said. "No one else was around at the time, and nobody reached the cabin quickly enough to put out the fire before the building was completely destroyed. There's not much evidence of it even having been there now," he explained.

Roger answered the usual questions then about the Sweetheart Silver Mine, which had been in operation about the same time as Pecker worked his claim. "Another mining concern, the Horseshoe Mining Consortium, sold some shares about this same time. But that idea apparently dried up before much was done. A man named Jeb Dickens had tried his hand at the promotion business for that one, maybe hoping to build Dyer Gulch into a city, but whatever his goal, he failed." Roger included his opinion about Mike Grant's fortunate lunch on a silver-laced boulder, saying, "Old Mike may have told his friend, Pecker, where he found his stake, but I doubt it. I think it more likely Mike just took his fortune for the gift that it was and decided to let others have a chance at finding their own strike. In a way, if the story is true about him killing Tarrington, Pecker got his revenge. No one else ever worked his claim, and the creek has been renamed for him. If the placer deposit that Mike Grant found scratching the surface lies near here, no one's the wiser. No silver was ever found here. It was all a crazy dream. The town site dried up before even the Rudefeha scandal down south near Encampment and the copper boom went bust in the early 1900s. Whatever happened to Pecker is unknown. He wasn't seen or heard from ever since."

"What about Dickens?" asked an elderly man.

"Unknown again. It's thought that he drifted away, maybe headed for California. Some folks said he had relatives back there and that he eventually died there. That's a good question, though. Someone ought to try to trace Dickens one of these days. It'd be a good research project."

He explained their next stop would be in Saratoga at the Hotel Wolf for lunch. The century-old hotel had once served as a stage stop on the road between Walcott and Encampment and hosted many a miner in its day.

Someone saw something glinting in the sunshine and pointed it out. "Probably fool's gold," Roger said, chuckling. "I don't even know if that story about the boulder is true or an old yarn that somebody made up because it sounded good. Nothing came from here but wagonloads of timber. The minerals and precious metals were found miles south of here. And the owners of the Sweetheart Silver Mine, the big mining concern, they went bankrupt, too. They clung to a false hope of swift riches and it cost them their lives."

Walking on down to the cars, sunlight played against Roger's eyes once again. The thought of being able to scrape a rock and earn your life's savings in one fell swoop appealed to Roger, even after the many times as he'd repeated the sorry tale about the hopeful miners plunged into despair. His grandparents, Edgar and Mary Baker, had often told him stories of the miners as he was growing up. He looked back toward the shiny spot. Nothing glinted there now. But that was what luck was all about, wasn't it? Seeing opportunity where others saw none. Roger hollered for his clan to stay together and keep the annual historical society trek on schedule. He glanced at the stately pines, listened to the whispering creek, and inhaled the sweet scent of mountain air. He sighed. His dreams of silver would have to wait for another day. As he climbed into his Blazer, sunlight on the windshield blinded him for a moment. He slapped the visor down, adjusted his sunglasses, and started the engine. He didn't notice the broken jelly jar jutting from the rock cairn, a frayed and yellowing scrap of paper clinging to a piece of glass and fluttering in the breeze.

Death Track

Dozens of men dangled from ropes tied round telegraph pole crosstrees. As Jimmy O'Malley watched yet another man driven to his destiny, he himself ceased to be standing on the rolling prairie among the motley canvas tents and buildings of Julesburg. Instead, he found himself again fighting the Battle of Franklin in the War Between the States. The stinging smell of gunfire burned his nostrils. Sweat trickled down his face. He blinked. The battle scene reeling before his eyes did not change. All around him lay dead and wounded soldiers. The man standing beside him shuddered once and fell in a bloody heap. Jimmy froze. Indecision cost him precious time. Should he help his companion or move forward into slaughter?

Standing there, hesitating, he heard a man shouting, "Come back, Jimmy!" He looked back to see General Jack Casement motioning for him to follow. In his hazy vision, bullets and cannonballs sailed through the air. The general stopped. "Jimmy! I'm waiting for you. Come, now!"

The short, wiry man continued gesturing to the taller, brawnier one until Jimmy at last shook off his stupor and followed the diminutive figure. He found himself again in Julesburg, Colorado Territory. Alkali dust tormented his nose and pressed against his lungs as if holding them in a vice. He once had followed General Jack through Hell and had emerged unscathed. Walking as if in a dream, where footsteps taken lose their ability to push a body forward, Jimmy trudged behind Casement and stopped at the push car which usually held the day's ration of supplies: spike barrels and ties. Today, the car overflowed instead with shovels. The general commanded, "Hurry along now, Jimmy. There's a passel of graves to dig." He exchanged Jimmy's Army issue rifle for a spade. "We're burning daylight."

Jimmy fell into step behind a group of fellow railroaders, each of whom carried a shovel. As the barren landscape of Julesburg came back into focus for him, he trembled. His mind's startling reversion to the sickening sights of the battlefield shook him to his core. Julesburg had made him feel uneasy from the start. Now, he knew his instincts had been right.

Having been a worker for General Jack since he began laying the rails west in '66, Jimmy had grown used to seeing land stretch out untouched before them, like a bolt of fine Irish linen. The once strange tent towns at end-of-the-tracks became familiar as they journeyed west. He hated the criminal element plaguing them all along the way. Fine men lost their heads to liquor or money or women and some did not even live to regret it.

The Union Pacific tracklaying crew had arrived in Julesburg just two days before. As with most end-of-the-tracks towns, the usual unsavory elements gathered there—prostitutes, thieves, crooked gamblers, and shady saloon keepers. The proprietors of the joints knew well the opportunities for profit inherent in catering to the railroad workers. General Jack had warned his crew of the wickedness Julesburg harbored, told of Indians burning the town and neighboring ranches in '65 and of the propensity for trouble offered by the forking of the Overland Trail and the nearness of the South Platte. Jules Beni's namesake trading post and stage stop had become known as a haven for horse thieves and other scoundrels, and the General—a man not given to showing worry—cautioned his men to be careful.

Sean Connaught, Jimmy's friend and fellow gandy dancer, laughed at Jimmy's notion that the town was sinister. As they emerged from the dining car that first morning, sated with the usual breakfast of beans, bacon, potatoes, fresh bread, and strong hot tea, Sean said, "You've been working too hard, my friend. These folks, they're only wantin' to make a living wage off of the likes of you, like all the others." Shaking his head, he walked to the push car to gather his supplies for the workday ahead. "All that talk. All talk, that's all. We have to look out for Injuns, that's all. Injuns are the ones burned the place down. The thieves, they have to live here."

Despite himself, Jimmy shivered. He sensed something ominous here but he couldn't put a name to why. Grabbing his own hammer and a handful of spikes, he hoped he was wrong. Even without Casement's warning, Jimmy would have felt the evil emanating from Julesburg. Thick with thieves, the place was. He'd be glad to be done with it. Jimmy whistled as he headed trackside. The better to ward off any demon spirits lurking nearby.

Soon his whistling faded into the much louder sounds of the clanging of metal against metal as the rail gangs fetched the rails and threw them down. Jimmy and the others pounded in spikes almost as quickly as the rails touched the ground, causing the sharp metallic ring of hammer against spike to numb his ears. General Jack set their tempo himself. Tracklayers were supposed to complete their jobs at the speed a man could walk. The rapid clip he'd dictated left no time for talk. Thus far, the crew managed a mile a day, sometimes more. Word was the General expected them to make three soon. Sweating, Jimmy paused for a moment to wipe his brow with his bandanna. Ten thousand spikes a mile. Were it not for Ida, he'd not have believed he could hold to the grueling pace. Thinking of her made the work go easier. Every spike he pounded brought him closer to Ida. The chugging engine of the locomotive trailing behind them and the steely squeal of the push car making its unending trips back and forth to replenish and release supplies punctuated their tiresome work. Wagons creaked along the route, too, as freighters hauled other supplies to the graders beyond track's end. Jimmy returned his handkerchief to his pocket and drove another spike home, trying to remember the exact words of Ida's last letter to him.

☾

Once the feverish workday ended, the men relaxed in the dining car after the evening meal. The men lingered over their tea and coffee, listening to Jimmy play his fiddle. Most of the time he brought his fiddle with him to the dining car. In the instrument's case he kept Ida's letters. He frequently read her words and composed his own by the light of the kerosene lamp illuminating the table. Jimmy read again the last letter he'd received from Ida in mid-June.

Dearest Jimmy,

I have only to close my eyes to hear the sweet strains of your fiddle music. Papa informs me that the railroaders have had conflicts with the Indians again. I do so hope you have not been harmed in any such adventures.

I long for the day when you will return to us, Jimmy. Papa suspects you might not. He says that a man like you might find the arms of another more comforting than mine, but I have reassured him I do not believe that of you. And Papa often mentions the terrors of drink. I do hope that such evils do not befall you, dear Jimmy.

Papa's legal practice causes him to work at all hours it seems. I sometimes fear for his health, yet he appears happiest when he is deeply engaged in some legal task. As for me, I find solace in my sewing and my singing. I sing in the church choir now. I cannot wait until you return and I can sing with you when you play your beautiful music on your fiddle. What lovely songs we can make together.

Your voice itself is like music to me. As you talk, it is like you are singing. I've tried to imitate the lilting quality in my own plain voice but I can't. And Papa doesn't like me to sound like that. He wishes me to cling to my American heritage rather than try to be Irish like you.

I have embroidered a handkerchief for you. I realize it is too dainty for one such as yourself to use but I hope this will serve as a kind remembrance of me.

With deepest affection,
Ida

Jimmy touched the fine linen handkerchief. Ida's embroidery stitches were neat and tiny. She had used black thread to sew his initials in the center of one corner. Stitched around the letters was a ring of sky blue flowers with yellow centers, probably worked to show a sampling of her considerable ability with different stitches. He kept the handkerchief in his fiddle case with her letters to protect it and keep it clean.

He did indeed know how her father felt about the Irish, especially himself. One evening after leaving the Lewis house, as he walked down the porch steps to the street, he had overheard Hiram Lewis tell his daughter, "I do not know what it is you see in that Paddie, Ida. I wish you would come to your senses and find yourself a decent man instead."

Jimmy could not hear Ida's reply. Her tone was much softer and her voice did not carry through the evening air as stringently as her father's. Jimmy, halted in mid-step on the final stair, stood listening. Hiram Lewis's voice again filled the air. "Love! You are far too young to understand love, Ida. And may I remind you, a common tracklayer is beneath your station, young lady. You will do better to seek the company of men of your class, like Oliver Edwards. I believe he is sweet on you."

With Hiram Lewis's words ringing in his memory, Jimmy wrote back to Ida. Her father had not been forced to seek physical labor to survive as Jimmy had. The worst of it had come during the potato famine, eking out whatever he could to keep Ma and himself alive. When she died, Jimmy came to America where he could do better. By the sweat of his brow he had. Lewis knew nothing of such labors and so could not respect them or the men who performed them. Lewis would soon ride the trains that connected the country from shore to shore, though, Jimmy knew it. But Lewis would never admit—let alone think about—the fact that he rode upon the breaking backs and aching shoulders of the men who had placed the rails mile by mile across this massive land. His was a life of ease. Jimmy yearned for the niceties of such a life, yet felt proud of his own honest hard work. He'd save until he could provide Ida a life like the one she'd grown accustomed to, even though he couldn't make it like the one her father made for her. He'd manage. Even though Ida loved to sew, he vowed he'd not have her mendin' clothes to buy their supper like his ma had done. Jimmy marveled at how Lewis, feeling as he did, allowed Ida to write to him. How she managed to keep his letters from her father, he did not know. She must have done so, otherwise he'd never had heard from her. He wrote:

Dear Ida,

> *The days pass long without you. We have this day arrived at Julesburg, a point 380 miles west of Omaha. General Jack drives us hard but our work is indeed important.*
>
> *Ida, I do plan to return to you. I believe the General will take care of things and I'll come out all right. Please do not worry. We have sparred some with Indians along the way but those matters seem small against the job laid before us. I feel as though precious time is racing through the hourglass and I cannot fill it full enough to spend as many happy moments in your company as I wish.*
>
> *I thank you for the beautiful handkerchief. I keep it in my fiddle case so that you are always near me in spirit. You are skilled at sewing. I hope that it brings you as much happiness as my music brings to me. The boys often have me play in the evenings after supper. Sometimes they even request your favorite tune, Camptown Races. I most often play me Irish jigs and sometimes Turkey in the Straw. If music could travel through the air, Ida, you would hear me fiddle as if standing near you on your porch in the evenings. Listen well when the stars appear and let my music fill your heart.*
>
> *Yours as ever—Jimmy*

He refrained from telling her his peculiar feelings about Julesburg. A letter didn't seem the proper place for that. Though he yearned to tell her many things, he couldn't bring himself to find words for some of his experiences. Soon after leaving Omaha, he discovered the vastness of the prairie could not hold words. So, instead of filling his letters describing what he saw, he reported mileages and commended the delicious pastries of the baker who merited his own private car to create his fine-tasting confections. He tried to make his letters cheerful so she would not worry about him. He did not tell her of the few murderous battles waged with Indian tribes along the route. And he did not tell her of the days his arms ached so badly from his labors that he could not hold his fiddle to his chin without trembling.

"Got yourself a handy packet of letters there, don't you, Jimmy?" Douglas Herlihan, a new crewman, asked, as Jimmy sealed the envelope.

"That I do." He held them together. They made a thick stack even in his massive palm. Ida Lewis had stayed with him all this time—nearly a year and a half now that he'd been laying track for the General. "She's a fine woman," Jimmy said to his bunk mates.

"There are surely some fine women in Julesburg. I intend to find me one or two," Douglas said, laughing.

"Be off with you then."

"Ida will never know, Jimmy. Come with us. We all need some refreshment, don't you know?" Sean coaxed.

"I'd know," Jimmy said in a strident tone, indicating the matter was closed.

"Ah, you're just like Casement. Word is he writes his wife every day. Come to think of it, I've never seen him take a drink. Have you?"

"No, I haven't," Jimmy replied, secretly pleased to be compared to General Jack. The General from Ohio who had safely led him from the Civil War battlefield had employed him since. He had been responsible for Jimmy's meeting Ida at a ball held in Omaha following the war. The Lewises were acquaintances of General Jack's. Jimmy knew that was the only reason Hiram Lewis had allowed Jimmy to speak to and dance with Ida that evening. Ah, Ida. The young blossoming lass with blonde curls and eyes the color of sparkling sapphires, dressed becomingly in blue silk gown and temptingly scented with orange blossom. Perhaps seeing his daughter's happiness had led Hiram Lewis to grudgingly allow Jimmy to court Ida before he left Omaha. His letters were, he had to admit, a way for him to remind Ida of his existence, for Jimmy had no doubt that the moment he had left Omaha, Hiram Lewis had begun campaigning for Oliver Edwards to court his daughter.

"Oh, come along for a change, Jimmy," Sean said. "What harm can there be in a night out?"

Jimmy replaced the letters in their hiding place inside his fiddle case. He returned the case to his berth in the bunk car. He joined the others on their sojourn to town, dropping his letter into the mail pouch along the way. As Sean had said, Jimmy found no harm in downing a glass or two of whiskey. The liquor eased the ache in his arms and made the days he spent away from Ida bearable.

☾

As the railroaders entered, the noise inside the Sagebrush Saloon crescendoed like a locomotive gathering steam. A boy of about fifteen pounded out tinny tunes on the piano in the corner. His music could barely be heard over the loud hum of conversations and laughter. Painted ladies, clad in scanty costumes, abounded. Some sat on the laps of men swilling whiskeys at tables while others sauntered around the bar, seeking opportunities. Jimmy fended off their advances and kept to his drink. Sean drifted into a card game. Douglas soon disappeared with a tall, voluptuous woman dressed in a paltry pink frock by his side.

The fracas began well after midnight. Douglas returned alone, cheeks aflame, planning to enter the poker game. He reached into his pocket to ante-up. His face took on a pinched look. He shouted, "She stole my wallet!" No one paid attention. Jimmy turned round from the bar. Douglas shouted again. Jimmy rose, aiming to calm him and prevent a fight, but he was too late. Douglas strode to the bar and demanded the bartender replace his wallet.

The bartender shrugged and said, "You're on your own friend. Maybe you didn't live up to your part of the bargain, eh? Did she need a little extra to make it worth her time?"

Douglas leapt to the bar and swung at the man. A chair-breaking, head-busting fight followed. Men took sides, some apparently for no reason other than to join in. Jimmy and Sean tried to stop Douglas but both men got pulled into the brawl and had to protect themselves. A single gunshot reverberated through the saloon. The fisticuffs stopped. Silence fell. People looked confused. One woman screamed. Soon a crowd of screaming women and cursing men scrambled outside.

Douglas lay prone on the plank floor beside the bar. Jimmy and Sean went to him, but it was too late. He was dead. Someone had put a bullet in his chest. They looked at the bartender. His derringer lay in plain view on the bar. "I don't take kindly to fights in my bar," he said.

Sean said, "Why you—" but Jimmy grabbed his shirt collar, effectively cutting off whatever curses might have followed. Eyes narrowed, the bartender looked Sean straight in the eye, hand hovering menacingly over the pistol.

"Leave it, Sean. No good can come from it."

Sean struggled in Jimmy's grip. "But he killed—"

Jimmy nodded, holding his friend back. "We'll carry Douglas outside. The general will be none too pleased."

☾

General Jack looked as furious as Jimmy had ever seen him. He was angrier than Jimmy recalled seeing him during the war. They stood together at the top of a gentle rise of land above the river. They had dug a makeshift grave for Douglas and planted a wooden marker at his grave. Two other men had been killed in the night. The trio of graves made a forlorn picture.

"This has got to stop," Jack Casement said through clenched teeth. He pivoted on his heel and strode to his office car.

That day, work progressed much more slowly than the steady walking pace the tracklayers had achieved most of the way from Omaha. Jimmy pounded extra spikes for Sean when he could. Sean could not pound many. Although he remained quiet, Jimmy knew Sean suffered in the hot sun. The pounding and all the other noises could not have been easy for him to take when his head undoubtedly hurt like the dickens. At lunch time, Jimmy felt certain Sean would stop working altogether and return to his bunk. But that luxury was not to be. Casement appeared in the dining car. He motioned to Jimmy and Sean and several others to follow him. He led them to the bunk car containing rifles. "Arm yourselves," he commanded.

"Indians again, sir?" asked one of the men.

"No." Casement explained that he had that very morning wired Grenville Dodge for permission to take care of their current situation in any way he saw fit. "We cannot fall behind on the building of this railroad, men," he said. "The ruffians of this town are interfering with my crew. Killing my men and injuring others so that they cannot do their jobs." He pounded the table with a scrawny fist. "Our work must continue at all costs."

Pacing before his select civilian army, he said, "Some scoundrels here purchased land from the Union Pacific but will not pay for it. We cannot allow this dastardly behavior to go on. We must stop them from taking over the town or we will face this same evil at every point along the route." He paused, taking a deep breath. "In one hour, a train will head for Omaha. I told the rascals to either be on that train or to ride their horses out of this sorry excuse for a town. If they do not comply with my request, we will stop them by force. Do you understand?"

The silence hung like an oppressive fog in the car. No one spoke. "Then wait for my return in the dining car."

When he left, the men spoke in whispers. The hushed tones may have been in part due to the lingering effect of hangovers, but Jimmy thought it more likely their quiet talk indicated concern. Knowing General Jack as they did, every man in the group realized the cost of events that would surely follow.

The train departed for Omaha with but few passengers. No one saw horses or wagons leaving town. Even the stage stop sat silent.

When Casement returned, he led the men on a march through Julesburg. Thirty men, bearing rifles, policed the streets as if they were once again soldiers. Some patrolled near the buildings. The warehouse, stores, saloons and gambling dives and even the theater, so crowded last night, stood eerily mute. The stillness was disturbed only by the footsteps of the railroaders, an occasional cough, and the intermittent flapping of tent canvas in the meager breeze.

Casement stopped them in the middle of the street. Jimmy felt the stares of people from inside the buildings surrounding them. Had General Jack gone crazy and led them into an ambush?

"I got one, General," hollered a man, dragging a struggling, well-dressed figure from the theater. He pulled his prey to stand before Casement.

"I told you and your kind to leave town," Casement growled, looking up into the eyes of the fiend, who stood several inches taller than he.

"I'll be damned if I'll let a puny squirt like you run me out of town," the tough retorted.

Casement nodded. A somber look came over his face. "Yes, you will," he said gravely. "Call out your cronies." The man ignored the command. Casement barked his order a second time. "Call out your cronies." The railroaders glanced around at the buildings. No sign of people. "Call them out or we will go inside and get them."

At this, shots rang out. The railroaders ran for cover, hugging the sides of buildings. They waited. As with most battles Jimmy had endured, this one began when someone got impatient and fired a shot. The rogues of Julesburg proved no match for the Union Pacific fighters, many of whom, like Jimmy, had fought in the war and were no longer afraid of battle.

The rascals who weren't killed by gunfire were led to the telegraph poles parallel to the railroad tracks. A scantily clad woman emerged from the saloon clinging to a man wearing only pants and no shirt. His suspenders hung loose around his hips. He tried to shake the tearful woman off, but she only tightened her grip. He gave her a final shake, tossing her against the door frame. Jimmy thought she was the woman in pink Douglas had chosen the night before. The man, snapping his suspenders in place, joined his criminal cohorts. He said nothing. Despite the wailing woman, he appeared to be peacefully facing his fate.

Instinctively, Jimmy turned to guard the backs of the railroaders as they marched the rascals through town to the edge of the tracks. He'd watched a similar show during the war. Only at that time, the woman attacked from behind, then clung to her man. She was shot when he was. The both of them fell together, blood soaking the ground by the cabin door. Jimmy hadn't even realized that he'd shot his rifle at the time but the barrel was warm to his touch. He and another soldier had reacted at the same instant. The memory of the woman dying atop her lover never left him. Jimmy shook off the unsought gruesome image. When he turned back, several men already hung from the telegraph poles. Dozens of men dying before his eyes. Some of the crosstrees held two bodies. For several moments he relived the Battle of Franklin in his mind, until Casement's order to dig graves jolted him from the horrible memories.

Trudging toward the rise where they had earlier that morning buried their young friend, Douglas, Jimmy and Sean followed other rail-roaders to their grim task. They found no need for words. Open space surrounded them. There was no need to fear attack now. The matter, as General Jack intended, had been settled.

Jimmy was the last to reach the makeshift cemetery. He heard the worn cloth of his work shirt rip and at the same time felt an odd burning sensation in his back. He fell to the ground, choking on dirt, grasping wildly for something to hold onto, something that could help him forget the tortuous alkali plain extending all around him and the sudden intense pain besieging him. Jimmy had not heard the gunshot, but Sean did. He whirled to see where it had come from.

"Jimmy, Jimmy, my God, man," Sean said, dropping to his knees next to his friend. "I don't know where it came—"

Others in the crew knew. They ran after a woman, grabbed her, and wrenched a pistol from her hands. She struggled against their grasp. She spat at Sean. Looking down at Jimmy, she said, "I'd have killed the lot of you if I could. You murdered my husband. You murdered my hus-band." Jimmy looked up, recognizing the woman who had collapsed in the doorway of the saloon.

How will I tell Ida? he thought. Then, mercifully, the world blackened.

☾

Sean took Jimmy's fiddle case and few other belongings to General Jack. The general wrote a letter to Ida Lewis informing her of Jimmy's death and included it with the package, along with a letter she had written to Jimmy, received that very day and unopened. Rather than send the package by mail, he entrusted its care to a messenger who traveled on the next train to Omaha.

The next evening, just as twilight faded and the torrential rains of a fierce thunderstorm dwindled, Hiram Lewis invited the young man into his home. When he learned the messenger's package was for Ida, he called her to come join them downstairs. She saw the man and slowed her steps as she came down the stairs. He placed the package on the table.

"From General Jack Casement, miss. He asked me to give this package directly to you."

Ida looked at her father, who nodded. Opening the package, she found the letter from Casement. She gasped. Hiram Lewis put a hand upon his daughter's shoulder. She handed him the letter. He read aloud Casement's condolences, his distress over losing one of his best workers, and his wish that Ida keep the belongings of Jimmy O'Malley, who spoke of her often and counted the days between her letters.

Holding the table to steady herself, she removed the fiddle case from the box. Opening it, she found the handkerchief she had made. Tears washed her cheeks. She touched the fine, varnished wood of the instrument. After a moment, she reached to pull the case closed. A thick packet of letters fell onto the fiddle strings, making a soft discordant sound. Jimmy had kept each and every one of the letters she had sent to him. They were packed into the lining, even under the instrument itself. She felt her father's grip tighten on her shoulder. "Oh, Ida. I am so sorry. So very sorry, dear," he said, his voice as gentle as she had ever heard it since the death of her mother. On top of the fallen pile was her last letter—the one in which she told Jimmy of her father's decision that she marry Oliver Edwards whom she did not love and her reluctant agreement to do so.

The messenger, watching Ida's grief unfold from an appropriate distance, said, "General Casement asked me to be certain you looked inside those envelopes, miss." She turned to the man as if seeing him for the first time, then did as he instructed. Each envelope contained varying small amounts of money. Jimmy had indeed been saving for them to begin their future together. She showed her father. Hiram Lewis let out a low whistle, shaking his head. "I'd never have thought that of an Irishman, Ida," he said.

The messenger departed. Ida, clutching Jimmy's fiddle case to her breast, followed and stood on the porch. The cool air chilled her. The stars were beginning to sparkle in the sky. She leaned against the porch rail, listening. She heard only the creaking of carriages, the neighing of horses, and the alternating voices of neighbors sharing conversation. She closed her eyes. Ida strained to hear the familiar tunes of the fiddle but could not discern any such sounds. Yet as he had promised, her heart was indeed filled with Jimmy's music.

☾

Author's Note

General Jack Casement and his brother, Daniel, earned the contract to lay track for the Union Pacific in 1866. Jack and his wife, Frances, who remained at their home in Painesville, Ohio, corresponded with each other regularly during the years he worked for the railroad. Their letters, Accession No. 308, are kept at the American Heritage Center, University of Wyoming, Laramie, Wyoming. Jack Casement achieved his rank as a general through bravery exhibited during the Battle of Franklin in the Civil War. See also John White, Jr.'s "Making Tracks: Jack Casement's Triumph," *Timeline*, March–April 2001.

Sources on the Julesburg conflict vary regarding what actually occurred in the summer of 1867. Some report that Casement had the hoodlums hanged and others state that the toughs were shot. All agree a cemetery sprang up soon after Casement issued his ultimatum. Some sources also indicate that this event was actually a legend, noting scarce newspaper accounts and little information from the railroad itself regarding the matter. Frances Casement wrote a letter to her mother in June 1867 describing her trip to Julesburg and the end of the tracks but she did not mention any such conflict. For more information on Julesburg and the railroad's track-layers, consult Maury Klein's *Union Pacific: The Birth of a Railroad 1862–1893* (New York: Doubleday & Company, 1987), John Debo Galloway's *The First Transcontinental Railroad* (New York: Simmons-Boardman Publishing, 1950); James McCague's *Moguls and Iron Men* (New York: Harper & Row, 1964). I am indebted to Bill Kratville, consultant with the Union Pacific Railroad and Museum in Omaha, Nebraska, for his assistance with additional details regarding the working men's lives.

The Timepiece

HAZY BLUE CIGAR SMOKE FILLED THE INTERIOR OF THE JACKPOT SALOON even though few customers crowded against the bar. David Kingman, seated at one of the room's rickety tables, pondered his next play. He held two deuces and a three, four, and five, each in different suits. This was not the hand he'd hoped for. He could discard the sure thing—a deuce—and hope to draw a six or keep the deuces and try for three new cards. The new three would unlikely be three of a kind but he might draw another deuce. He tried not to let anxiety show on his face. If he were only playing for his own enjoyment, he'd toss the deuces and try for the straight. But today he played for Sylvia Wilkins. If he chose the wrong move, Sylvia's land could be lost to her forever.

Angus Nielson tapped his cards against the table. Eyeing David, he pursed his lips and said, "Any time you feel like playin', Kingman." His voice sounded gritty. He smoked fancy cigars one after another as if they'd soon go out of style.

David looked up from his cards and met Nielson's eyes with what he hoped was an even glance. Sylvia's brother, Cole Edwards, seated across from Nielson, cleared his throat, coughed a bit and said, "Take your time, David." He realized the importance of the game. It was through Cole's folly that Sylvia's land had come down to the luck of the draw in the first place. He'd lost the land to Nielson in a card game.

That Nielson had consented to play another was a small miracle on its own, and letting both David and Cole play against him and his partner, Web Gray, was a mighty big concession on the part of the professional gambler. Gray stayed quiet.

David swallowed hard. Throwing the deuces in the discard pile, he asked for two new cards. Sylvia's parcels lay in the hands of fate now.

☾

Leave-takings hurt the most. Sylvia sighed as she made her way down the aisle of the rail car. She stepped past other travelers. This was a motley group with some dressed in their finest as she herself had done and others looking as if they hadn't a belonging in the world except what they wore.

Sylvia found her seat by the window. Looking out, she saw Cole sitting in the wagon watching for her. She placed her gloved palm to the sooty cool glass of the window as if she could touch his hand. Even knowing this was not possible, the feeling of connection and the pull of her heart begging her to stay lingered. Cole saw her signal, removed his hat and waved it wide so she could see. Unbidden tears stung her eyes. She loved her brother and she'd miss him terribly for these weeks she'd spend in Cheyenne.

The whistle blew and the train inched forward. As Sylvia traveled west, Cole would return north to the homestead they were making. As the locomotive gathered speed, Sylvia realized she missed Cole, but her tears were shed perhaps more for the land she was leaving. The homestead was her security now, and the Lord knew she could hang onto the land. Those acres of Nebraska property would never desert her, never disappoint her in the brutal ways of men. She left her hand against the window until the train was well past the Kimball depot.

Sylvia settled herself in her seat. This was a time for looking forward, she decided. Traveling the long miles to Cheyenne, she could let the past drift away behind her. Working for the Kingmans would afford her the opportunity to save enough money to purchase more land. The

hope for that drove her now. If a woman owned land, she had all the
dreams she could ever hold.

☾

The Kingmans lived on Cattle Baron's Row in Cheyenne, Wyoming
Territory. The name fit because the street boasted so many elegant man-
sions, several of them owned by wealthy cattlemen. The Kingman house
stood on the corner, a two-story brick. A rich walnut staircase, large
enough in Sylvia's mind to contain a whole herd of cattle, and an
ornate crystal chandelier worthy of royalty were the prominent features
in the wide entrance hall. If the foyer were any indication of the opu-
lence of the rest of the house, Sylvia expected dusting to be one of her
main chores.

"Good afternoon, Sylvia." The soft, commanding voice came from
her left.

"Good afternoon, Mrs. Kingman."

"You're looking well. Your traveling suit becomes you. I trust you
had a pleasant journey."

"Thank you. Yes, Ma'am."

Emily Kingman smiled. She was a statuesque woman, always well
dressed and neatly groomed. Her hair was beautifully silvered yet she
gave no impression of age. Sylvia, pleased at the older woman's compliment, self-consciously touched a hand to her own brown locks, running
her fingers across the tortoiseshell comb her mother had given to her.

"Well, then. There's plenty of dusting for you today, dear girl. And
you might also check with the cook. I'm sure he'll expect your help for
the ball tomorrow evening."

"I'm sure it will be a grand event, Mrs. Kingman," Sylvia said.

"Oh, indeed. I'm looking forward to it but the details could wear a
body out. If it weren't for David, I don't know how I'd manage." She
strode from the room. Had she not said anything, Sylvia would never
have guessed Mrs. Kingman worried at all. She appeared confident and
poised rather than anxious.

Sylvia climbed the magnificent staircase to go to her room and change clothes. Though she'd worked here for several weeks, she had yet to meet David, Mrs. Kingman's only son. He apparently was always busy supervising his mother's business and the funds left to her by her husband. Though Elias Kingman had been a rancher most of his life, he had sold his cattle and most of their ranch property to build this Cheyenne mansion for his wife, who didn't like the stockman's lifestyle. The other servants often talked about Elias's decision, and their stories made his choice more colorful by adding rumors that he had only speculated on the house and had intended to sell it to buy more cattle eventually but that poor health had beat him. Sylvia liked to believe the more romantic version of his giving up his dream for his wife. Whatever the case, Elias had certainly done well.

Sylvia's small, simple room doubled as the sewing room. A sewing machine and a dressmaker's body form—today cloaked in a sumptuous navy satin gown—and yards of other fabric lay scattered about, filling about one-half of the space. She quickly changed her clothes, putting on a simple black cotton frock and covering that with a plain muslin apron, and returned downstairs to see to her work.

A shaft of sunlight shone down onto the end table she polished, sparkling against the particles of dust in its beam. A shadow broke the light. Sylvia looked up to see a man silhouetted in the delicate afternoon light, a tall figure with wide shoulders wearing a cowboy hat. She'd been so intent on her work that she hadn't even heard the door open. The man, clad in cotton shirt and denim trousers, removed his hat.

"I apologize for tracking in more dirt, Ma'am," he said, his deep voice echoing like thunder rumbling across the prairie.

Sylvia said, "I'll look after it." She immediately guessed that this was David Kingman. He had reddish-blond hair and a moustache and a charming smile. His face looked ruddy, as if he spent long hours outdoors.

"Much obliged," he said.

He lingered for a moment, studying Sylvia in a not unpleasant manner. She returned her gaze to her dusting cloth. As he strode toward his mother's study, Sylvia saw the same confident bearing of Emily

Kingman in his movements. Sylvia moved to the closet under the stairs to find a broom, surprised at how differently she had pictured him. David Kingman was most certainly not the satin-vested businessman she'd expected. As she swept the dirt that had fallen from his boots, Sylvia felt relief. She liked his obvious attachment to working the land and was glad to learn he had good manners.

☾

"The navy satin suits you, Sylvia," Mrs. Kingman said.

Sylvia blushed. The dressmaker had asked her to try it on prior to allowing Mrs. Kingman the privilege in order to remove excess pins. But the dress fit like a dream, and looking in the mirror, Sylvia imagined herself swirling at the cattle baron's ball. She fingered the tortoiseshell comb that held her dark curls in place atop her head.

"Yes, indeed," Mrs. Kingman said, coming to stand behind her and gaze at her reflection in the mirror. "You look beautiful, dear."

"I'm sorry, Mrs. Kingman. We wanted to remove the extra pins so you wouldn't be scratched."

Emily Kingman chuckled. "As if I've never been scratched. What nonsense. All the same, I'm glad you tried on this gown. It's fun to see it worn by another person."

At that moment, David Kingman entered the room. "Mother, I need to talk with you about the Chugwater property," he said. He stopped when he saw Sylvia and the seamstress. "Oh, I am sorry. I didn't realize—"

"No, no, no, David. It's quite all right. Sylvia is modeling my gown for me. Don't you think it becomes her?"

Sylvia's face felt as hot as the dressmaker's iron. If she could have seen her toes at that moment, she wouldn't have been surprised to see them turn red as cherries as well. David gave her an slow, appreciative look. Their eyes met in the mirror. "Yes, quite regal."

"Thank you," Sylvia managed, in a voice a few steps higher than its usual range. His eyes—the color of the whiskey Mrs. Kingman kept in a crystal decanter—and the slow smile that lifted the corners of his moustache unnerved her. She moved her hand to her throat, fiddling with the delicate lace of the high collar.

Mrs. Kingman turned to her son. "Now, what was it you wanted, dear?"

"About the Chugwater property," he began.

"Oh, yes. Why can't that wait, David?"

"Mother, will you never realize the importance of land?"

Emily Kingman chuckled. "Oh, I realize plenty, David," she answered him. "You could own the whole continent and never have enough land. Let's talk downstairs so these women can finish their jobs."

When the Kingmans departed, the dressmaker shook her head. "This dress won't be good for Mrs. Kingman even if it was made for her. It looks like I made it for you." She turned Sylvia this way and that, examining her work in the mirror. "Or perhaps," she said, a wry smile brightening her face, "you were made for this dress." The dressmaker tugged at a sleeve. "I think he fancies you," she said, patting Sylvia's arm.

Sylvia, still blushing from David's frank admiration, didn't respond, but allowed herself a couple more glances of the beautiful blue gown. She could still feel the warmth of David's eyes upon her, something that made her happier than she'd felt for a long while. But the feeling would fade, David was not in her league, and the dress did not belong to her. So she willed herself to become Sylvia the servant girl once again and tried to imagine Mrs. Kingman wearing the gorgeous gown at the Cattle Baron's Ball instead.

☾

At the ball, Sylvia, clad in standard black dress with muslin apron, helped to see that glasses and dishes were taken away promptly so the guests could enjoy themselves properly.

The guests were dancing a quadrille when she made another round of the second floor ballroom. She noticed Mrs. Kingman clothed in a brown satin dress, and felt a hand at her elbow.

"She said she prefers brown. It brings out her eyes," Following her glance, David Kingman nodded at his mother. He stood behind Sylvia.

"Oh, your mother looks lovely in anything."

He smiled. "Yes, she is a handsome woman."

"I must get on with my chores and get out of your way." Sylvia moved to take the tray filled with dirtied dishes but David took it from her hand and sat it down on the floor next to the wall.

"Not just yet. You can watch for a moment or two."

She hesitated for a moment. "All right. Thank you."

As the men held out their hands and bowed and the ladies twirled, their flowing gowns making beautiful swirls of color against the wood of the room, the music swelled. David took Sylvia's hands in his own and twirled her around in the corridor.

"But someone will see us," she whispered.

"Does that matter? Don't you like to dance, Sylvia?"

"I love to dance," she admitted. She hadn't danced since her wedding so many years ago. She relaxed a little and allowed him a smile. When the music ended—far too quickly—she thanked him and reached for her tray. "I'm sure other ladies wait for the pleasure of your company, Mr. Kingman."

He held her hand for a moment longer. "That may be, but they are none of them finer than you, Sylvia. My mother speaks very highly of you. She says you are a homesteader, is that right?"

"Yes, thank you," she said, certain her fiery face gave away her feelings. "I must be about my work now." He released his grip on her hand as suddenly as he had grasped it, and as she made her way carefully down the steep stairs, she had the oddest feeling that David Kingman had not taken his eyes from her. She enjoyed being with him far too much, and as she descended toward the kitchen, she knew what she must do. The bonus she'd receive for working during the ball, added to what she had already saved, would be just enough to purchase another parcel. Sylvia had completed her domestic duties. In the morning, she'd return to Kimball on the train. Now her land awaited her.

☾

The wagon creaked and rattled as they reached the homestead. Sylvia drank it all in with her eyes, imagining the grassy prairie filled with abundant crops and cattle and replacing the tiny sod house with a fine frame one. A saddled chestnut horse grazed outside the house.

"Were you expecting company, Cole?" Sylvia asked.

Her brother pulled the reins, and their team stopped. "No."

He climbed down from the wagon and lifted Sylvia down. By that time, a man had come to stand in the door of the soddie. He leaned against the frame, his arms crossed against his broad chest and legs crossed, black boots shining. Sylvia's first impression was that all about this man was dark, because his hat and his trousers and jacket were all black. A diamond glimmered from the silk cravat at his throat, setting off his silvery gray vest. Cole's tightened jaw and pressed lips told Sylvia he did not like the man, who, on closer inspection, had buckskin-colored hair and wintry blue eyes.

"Hello, Angus," Cole said.

Angus Nielson removed his hat in deference to Sylvia. "Hello, Cole. Aren't you going to introduce me to your lady friend?"

Cole frowned. "Sylvia, Angus Nielson. Angus, my sister, Sylvia."

"Pleasure," he drawled. He had not moved from his position inside the door.

"What are you doing here, Angus?" Cole asked.

Angus shook his head and smiled at Sylvia. "Is that any way to treat a guest? Come now, Cole, after our game the other night, I would have thought you would have been pleased to see me."

"You thought wrong."

Sylvia watched her brother. So, he had been gambling again. She sighed. He would never learn, and she regretted not having been here to stop him.

"But Cole, seeing's as how this is my property now, I wanted to look it over."

"This is not your property, Mr. Nielson. My brother and I own it."

"Ah, the lady speaks," Angus said. "Surely Cole has told you?"

"Told me what, Cole?"

Cole's jaw muscle twitched. He kicked at the grass. "I lost our land—mine and yours—in a poker game. Angus won."

Sylvia grabbed Cole's arms. "No!" She shook her brother. "Cole, you didn't." Her voice cracked. When he finally met her eyes, she saw the truth. "How could you?"

"Don't blame him too much, little lady," Angus spoke again from the doorway of the soddie. "He faced insurmountable odds, gambling against a professional like myself."

"Syl, I—I wanted to make extra money so we could buy more. I swear it. I didn't want you to have to be working so hard. But the cards went against me."

"Oh, Cole. Will you never learn that the cards will always go against you?"

Angus chuckled, a grating sound, like sandpaper scraping against rough wood. "Ma'am, I can attest that the cards don't always go against a man. That's what makes gambling so glamorous. There's always a chance that luck will favor you."

"Cole, you had no right to gamble with my property. No right." Sylvia's anger vibrated through her whole body. Her hands shook as she straightened her skirts. She took a deep breath and faced Angus Nielson.

"I want it back. I want my land back, and I want you to leave, sir."

Angus raised an eyebrow. "I see, but it is mine now, fair and square."

"Cole had no right to gamble with my land," she said. "Surely a reasonable man such as yourself can understand that much."

Angus allowed a slow smile to spread across his face. "What might you be willing to do to get your precious land back?"

Sylvia pressed her lips together. "I shouldn't have to do anything at all. You won it under misleading circumstances and I want it back."

"Well, Ma'am. A poker game to me, is quite serious business." He ran his hand along the door frame. "But seeing as how you didn't realize what your brother had intended, I can make an allowance or two. I would certainly let you stay here in your soddie until other arrangements could be made."

"How much?"

"Pardon me?"

"How much?" Sylvia repeated. "How much money must we pay you to have our land returned?"

Angus chuckled again. "Well, now, Cole. Your sister's got spunk, hasn't she? What did you have in mind?"

"Same amount we paid for it originally."

"Mmm. I think it perhaps is worth more. You've got a soddie built here now and I believe Cole mentioned a tree claim as well."

Sylvia sighed. "I can't pay you more."

Angus put on his hat. "That is a shame, Ma'am." He looked at brother and sister. "I see that you have some things to discuss this evening. I'll come back in a couple of days, after you've gotten used to the idea."

He strode past them, mounted his horse and left.

"Cole, how could you gamble my land? You silly coot!"

"Now, Sylvia, don't have a conniption. Your dowry money bought it so I figured I could offer the whole of the property."

"Father gave me that dowry money. It was not yours to use."

"How do you figure that? Our father earned it, so it belonged to both of us, especially since you won't be needing it now. I'm just glad old Abner didn't take it when he ran off."

Sylvia didn't need his reminder of her failed marriage to Abner Wilkins. As he intended them to, Cole's words hurt because of the truth that rang through them. She stayed silent.

After a long moment, Cole said, "I'll get it back."

"I'd like to know how. That man is not going to give an inch. Do you expect to gamble again to win it back?"

"I could try."

Sylvia harrumphed. "You could, but then we'd wind up losing anything else we own, which without the land, Cole, is nothing."

"You're still working for the Kingmans. That pay will help us buy new land."

"No, Cole, it won't," she retorted. "I finished my duties at the Kingmans because I'd saved just enough to add another parcel to this acreage. I'll not go back. That's my money. I earned it, and I will not share it with you now." Sylvia glared at her brother. In the space of one afternoon, she'd lost everything. Her land, her job, her trust in her brother. Tears welled in her eyes. Pride stopped her from fighting further. She didn't want him to see her cry. She turned on her heel and stomped into the house.

☾

Sylvia did not speak to Cole the next day. He had gone to a neighboring ranch to see if he could find work. She had not slept well. She felt anxious and edgy. Her mind reeled. As she tended her daily chores of cooking and cleaning, she tried to find a solution to her problem but could not. She couldn't go back to working at the Kingmans because she dared not face David. She could perhaps find another employer in Cheyenne, but to do so now, she would have to live there. The likelihood of facing David was too great. And after her sad experience with Abner—who deserted her without any warning—she did not feel she could ever love another man. She could use her meager savings to purchase another piece of property, but she had already fallen in love with this land, the land they had chosen at the top of a windswept hill near the limestone hills speckled with pine trees. Any other land would not be as good. Cole had eliminated her chance of helping him prepare their land for crops and cattle. And she most certainly would not back-trail to Ohio after having come this far.

She rested for a moment, drinking a cup of coffee before she prepared to water the few apple trees she and Cole had planted when they arrived. She dreaded facing the trees for she had fallen in love with them, too. Her only option, she decided, would be to swallow her pride and find another job in Cheyenne. Maybe there, her dreams of owning land would fade. That had happened to others after all.

Sylvia walked outside, startled to see someone approaching on horseback. She leaned against the wall of the soddie, grabbing her apron and wringing it with her hands, fearing the presence of Angus Nielson.

Instead, as the figure drew near, she realized it was David Kingman. She let go of her apron, brushed a stray lock of hair from her face, and straightened her skirt.

David dismounted. He removed his hat and stood before her, as handsome as she remembered.

"Hello, David. What brings you here?"

He lifted a package from his saddle bag. "I'm on an errand for my mother."

"I see," she said. "Then please come inside where it is cooler, and we can visit." Sylvia ushered him into the dark interior of the soddie. She motioned to the table. "Sit down. Would you care for a cup of coffee? My brother, Cole, will be home soon." She poured two coffees and then sliced a couple of pieces from the loaf of bread she'd baked that morning and placed butter on the table. "He's visiting neighbors this morning." Sylvia felt somewhat uncomfortable having a man inside their home without Cole there, but her father's rifle stood by the door and she knew how to use it. Besides, David had been nothing but kind to her.

David placed the package on the table. "Please," he said. "Open it."

Puzzled, she removed the twine and brown paper from the rectangular box. When she removed the lid, she gasped with surprise. She wiped her hands on her apron before touching the object inside. "It's the navy satin gown," she said.

"Yes. My mother wanted you to have it, and you left in such a flurry after the ball that she hadn't had time to give it to you."

"It's beautiful," she said. "But I cannot accept such a gift."

David reached for her hand. He held it in his own for a moment. "I couldn't tell you that day, but Sylvia, you looked so lovely in that gown that I couldn't breathe," he said.

She luxuriated in his comment and the warmth of his hand on hers for a brief moment. Then she stood.

"I cannot allow this flirtation to continue, David. I must be honest with you. I am a married woman." His sharp intake of breath hurt her. "My husband abandoned me some time ago."

"I am sorry."

"Don't be. Others carry more difficult burdens. I had my chance but all went wrong. The past is behind me now. I am trying to obtain a divorce. There will not be another."

David felt pleased that she would soon be free but her words frightened him. "Perhaps you'll be able to love another one day," he ventured, but watching her face he saw her stubborn refusal to even consider such a thing. "Your view of love is not irrational after the pain caused by a coward who had not the decency to end your marriage in a more straightforward manner," he said. He could not keep the anger out of his voice. He liked Sylvia too much. "What kind of man would leave such a fine woman to fend for herself? That is why you came to work for my mother, isn't it?"

She nodded. "In part. I wanted to buy this land for myself and for my brother. You understand, I think, that land is the best security a person can have."

"And you managed enough funds to purchase what you need?"

"I had thought so."

"But?"

She waited long moments before confiding in David. "My brother gambled my land without my knowledge and lost. So now I'm trying to purchase my land back from the gambler Angus Nielson."

She hadn't meant to tell him, but she could not stop herself. "I'm afraid I cannot accept the dress. I don't accept charity."

"It's not charity, my mother wanted you to have it. She's never worn it. Said it looked much better on you than it ever would on her and that you should consider it a thank you for your good work." She started to protest but he interrupted. "I cannot take it back to her. She'd be forever insulted."

Sylvia took the dress. "Thank you. I'll never forget how kind your mother was to me."

"She'll be glad to hear it."

A silence fell between them.

David stood. His quiet voice broke the stillness. He said, "Few women understand the importance of land, Sylvia. It's a strong woman who knows her own heart so well."

She felt happiness course through her at his praise. Here at last stood someone who understood her passion for the land. But her short-lived joy was tinged with the sadness of loss. She felt equally certain that she would never again see David Kingman. She regretted that more than she could say.

David thanked her for the coffee and tasty bread, mounted his horse, tipped his hat to her, and rode away. He did not tell Sylvia he had also been at the card game in which her land had been so cruelly lost. At the saloon in Kimball that evening, he'd been looking forward to a bit of relaxation. He had been scouting property himself that day, hoping to find some good land that would compliment his mother's Chugwater acreage. His hand had not been good enough to earn the prize of Sylvia's land but he dared not tell her that he had been a party to the scheme. He had not connected Cole Edwards to Sylvia until now. As he rode across the unfettered prairie, an idea grew in his mind. He had a few things to discuss with Cole. And with Angus Nielson, if he could find him.

☾

David drew the five of hearts and two Jacks. He was better off than he had been. With a flourish he laid his cards face up on the table. "Two pair," he said, in a voice he hoped sounded confident.

Nielson said, "Nope. Ain't got me beat." He showed three of a kind—tens.

Cole threw his cards into the pile without showing them. "You've won it, Nielson," he said.

Nielson did not laugh with glee as David had expected. Instead, he said, "It's not always the winnin' I love, but the thrill of the game, gentlemen."

David and Cole stood. "We'll fill out the paperwork soon as the clerk's office opens on Monday," Cole said.

Nielson shook his head. "No need."

The two men stared at the gambler. Nielson gathered the cards together into a neat deck and tapped them on the table. The silence lingered until he said, "I admire your courage, David. Not many men would risk a woman's land like you did. She's a lucky lady indeed to have you." He rose from his chair and stood beside them. "Because of that, I'll give your land back." At their looks of surprise, he continued, saying, "I'm an honorable man and I dislike the way this came about." He fixed Cole with a flinty stare. "And I want to make it right for the lady."

Cole stared at his shoes. David bit back a smile at the gambler's rebuke. Cole deserved worse than that for having risked his sister's land—her dearest possession—after all.

Nielson kept talking. He gestured at David's pocket watch, hanging from a fob on David's vest. "Maybe we can trade the land for your pocket watch."

David held the timepiece in his palm, watching the second hand tick away the time. "It's not an even trade, I'm afraid," he said, sighing. "I'd still owe you. The watch's value is mostly sentimental." He looked into Nielson's curiously pale eyes. "This belonged to my grandfather. It's not anything fancy, not even a gold case. An Elgin."

Nielson nodded. "Then I'd say it would be a fair trade indeed. Land is precious, as Mrs. Wilkins knows. So by trading me something precious in return"—he opened his hands and held out his arms as if expecting to capture a windfall—"we're even."

David gazed at his watch for a long moment. Perhaps this was a small price to pay for a woman he loved. He believed his grandfather would tell him so if he were here to offer advice. He released the watch from its chain and handed it to Nielson.

☾

Sylvia saw the men approaching and ran out of the house to greet them. Caught in the middle of punching down a batch of bread, she wiped her hands on her muslin apron. She clutched the apron as she saw their dispirited expressions. Meadowlarks sang their pretty tunes and the prairie grasses rustled in the morning breeze as if nothing of import were happening.

David dismounted first and came to stand beside her. He removed his hat.

From his action, Sylvia knew the result of the game. She ran into the house so he wouldn't witness her tears. She stood with her back to the men, who followed her into the coolness of the house, grateful for the loaf of bread and the physical release that punching down the dough offered. Cole cleared his throat. She did not turn round.

He said, "David won your land, Syl."

She punched the dough again and rolled it against itself. Then his words sank into her mind. She took a moment to compose herself and turned to face them.

"I can't believe," she began. "You—you won?"

David started to explain the details of his "win" but Cole interceded, saying, "Yep. Fair and square. Your land belongs to you now, Syl." He frowned. "And I guess I should say I am sorry for causing you such worry." She hugged him tightly, saying, "Cole, you should be!" She released her brother from her embrace and looked at David. "But if you won, David," she said evenly, "then this land belongs to you."

David shook his head. "No, ma'am. It's yours. You are the one who bought it. I merely helped Cole out of a bad spot."

"And we'll not be beholden to you in any way?"

"I'm not that kind of man," David replied. He didn't speak of the consideration he had in mind. There would be plenty of time for that in the future.

"Well, then sit down and eat breakfast with us, Mr. Kingman. I'm mighty glad your gambling skills are so fine. Feeding you a meal is the least I can do for you."

☾

Sylvia finished watering the last of the apple trees in their tree claim. The hot July afternoon pressed on her. She removed her sunbonnet, pushed a stray strand of hair behind her ear, and dabbed at her sweaty brow with her apron. The walk from the well Cole had dug for the house wasn't far from the trees but the dry heat made the journey miserable. Cole hadn't yet given up his penchant for gambling but at least he had learned not to fritter away her belongings, and he was trying desperately to make amends by working extra hard to make things nicer for her. She fiercely wished she and David hadn't planted so many additional trees but daily thanked the Lord for the presence of water underneath their land. The nearest creek was miles away and the recent weeks of heat dried up any chance of finding water in the cedar-dotted draws. As she stood hoping that the apple trees—not even as tall yet as her own knees—would grow despite the weather, David came walking toward her.

"I've a package for you, Sylvia. It came in the mail," he said. He handed her the small box. She turned her water bucket upside down and sat on it.

"I don't recognize the handwriting," she said, examining the address. She opened the package. She took out a letter in the same handwriting and gasped.

"What is it, Syl?" David asked, concerned about his bride's unexpected reaction.

She held up his grandfather's pocket watch. He reached for it.

"Read the letter," he said, a muscle in his jaw tightening. Had Angus reneged on their agreement? He surely couldn't mean to take Sylvia's land from her now.

"It says, 'Heirlooms belong in their rightful families. Please consider this my wedding gift to a fine couple. You should keep this, Sylvia, as a reminder of Mr. Kingman's abiding love for you. Such affection is rare indeed. Don't gamble with it.' And it's signed, Angus Nielson." She saw David's relief. He still held the watch gingerly in his palm.

"David," she said. "How did Mr. Nielson know we were getting married? Did you tell him? That was arrogant of you, wasn't it?" Sylvia was thinking of the months between the game that sealed the fate of her land and her acceptance of David's proposal. If David had told the gambler of their plans to marry, it would have been before she herself knew. They'd gotten married quickly with little fanfare because her superstitions had gotten the best of her. She'd done everything right the first time and things had turned out badly. This time, she had tried something different. She had worn the navy satin dress. "How did he know?" she asked again.

David blushed, shaking his head. "They say some gamblers have a good sense of people. I guess Angus sure does." He gave the watch to Sylvia. She moved to hand it back, but he closed his calloused hands over her rough, red ones. "Nielson's right. You should keep the watch. I've already won my fortune." He looked at her for a long moment. Sylvia rose, holding the precious timepiece. They shared a lengthy kiss before walking arm in arm toward the house.

The Legend of Lover's Leap

Just above a pretty little valley, on a higher plain, rose a great limestone bluff. The naked rock bluff jutted from a green knoll sprinkled with cedar trees and flecked with spiky yucca plants ready to burst into bloom. The rock's rough triangular shape gave the impression of a serpent's head ready to strike. Little Lark imagined that peaceful spirits had frozen the serpent in place before he had been able to finish his task. Having been warned of the presence of rattlers and the dangers inherent in being bitten nearly every time she exited her family's tipi, she had decided rattlesnakes must protect the area from intruders on behalf of their brother jailed forever inside the stone.

Little Lark gazed at the bluff as she walked through the soft June night to the watering hole, watching for movement and listening for the unmistakable buzz of those dangerous rattles. Moonlight made even the thin, sharp leaves of the yucca plants look silvery and touchable and transformed the hilly landscape into a tanned buffalo hide like those she had grown so skilled at making. Other smaller limestone bluffs were barely visible in the pine-studded canyons to the west. The Great Bluff stood alone, its shadow darkening the watering hole.

Little Lark's footsteps creasing the grass startled a cottontail from its hiding place near a pine tree. She herself jumped when she noticed the movement from the corner of her eye. Smiling at her folly, Little Lark stopped at the small watering hole—a deep crevice in the rocky hills filled with melted snow and captured raindrops—just enough for the tribe's needs as they camped nearby. She knelt, dipping her jug into the pool. Doing so, she became aware of a shadow falling across her. Hand trembling, she focused on filling the vessel. A musky male scent mingled with that of pine and grass, moist dirt and water. Little Lark finished her task and rose, attempting to mask her fearful anticipation with confidence.

Next to her stood Eagle Feather, one of her father's young warriors. Little Lark's heart filled with pleasure. She liked Eagle Feather and believed he felt the same. She noticed the smooth way he had found to walk next to her while the tribe traveled from camp to camp. She had hoped for this moment, yet now found herself suddenly and intensely shy in his presence. She stole a glance at him. He was a few inches taller than she, muscular from his work with the tribe's ponies. Dark hair framed his square-jawed face, and a hint of a smile lifted his lips. His brown eyes were kind.

He greeted her and his deep voice thrilled her. "I have been waiting for you, Little Lark," he said. "You come later tonight than other times."

She spoke quietly. "I did not wish to wake my parents. They would worry."

"You are good to care for their feelings."

She smiled but did not reply. Eagle Feather continued, "I have done what I must in the Warrior Society, Little Lark. I have only to count coup and then I can marry." Eagle Feather took her hand, cool from filling the water pot, in his own much warmer grasp. "I had hoped to do so sooner. Perhaps the hunting expedition will provide me the opportunity." Little Lark looked down at the pond, then shyly raised her gaze to his again.

"You are a strong warrior," she said, looking into his eyes. "You will do what you need to do."

They were alone. A silence fell between them. Eagle Feather reached out, stroking her long dark hair. She'd loosened it from its braids before coming outside on this night. Eagle Feather drew her close to him and kissed her.

Little Lark trembled in his arms like the doe he'd frightened in the draw that morning.

"My father," she whispered. Following their recent argument, her father, Chief Soaring Hawk, had forbidden her to meet Eagle Feather. He was the reason his daughter had disobeyed tribal rules. She had left the tipi where women were segregated during the time of the month when their mysterious powers peaked. Her presence near the warriors at that particular time might have caused their arrows to go awry of targets or worse. The chief—who feared that this time when women bled could cause insanity and even death among his warriors if they came near—had not yet forgiven either one of them. In his eyes, the young couple had tempted demons. Why the demons had not yet caused harm remained a mystery.

"I will show your father I am worthy," Eagle Feather said, touching her cheek. "He should be proud of you, Little Lark. Such bravery is not often seen in a woman. Your spirit is strong."

"My father did not believe I was brave," she said. "He thinks I endangered our tribe."

Eagle Feather shook his head. "No harm came to us."

A frown crossed her face. She looked at her moccasins. Eagle Feather caressed her cheek where moonlight shone against her smooth skin. Little Lark did not look up but reached up with her hand to hold his.

Eagle Feather longed to hold her in his arms but the time was not right. He must first prove himself to her father, Chief Soaring Hawk. He would return from the hunting expedition with several buffalo. That would at least build respect between him and the older man. Then he must count coup, must touch an enemy, a white man, to prove himself as a warrior. His success would exonerate Little Lark as well. Her father would be so impressed with Eagle Feather's accomplishments that he would forget his daughter's indiscretion. After that, he and Little Lark could be married.

A rustling of grass alerted them to another's approach. With reluctance, Eagle Feather let her go, holding her hand until she had to stretch her arm and pull away gently. Little Lark nodded to the visitor, Gentle Flower, come to fill her cup, as she made her way back toward camp. Eagle Feather reached into the water, cupped his hand, and sipped the drink from it. The woman dipped her vessel into the water. Eagle Feather, unruffled, stood and walked away. Eyes heavenward, he gazed at the stars, finding the Big Dipper easily and believing it held many moons of promise for him. Watching his calm behavior from the path and delighted at his rebuff of Gentle Flower, whose name did not fit her personality and who wanted Eagle Feather for herself, Little Lark smiled with joy.

☽

The next morning, in the pale dawn light at Fort Laramie, freighter Tobias Johnson packed his wagon. "Moving on," he told the sutler. The man nodded, helping him secure the load. Patting a bag of flour, he said, "Watch yourself on the plains, now."

"Always do."

"See to it," the man said, his tone somber. "The Sioux are traveling and looking for buffalo. There's been lots of ponies stolen around these parts."

Tobias snorted. He tugged on the line holding his two nags to the wagon. "And you're worried they'll take these fine mounts? Then they must be desperate." He spit a stream of tobacco at the horse's feet.

The sutler disliked any man who tore down his work horses so. Disguising his disgust, he said, "As I said, watch yourself."

"Maybe they'll trade me something fine for this here whole load." Tobias tilted his head. "With Injuns, one never knows. See you on the return trip." He climbed into the wagon. Shaking his head, the sutler watched the grizzled freighter begin his journey.

☽

Several days passed. Little Lark's tribe began to make preparations to move on. The watering hole had dwindled from use and the early summer heat. Little Lark and Eagle Feather continued to meet clandestinely at the watering hole. One night, after everyone in camp had fallen asleep, Eagle Feather crept into Little Lark's tipi. She awakened at the sound of the rustling as he crawled beneath the hide that covered her. His body warmed hers. He put a finger to his lips, reminding her to be quiet. Inherent in his gesture was also a question. *You do not want to wake your parents, do you?* If she did awaken her parents, she told Eagle Feather she did not want him. Remaining silent, she smiled and took him into her arms. Through this quiet embrace and acceptance, Little Lark agreed to marry her handsome young man.

Unbeknownst to the young lovers, Little Lark's mother reached out for Little Lark's father, Soaring Hawk, putting a finger to her lips as Eagle Feather had done. The chief frowned. Little Lark was their only child, and although he liked Eagle Feather, he found no warrior suitable for his daughter. However, his wife's ministrations were most persuasive and he soon forgot his concerns.

In the morning, Little Lark awoke alone. Their night of great promise was over, yet she felt continuing joy at their union. She and Eagle Feather would inform her parents of their intention to marry on this night. Her parents said nothing, but Little Lark sensed her father's distraction. She wondered if they knew of her activities. They had been separated only by the hide hung between their sleeping areas. When another warrior came to inform Soaring Hawk of the poor condition of some of the ponies, and the difficulties of the long journey ahead in the days to come, Little Lark decided her father's aloof manner came from his continuing disapproval of her actions and from his overwhelming responsibilities.

☾

Later that day, a white freighter arrived in camp. He wore a dirty hat and clothes soiled with trail dust. His face was burnt and wrinkled like a piece of deer meat cooked on the fire. The noise of the creaking wagon wheels scattered the rambunctious young children playing amidst the tipis of the Sioux camp. Little Lark stirred soup. She wanted to make something special for this night of her announcement with Eagle Feather. She watched the man approach. He used wide hand and arm gestures, showing those gathered around him his wares in the wagon. Tribal members gathered round for a moment, but most returned shortly to their tasks. Soaring Hawk was summoned. The men talked. To Little Lark's surprise, her father invited the ugly white man into their tipi.

Little Lark shifted her attention from the soup that now had cooked thoroughly and was available for anyone who wished to eat it. She entered the tipi, wrinkling her nose at the sweaty smell of the white man, mixed as it was with tobacco and whiskey and other unwelcome scents that brought tears to her eyes. She nodded to her father and mother and went to her place. She fingered the intricately-beaded moccasins she'd made to wear for her announcement and the upcoming wedding. They were some of her finest work yet.

In the place near the fire, Little Lark heard the men arguing.

"No." Her father spoke in his most authoritative tone. The argument was settled.

However, the white man continued to talk, in a whiny, high-pitched voice, punctuated by guttural sounds and throat clearings.

"Now, Chief," Tobias Johnson said. "I know things here have been rough on your tribe. I can help you. Folks in this area are up in arms over the fact that you're stealing their ponies—" (At this insult, the white man reached out his hand, palm outward, stopping her father from interrupting him.) "—You know it and I know it. That's what you Injuns do. So anyhow, I can lead you through the places where the white men ain't and save you lots of trouble. I know right where the buffalo are staying just now. I can save you days of wandering and lookin'. I can even give you supplies from my wagon." He made a sort of laugh, and said more quietly, "That is if your braves and women ain't stolen what's already there."

Soaring Hawk tightened his lips. To Little Lark, it was clear her father meant to listen to the man's gibberish to humor him. Soaring

Hawk would soon send the man away, and he'd be lucky if the chief didn't send a few warriors out to kill him. From the insults and the tone, she felt surprised her father hadn't already slit the man's throat. He could do it easily enough. He had done so in the past as his own coming of age and counting coup, but her father was even-tempered. He considered actions before taking them.

Their need for supplies was great. Soaring Hawk went outside and pointed to the wagon. The tribe would need that, but what he really wanted was ponies. Several of the ponies they had brought with them had gone lame. Though Eagle Feather watched over the ponies, the horses had grown tired on their journeys. They needed fresh horses for the buffalo hunt and especially if they neared encampments of the white men.

"In return," the white man said, "I'll take her." He pointed at Little Lark. She had followed to watch and now stood just outside the tipi. She looked up in amazement at her father. He shook his head. The white man crossed his arms, leaning against the wagon. "No deal then, chief. I can get you ponies." At this word, he patted the behind of his horse. He again pointed at Little Lark. "I'll leave you the wagon and bring you the ponies. Then I will vamoose with her. Otherwise, no ponies." He mounted his wagon, acting as if he would leave.

Soaring Hawk waited for a long moment. When the freighter shook the reins and his horses moved forward, the chief told him to bring the ponies. Little Lark returned to the tipi, tears staining her cheeks. She had heard enough of the conversation to believe she had just been sold for ponies. She would not go. She and Eagle Feather must plan their escape and go tonight, before the evil deed could be done. She did not understand her father's trading. Her mother put hands on her daughter's cheeks, and said, "Child, your father knows what he is doing. You must learn to trust."

Little Lark shook free of her mother's embrace. "I will not go with the white man. I will not."

Her mother frowned. "You must do your father's bidding, Little Lark. You cannot see it but he has your best interests at heart. I cannot tell you more than that." She dared not tell the girl that her father never planned to exchange her for horses. Instead, when the freighter brought the ponies, the warriors would kill him, thus providing Eagle Feather the opportunity to count coup and allowing the young lovers to be married soon. Little Lark proved a worthy lure for such a plan. Had she known, she might have mentioned the idea to Eagle Feather or another friend. Soaring Hawk, still stinging from Little Lark's betrayal of the rule of women, had not regained his trust in his daughter. He could not take the chance that word of his deceit might spread through the tribe. For then the plan might also fall upon the ears of Tobias Johnson, and the ponies they so desperately needed would not arrive.

"He looks after only the interests of the tribe," Little Lark retorted, as if reading her mother's thoughts. "He does not like Eagle Feather. This is his way to stop me from marrying him."

"Little Lark, you must understand your father loves you."

"Then he should understand I love Eagle Feather."

"You have not yet gotten over the argument with your father."

Little Lark's lower lip jutted out. "I did nothing wrong."

Her mother nodded. "Ah, but you did. You might have caused great harm for the hunters."

"I only wanted to watch Eagle Feather."

"I know, child, but women are not to go on the hunt. And especially during their time of the month." She paused and raised her hands skyward. "I am thankful that your powers then did not fault the aim of our men shooting arrows."

Little Lark continued to pout. She had not only disobeyed the tradition that only men participated in the hunts but also had denied the basic mystery of her womanhood to do so.

"Nothing happened. I was not hurt, nor were our hunters. I did no harm—"

Little Lark's mother hushed her. "You must learn patience. And you must abide by your father's wishes."

Thus scolded, Little Lark ran from the tipi, approaching the Great Bluff. There, she found a ledge where she could sit and think. The rock embraced her, sheltering her from the wind and providing some warmth as its pale surface reflected heat from the sun. She cried until her tears would come no more. Sitting there, she heard the *scree scree scree* of the frightened killdeer and the throaty songs of the meadowlarks, for which she was named.

☾

Before sunset, Little Lark rushed to find Eagle Feather to tell him of her decision. But she could not find him. He was not with the ponies, and he was not at his family's tipi. His mother told Little Lark that he had gone out hunting that morning with others in the Warrior Society. He would not return that night.

Little Lark spent the next day anxiously watching for Eagle Feather, and with fright in her heart, for the white man. Eagle Feather had to return before the white man came to take her away. She prayed that Eagle Feather would find many buffalo, and thus impress her father. She did not speak to her father. Although she had hoped he would talk to her, would tell her there had been a mistake, he did not speak with her either. The chasm between them grew wider. In her anguish, Little Lark again retreated to her special place on the side of the Great Bluff. She could see for miles, almost as if she were flying in the air with the birds. This still did not make her heartache cease.

She waited throughout the night and all the next day. That evening, Eagle Feather and the hunting group returned with many buffalo. Eagle Feather proudly showed his three conquests to Little Lark and her father. Little Lark watched with pain in her heart. The buffalo would feed and clothe the family but Eagle Feather's contribution fell short of the white man's. Tobias Johnson had arrived in camp that afternoon with twenty fine ponies secured from Fort Laramie, so he said. He waited now to dine with Little Lark and her family. Then he would take her away.

"A fine showing," Soaring Hawk said.

Eagle Feather motioned to Little Lark. "For your fine daughter," he said.

Soaring Hawk replied, "My daughter has been pledged to another. You have yet to count coup." He could not bring himself to admit his plan in the presence of his daughter. He wanted to wait until the warriors had rested some from their endeavors before killing the white man. The morning would bring certain opportunities.

Eagle Feather's eyes darkened. He frowned, confusion drawing deep lines across his forehead. He looked to Little Lark in hopes she would dispute this claim. Instead, he found confirmation. Soaring Hawk said nothing more and left them alone.

Tears rolled down Little Lark's cheeks. The wind riffled her hair, making it look like a dark river in the moonlight. The strengthening breeze danced between them. Neither made a move toward the other. They looked at each other for long moments. Eagle Feather closed his eyes. Her image remained in his head. When he opened his eyes again, expecting to ask her what had happened in his absence, Little Lark had gone. Disheartened, he went to his pony, Sun Dancer. Sun Dancer nickered softly and nuzzled his hand. Eagle Feather stood with his horse, tempted to run away himself. He did not understand the chief's harshness. He stood there among the ponies long enough that the stars changed position in the sky.

The wind had grown, blowing in a storm from the west. This strange storm, causing a breeze to rise to full-blown wind in the night, already obscured the stars of the western sky. Looking up toward the Big Dipper, once a symbol of promise and now only an empty vessel, Eagle Feather caught a movement from the corner of his eye. Then he noticed her in the darkness. A patch of wan moonlight barely illuminated her figure. She scrambled up the side of the Great Bluff, running between the yucca plants blooming like lighted torches, grasping at grass when her feet slipped, and reaching for purchase as she ascended the slope. She turned toward him once. Tears like sunlight sparkling against dewy grass silvered her cheeks.

Eagle Feather watched for a moment, sensing something was wrong, then realizing Little Lark's intentions. His split second of indecision cost him precious time. Eagle Feather ran to catch up, but even with his strength, she had gotten too much of a head start. He reached the top of the rock as Little Lark sprinted across to the end of its flat summit. She screamed as she leapt into the arms of the wind. Eagle Feather fell prone against the still warm rock, arms outstretched as if he could still catch his love. The wind rushed across him, riffling the feathers in his headband, almost as if she had granted him one final earthly caress. The wind carried her hollow moan far away. Silence came again. Even the distant buzz of a rattlesnake did not frighten the grieving Sioux warrior. Eagle Feather's tears flowed throughout the night, filling a dip in the rock.

☾

"Very good, Katherine," Richard Peters said. "I like your story. You've obviously done your research into the time period to flesh it out. Quite imaginative. Of course, this is just legend," he told his students. "We really don't know if an Indian woman jumped from that rock because she was distraught over her father's decision that she had to marry a white man. But it keeps us spellbound, doesn't it?"

"I have a question, Mr. Peters," Katherine said, leaning against the podium. When he nodded, she continued, "Whatever happened to her moccasins? What evidence is there to prove she lived there or to prove that the Indians came through?"

"Precious little," her teacher answered. "To my knowledge, there's not been an archaeological dig to prove or disprove their presence at Lover's Leap. It's private property. As to her moccasins, I couldn't say. They were probably placed on her feet when she died and deteriorated as her body did. The evidence for this legend, like most of them, I'm afraid, is mostly hearsay. Oral histories. Stories passed down from one generation to the next. And in this case, we are relying, quite frankly, on the memories of the white settlers who lived in this area rather than upon any Indian stories. So we don't know their side of the events that may have taken place."

Katherine sat down. Another student rose to tell his version of how the Great Bluff became Lover's Leap. Katherine stared out the window. Lover's Leap was only two miles away, but the rolling landscape rose dramatically in that short space, obscuring the view. Riding the school bus from her ranch home seven miles away, Katherine passed the limestone outcropping daily. Following this assignment, its significance seemed greater to her. Apparently only the one suicide had occurred. The Indian maiden's death marked the rock as a sacred spot, if not for the Indians, most certainly for the white settlers. Katherine believed telling stories about something was a special way of cherishing. Since Lover's Leap figured prominently in the area's history—even if the whole thing was legend and not fact—the white settlers and their ancestors clearly cherished the pale limestone ledge.

Mr. Peters explained that he planned to send the students' renditions of the legend to the elderly rancher who owned the site. A week later, Mr. Peters read the rancher's invitation for the students to come climb the rock, and the field trip had been set to take place the next day. Once atop the flat top of Lover's Leap, a site that always made Katherine think of an iron laid upside down on its handle instead of its pressing side, the climbers could see what appeared to be the entire county. Miles and miles of gently rolling hills tinged with green melded into the bluish white horizon. Wind whipped their jackets against their hips and shoulders. The sheltering trees and meadows lay far below.

Elmer Higgins, the rancher who owned the property, explained that he'd never stood here on top of the bluff without the wind blowing. He said, "My family's owned this property for nearly a hundred years now. Sometimes the wind wails like a woman possessed, especially during the winter, even down yonder at my house." He motioned below and off to the left. His house and buildings could just be seen peeking out from a stand of elm trees in the meadow.

Katherine and her classmates remained quiet throughout the tour as if maintaining a respectful silence for the dead Indian woman. The other students thanked Elmer Higgins and trotted along toward the school bus, but Katherine stayed a moment longer.

"Do you think it's true, Mr. Higgins? The legend?"

He smiled at her, cocking one eyebrow in thought. "I don't know, young lady," he said. "But sure seems possible, don't it?"

Katherine took a bouquet of tulips she'd gathered from her mother's yard from inside her jacket and laid them at the base of the great limestone bluff. She stepped back from her memorial offering, rewarded by a nod from the rancher and by the cheerful trilling tune of a meadowlark. The bird's song carried across the prairie on the wind, clear and strong.

☾

AUTHOR'S NOTE

I was raised in western Nebraska in Banner County where Lover's Leap is located on private property about two miles south of Harrisburg. The legend is oft told of a Sioux Indian maiden pledged to a white man for ponies. She loved an Indian brave instead and killed herself by jumping from the bluff rather than be forced into an unwanted marriage. In this story, I hoped to flesh out the legend, which has always haunted me. The rancher who owns the property in my story is fictional.

Prairie Music

A GUST OF WIND PUSHED LAURA WHITAKER BACKWARDS. STARTLED, she drew herself up and disembarked from the train. The tails of her finest blue bonnet slapped her cheek. Daniel, grumpy from being awakened from deep sleep and chilled by the autumn air, began to cry. He struggled in her arms, pushing against her shoulder with his surprisingly strong toddler's touch.

"It's all right, son," she said, shifting Daniel's weight to her other hip. She rubbed his back and he settled against her shoulder. "We'll soon find Daddy, and all will be well."

From the platform, Laura could not see much of Laramie City. A scattering of buildings, some tents amassed near the railroad tracks. Late afternoon sunshine burnished the steel tracks and wooden crossties. The annoying wind peppered her face with grit. The scents of sweet burned coal from the train's smokestack and the sour odor of cattle manure mingled.

Laura searched the sparse crowd for Walt's face. She did not see him. Others intent on finding their loved ones or hurrying to important appointments jostled her. Daniel whimpered. She smoothed a strand of his curly blond hair. "Maybe he had to work," she said aloud, though more to comfort herself than her child.

She made her way through the group of people collecting their baggage. She heard stray bits of conversation, muffled laughter. Not knowing what else to do, she stood beside her trunk and waited. Daniel fell quiet. She watched as other families happily embraced and chattered amongst themselves. The crowd, as if encased in an invisible bubble of merriment, moved away from the platform, away from the depot, away from her.

The conductor noticed her confusion. "Ma'am, may I help you?" he asked.

She pressed her lips together. "Yes, I hope so. My husband was supposed to meet us here, but he—he was unable to come, sir." She bent down, Daniel's weight pulling her forward, and reached into her bag. She pulled out an envelope with her last letter from Walt. "He lives at this address. Perhaps you could tell me how to get there?"

She tried to keep worry from her voice. She had not considered the possibility that Walt would ignore her telegraph letter and miss their arrival.

The conductor smiled. He pointed to a brick building a couple of blocks away. "That's very near here. It's just inside that building. You could walk without difficulty—" He stopped, seeing her concern. "I see you have too much to carry. I could arrange to have your trunk delivered if you'd like."

She smiled. "Yes, thank you." She tore the address from the envelope and gave it to him. Then she reached into her bag again and found some extra coins for his effort. He graciously declined. Laura disliked leaving her precious belongings in the care of a stranger but she was forced to trust him.

She descended the steps from the platform and walked toward the building. The streets were dusty. She couldn't hold up her skirt while carrying Daniel. She put him down. He could walk for a ways on his own. Her dress felt sweaty where the toddler had cuddled her. The wind blew dirt into her eyes. She blinked and tasted bitter dust. Had it been considered ladylike to spit, she would have done so.

She dreaded what foul things the wind teased into the air. This town was not at all as she had envisioned it. Not at all as Walt had led her to believe. His insistence on the delight of the wide-open spaces and the freedom and fortune they would find in the west had brought her here to join him. Instead of the beautiful homes and grassy knolls and trees she had expected, the streets here were practically barren. The town gave the appearance of having been rapidly slapped together. Livestock roamed the streets as if they lived there rather than in pens. Hogs squealed and cattle lowed as she passed. She saw few people, but numerous wagons and horses filled the streets. Her uneasiness grew as they reached the building. Where was Walt? Why hadn't he come to meet them?

Daniel, enchanted by the mules driving a passing wagon, pulled free of her grasp and ran into the street. She ran to follow him. "Daniel! No!" But her little boy ran into the middle of the street, mindless of the wagons and livestock posing life-threatening danger to him. A wagon, wheels creaking and horses whinnying, sped toward him from the other direction.

A man darted out from behind them, passing Laura. He pushed Daniel. The wagon passed between Laura and her son. She closed her eyes. The wagon driver cursed. "That kid coulda upset the whole she-bang!" His words carried to Laura. She opened her eyes in time to see him round a corner.

Daniel sat happily in the arms of the man who had dashed to his rescue. To Laura's consternation, Daniel giggled. Forgetting a street separated them, she scolded, "Daniel Whitaker! Don't you ever do that again!"

Carrying Daniel, the man crossed to her. "Ah, the little one's all right, Ma'am. Gave us a fright though." He returned her son. He took off his woolen cap and held out his hand. "My name's True Malone." He was tall and slender and wore a plain blue wool shirt and black trousers held in place by suspenders. The wind tousled his straight blond hair. His round eyeglasses accentuated the roundness of his blue eyes. They almost matched the shade of Laura's blue traveling dress.

Laura extended her own hand. "Laura Whitaker. And you've met Daniel."

"My pleasure."

"We are indebted to you now, sir."

True smiled. "No, no. No repayment necessary. Better keep an eye on him. This place is hard on youngsters." He looked at her. "Begging your pardon, but you look weary."

Daniel's near-death escapade had loosened Laura's reserve. She spoke more freely than she might otherwise have done. "We've come from Omaha on the train."

He nodded. His gaze intensified. "Are you waiting for someone?"

"Yes. We're waiting for my husband, Walt Whitaker. We were going to the boardinghouse when Daniel had his mishap. The conductor is bringing my trunk."

He frowned, looked down at his boots, and rubbed his stubbly jaw with his hand. He didn't speak right away. "Did Walt know you were coming?"

"Yes. I sent word. What is it, Mr. Malone?" Laura asked. Something in his tone unnerved her. Since she and Walt had been separated these past six months by hundreds of miles of land and Walt's dreams of success and opportunity, she had worried. Perhaps he'd found being on his own to his liking. Worse yet, perhaps he'd found another woman to share his new life.

True replaced his cap. "Might I accompany you to the boarding-house?" he said. "I was on my way there myself." He motioned her toward the building.

Once inside, events blurred for Laura. True introduced her to Georgia Drake, who operated the boardinghouse. A kindly appearing elderly woman, her face contorted when True said Laura's name.

"Oh, my dear. I am so sorry. Please won't you sit down and make yourself comfortable." She fluttered around Laura and Daniel like a lone bumblebee worrying the last blossom of alfalfa. She brought hot tea for Laura and cookies and milk for Daniel. Georgia wrung her hands in an embroidered towel. She looked at True and shook her head. "I'll go get the minister."

True sat down at the dining table opposite Laura. Daniel gobbled cookies as if he hadn't been fed for days. "Daniel," Laura whispered.

"Mind your manners." To True, she said, "Why did Mrs. Drake need to find a minister?"

True began to speak but could not. He cleared his throat. "I'm sorry. I'm sorry to have to be the one to tell you. Walt's dead. He was killed in an accident yesterday."

Laura blinked her eyes. She peered with disbelief at True.

"I did not receive a telegram," she said, realizing as soon as she spoke that she could not have received the news. She and Daniel would already have been traveling. Her aunt, with whom they had stayed while Walt came west, probably sent one to the Laramie station when she received the news. But Laura had only just arrived.

True said quietly, "Ma'am, there wasn't time for a telegram."

Laura took a deep breath. "What happened to Walt?" She didn't cry. She felt stunned by the unbelievable news, and half unwilling to take this stranger's word at face value. But Mrs. Drake had sought the minister. Two people wouldn't dream up such a morbid story.

True wiped imaginary crumbs from Mrs. Drake's lacy tablecloth. When he looked up again, he did not turn his gaze to Laura. He watched a far off place instead. He said, "He slipped and fell beneath a rail car. Several of us were there. There was nothing—we couldn't help him."

Surprising herself, Laura did not cry. She said, "I'm sure you did your best." Her words were spoken so softly True strained to hear them. She had surprised him by not bursting into tears or going into hysterics.

"Mrs. Whitaker, I worked with your husband. He was a good man. I'm sorry for your loss." He cleared his throat again. "We've lost many good men in similar accidents. They live on in the trains heading west. At least, that's my belief."

"Thank you, Mr. Malone, you've been quite kind to us."

"Please call me True."

"Then you must address me as Laura."

Mrs. Drake came in with the minister then. True and Mrs. Drake departed and the minister, a short, round man with a fringe of white hair, took Laura's hand. After they prayed together, they worked out arrangements for Walt's burial.

❨

Mrs. Drake brought a light supper of roast beef and potatoes to Laura and Daniel after she'd gotten them settled in Walt's room. She had removed his things after the accident and told Laura she could have them whenever she was ready. Then she left them alone.

Daniel, filled with cookies, had napped earlier. His ravenous appetite was unaffected by their circumstances. Laura took a few bites of the food but could not eat. She felt tired but could not rest. The conductor had brought her trunk but she didn't feel like unpacking it.

She carried only enough money to bring them here. She longed for Walt and at the same time felt angry with him. She could not afford to return to Omaha. She was not sure she could afford a proper burial but she must try. She could not return to Aunt Emma's. Pride prevented her from asking Aunt Emma for funds to return home. Laura's thoughts rolled in her head like the tumbleweeds she'd seen scattering across the prairie.

The wind had not calmed since their arrival. The window pane rattled against its frame. A chilly draft wafted from the sill. Laura walked across the room to secure the window to no avail. Lacy curtains did not improve the view. Laura saw only the railroad tracks that had led to Walt's destruction. She stood there for a long while, though she did not know how long.

Daniel tugged at her skirt. "Hear, Mama?"

"What, son?"

"Hear?"

"It's only the wind. Don't be afraid."

Frustrated, Daniel shook his head. "Hear?"

She didn't know what her son was asking her. He cocked his head. His eyes drifted toward the door. Laura listened. Muted fiddle music carried from the parlor downstairs.

"Oh, yes, Daniel. Isn't that lovely?"

Daniel wanted to go see. Laura objected several times but finally agreed. She picked him up, straightened her dress, and took him down to the party. She half believed she might find Walt there. She scanned the seated strangers, hoping to see her husband smiling, brown eyes sparkling, and tapping his feet, but to no avail. She bit her lip. Walt was not here.

True's eyes lighted when they entered the parlor. He had changed into clean clothes, neatly pressed, though he still wore a shirt and trousers with suspenders. His hair was slicked down with oil. He was playing "Jim Crack Corn." He appeared to be part of his fiddle. He tapped his foot and bent and swayed to the rhythm of the music. Laura held Daniel and stood in the doorway until he finished the song. They entered and sat down in empty chairs across from Mrs. Drake, who smiled and looked away. Several other people applauded True. Laura guessed that they were regular boarders. Some might have come here to wait for the next train.

When the applause quieted, no one spoke. There was no need for introductions, Laura knew. She felt certain that the boarders knew her as the woman who hadn't even known of her husband's demise. She suddenly felt uncomfortable. Perhaps it was unseemly for a woman in mourning to sit among those finding pleasure. Most women would have been shedding tears by the bucketful, not seeking company. She had not cried. She would not cry in front of strangers. Laura realized she should have worn her black dress. She sighed. She had not the strength nor the desire to change her attire.

True said, "And here's a tune some of you might know." He had a deep voice. Deeper than that of any man she'd heard before. His voice sounded strong and soothed her, much like leaning against the trunk of a sturdy cottonwood tree on a river bank made her feel safe. Again he made the room a happy place, playing "O Susanna." The lilting music lifted. The stale air of the parlor smelled of roasted meat and cigar smoke. Daniel snuggled close to her and shyly looked at the fiddler. Some of the boarders sang.

Laura was exhausted but the warmth of the parlor—mimicking a family with its circle of strangers gathered together by the music—comforted her. She closed her eyes. She could almost imagine Aunt Emma's parlor filled with cousins and friends. Walt would be there. Even the thought of his name stung her heart, but she was too tired to weep. She rubbed Daniel's back and concentrated on the fiddle music. True introduced another favorite, "My Old Kentucky Home," explaining that he was from Kentucky.

A fiddle string broke. The eerie twang startled Laura. She jumped.

"Oh!" She said. Daniel, held in her arms and jostled awake by her quick movement, began to cry.

"Oh, I am so sorry. Please continue your beautiful music. We'd best say good night."

Mrs. Drake said, "It's all right, dear. Grief affects us all in different ways." She stood also. "Might I come help you with the baby?"

But Laura, aware of the stares of the boarders and of True's eyes upon her as well, declined. "We'll be fine, thank you." She rushed from the parlor. True followed and stopped her in the corridor. He handed her the fiddle string. "Take it," he said, placing it in her hand. "Let it bring you happy memories."

Back in their spartan room, when Daniel finally slept, Laura realized why Mrs. Drake used the word *grief*. Laura was a grieving widow. The words hit her as if they were a physical blow. She held the corner of the dressing table so that she would not fall to the floor in a heap.

In her heart, she was still married to Walt. She would remain true to her wedding vows forever, for that is what she had promised before God. As was her custom at the end of the day, she washed her face. But she did not look at her face in the mirror. She always did so, to see the cheerful features of a happy wife. Tonight, she held a towel to her face to pat it dry. She did not want to see the face of a widow looking back at her.

❨

She spent a restless night. Sleep would not come. And neither, to her amazement, had tears. It was almost as if, having not seen Walt for so long, she must only wait a few days longer.

Daniel slept well and awoke with plenty of steam to see him through the day. They were ready well before Reverend Martin arrived in his wagon to drive them to the cemetery. Laura had donned her black dress and

dressed Daniel in his finest Sunday clothes. They had eaten a light breakfast. Mrs. Drake fussed over them as she had the day before. Laura wondered if Mrs. Drake had adjusted the dining schedule of her other guests
to accommodate them. She offered to keep Daniel with her while Laura
went to the cemetery. Laura accepted gratefully. Daniel did not understand what was happening. After his near accident yesterday, Laura feared
another such occurrence while she was preoccupied with Walt's service.

True met them in the dining room. "If it is all right with you,
Laura, I'd like to play a tune for Walt." He wore the same clothes he'd
worn the previous evening.

Touched by the gesture, she could only nod. True rode with them
in Reverend Martin's buggy. The cemetery stood on a hill east of town.
A few scraggly cottonwood trees rimmed the graveyard.

A mound of dirt covered Walt's body. A wooden cross with his
name and the date of his death, October 13, 1868, carved on the horizontal piece stood at the head of his grave. Laura did not cry. She vowed
she would purchase him a proper headstone, but she did not know how
she could earn the money. She hadn't enough to pay for her and Daniel's
room and board.

"I do so wish this wind would stop," she said, unaware she had
spoken aloud.

Reverend Martin smiled kindly. "I'm afraid the wind is a part of
Laramie City, Mrs. Whitaker."

"I do not know how people stand it. Does it blow so every day?"

True placed his fiddle beneath his chin and readied his bow. "The
wind plays a different tune every day," he said. "You'll grow to like it if
you listen." They stood silent for a moment. The wind stirred a pile of
leather-colored leaves against a tall marble monument. "It's prairie music."

"It sounds more like a roar to me."

True closed his eyes. "Today the wind sounds sad, Laura. Blowing
a sad song. Surely is and rightly so."

Reverend Martin cleared his throat. "We should begin."

Laura heard the minister's voice, but she didn't hear the words. She
longed for the comfort they could give, but she could not concentrate.

Her husband, dead. Herself, his widow. Those words made no sense to her jumbled mind. She forced herself to stand against the wind, to mouth the words of the Lord's Prayer when Reverend Martin intoned them.

The melancholy sound of the fiddle lifted and fell in accompaniment with the breeze. True played "Amazing Grace." The hymn faded and the moaning wind filled Laura's ears again.

"How sweet the sound," True said, lowering his fiddle and bow.

She stood at the foot of her husband's newly made grave. She did not cry.

☾

Though she had not thought it possible she would survive even the first day without Walt, she managed for three weeks. She ached to hold him in her arms. At the same time she felt angry with him. She marveled at the way he had tempted her with his words of new opportunity in Laramie City. And living here, she had discovered that he lived in a boardinghouse next door to a brothel. Mrs. Drake sometimes fed the prostitutes, although she did so in her kitchen and never in the dining room where guests might see and take offense. Had Walt been tempted by their wiles? Laura could not bear the thought but with loose women so near and loneliness most certainly a factor, she could not deny the possibility.

Laura had managed through the unfailing kindness of Mrs. Drake and Reverend Martin. She had managed because she had to support herself and Daniel. She had managed because she had to purchase a headstone for Walt. She had managed because she had to earn their return fare to Omaha. She had managed because she had no other choice.

Mrs. Drake allowed her to cook to pay her room and board. Her specialty, baking powder biscuits, brought not only the prostitutes to the door early in the morning but many of the railroaders as well. Mrs. Drake paid her extra when they sold biscuits to the working men. Laura still searched their ranks for Walt's tall, husky body. She couldn't stop herself from looking for his mustachioed face and unruly blond hair.

On this morning, Amybelle, one of the fallen women, came downstairs and helped herself to a fresh biscuit. She slathered butter and Mrs. Drake's chokecherry jelly on it. Amybelle possessed little modesty. Her wrapper gaped open, exposing one plump breast.

"Amybelle," Laura said. "Would you please take care to cover yourself in front of my son?"

Amybelle laughed. She took a bite of biscuit, ignoring Laura's plea. Then she reached over and tweaked Daniel's cheek. "Ah, this one's a looker. He'll be learning it soon enough."

Laura stopped what she was doing, and with floury hands, gave Daniel a biscuit and sat him on a stool near the counter where she worked. He was soon busy with his food and paid no attention to Amybelle. She sniggered. In a sharp tone, she said, "You'll come down from your high horse one of these days soon, Missy. What would you do without the likes of us watching out for him while you're cooking?"

Laura had no retort. She pulled herself up and stood even taller. She could not escape the thought of Walt sitting in Daniel's chair instead of their son. She believed he'd been faithful to their vows as she had. Still, could a man resist such blatant offerings? Laura had no answer. She returned to mixing another batch, trying to turn her mind to thoughts of the day when she earned enough to purchase their train fare. She would pay their debts and leave this barbaric place behind forever.

Amybelle cursed the wind. Laura did not scold her for cursing in front of Daniel because she knew it would have done no good. Instead, she said, "I hate it."

Amybelle munched her biscuit thoughtfully. "I've heard some women have gone crazy because of the wind."

"I would not doubt it," Laura said. "The incessant howling is enough to torture anyone."

Amybelle laughed, a rough sound, like sandpaper against wood. "You'll either learn to like it or. . . ." Her voice trailed away. She finished her biscuit, drew her wrapper tight, and left Laura and Daniel in the kitchen alone.

❨

True visited them every day. His fiddle tunes delighted boarders nearly every evening when he came from work. He worked for the Union Pacific, Walt's employer. Laura looked forward to his visits. Sometimes he spoke with them in the kitchen at breakfast time before he left for work. Sometimes Laura sat with him when he ate a late supper. On those evenings, she cleaned the kitchen while Mrs. Drake watched Daniel in her room.

"You look tired, True," she said, on the evening of her exchange with Amybelle in the kitchen. "Hard day?"

He took a deep breath and sighed. "Feels like the harder we work the further behind we are," he said.

"I'll bring you supper in the dining room. Go sit and rest. I'll bring it right away."

But True declined. He pulled out a chair at the kitchen table and sat there instead. "It's less trouble for you if I sit here."

"But I'll disturb you with my cleaning."

True smiled. "No. You won't."

She filled a bowl with beef stew that simmered on the coal stove. She placed it before him, along with a plate of biscuits. "I kept them warm on the stove."

"Thank you," he said.

She wiped her hands on the muslin apron she wore to protect her calico dress, poured herself a cup of tea, and sat across from him.

"I've never thanked you, True," she said.

"No need," he said, closing his eyes as he tasted the stew. "Mmm. Laura, Mrs. Drake's mighty lucky to have you cooking for her."

"I'm the lucky one. And it's because of your intervention on my behalf."

True shook his head. "It's because of your cooking skills." He devoured two bowls of stew and several biscuits. They talked of happenings in town as they often did. But they didn't talk of the day when Laura and Daniel would return to Omaha, nor did they discuss the day when True would move on west with the railroad. There was still work to be done near Laramie City, and True's job would last as long as the work. Then he'd follow the tracks to a new destination.

"If it snows, we'll stay longer. But even those who live here say this has been an odd fall with so little snow. When it comes, they say, it'll stay 'til May," True told her once. They'd not talked of it since.

Laura learned from Mrs. Drake that True earned his room and board by fiddling for her customers. Otherwise, he would have lived in one of the scattered canvas tents that stood on the edge of town.

She waited until he had finished, then she took his bowl. She replaced it with an apple cobbler.

"I'd best get busy," she said, facing her evening's chores. She stood next to the stove, turned sideways to True. She shivered. "Oh, even standing by the stove, I feel the wind. Amybelle says it drives women insane."

True finished a bite of cobbler. "Don't listen to her, Laura."

"I wish it would cease its horrible howling."

True finished his cobbler and came to stand beside her. He placed his dirty dish on the counter next to her. "Amybelle doesn't know what to listen for," he said softly. The timbre of his voice made Laura's skin tingle. "Listen for the music, Laura. If you listen for the music, you'll find you can stand it."

She turned to face him. His round eyes were kind. "You might even begin to hear your favorite tunes, and if you do, you can hum them. They'll become a part of you."

"That's kind advice," she said. Haggard as he was from his tiring day of work, Laura thought him handsome. She wondered why he had never married but dared not ask.

Their eyes met. Neither turned from the other's gaze. Save for the continual keening of the wind, the soft sizzle of coal burning in the stove and the bubbling of the stew were the only sounds in the kitchen.

True reached out and touched her pale skin. "You're beautiful, Laura." A strand of russet hair—very nearly the color of the wood of his fiddle—had fallen loose from the roll curving above her neck and dangled at her cheek. She dared not admit how calming and soothing his touch felt. Nor did she dare explore further the tingling excitement she experienced at his touch. He moved forward and kissed her.

She had longed for a man's touch, for a man's kiss. The softness of his lips and his gentleness both delighted and terrified her. She reached up and placed her hand on his. When they broke apart, she moved his hand away. Laura held True's hand suspended in midair for the eternity of a heartbeat and looked into his eyes. Neither spoke. Time halted for an instant. She pulled his hand down to their sides. He held her hand and would not let go.

Quietly, Laura asked, "Why have you been so kind to us?"

"You needed help."

"But you stood to gain nothing from us, True."

He tilted his head. "Oh, I wouldn't say that. I've gained much. The delight of seeing your eyes sparkle when you forget your sadness for the briefest instant. The wonder in your son's eyes when he listens to my fiddle tunes."

"You've been paying us more than customary attention."

"I am grateful for your friendship."

She turned away. He resisted the urge to stroke her slender neck. He let go of her hand. "I dislike being indebted to anyone," she said. "And we are indebted to you for so many things. For helping us get settled when we arrived, for burying Walt, and for helping me find respectable work so that I may pay those whom I owe."

She reached to her throat, slim fingers curling around her grandmother's cameo pin. "I hope you didn't believe that I might pay you back in the ways of love." She trembled. They stood alone in the kitchen. What was to stop him from taking her right here and now if he so desired? No one would disturb them.

She turned her eyes to him again. "I cannot," she whispered the words. Laura believed that once a woman married, she was married for life. In her mind, she would forever be Mrs. Walt Whitaker.

His face crumpled, as if she had struck him physically. "I would hope that you would hold me in higher esteem than that, Laura." He lingered for a moment longer. She looked away. True left her standing there all alone.

☾

Amybelle brought news of the accident the next afternoon. Several men had been injured when two rail cars collided. One man had been killed, but she didn't know who. She whisked Laura away from the stove and soon Mrs. Drake and Daniel followed. Amybelle said, "They always bring the bodies along this street."

The wind took Laura's breath away.

Daniel tugged at her skirts. "Blow, Mama. Blows."

She picked him up, letting the wind strike their faces. "It's playing music, Daniel. That's prairie music. Can you hear it?" The wind played a woeful tune on this day. The sound made Laura uneasy. Her stomach knotted. She recalled True's words and listened. She could not hear a consoling tune.

She planned to explain her feelings to True in the evening. She had slept badly, knowing he misunderstood her words in the kitchen. She valued his friendship but it was too soon for her to seek the company of another, if she would ever find that possible.

The grass rustled and a whirlwind of dust swirled leaves across the street. She smelled smoke on the breeze. A dry, ragged cottonwood leaf fell by her feet. A wagon appeared at the end of the street. Laura did not need Amybelle to tell her who had been killed. Her heart pounded in her chest. She hoped her intuition was wrong. The buckboard driver saw them standing there. He shook his head as he approached. "No music today," he said.

"True's music?" Daniel asked, making the word sound like "moose kick."

Laura bit her lip and nodded.

"True's music," she answered, as the horses' hooves tapped against the ground and the wagon carrying his body rolled past.

☾

The moon was still visible in the western sky. A trio of stars lingered near it. Though the moon gave little light, the harsh blue of November's dawn broke the horizon. Laura held the broken fiddle string True had given her that first night when it snapped and slithered across his instrument like a snake. She walked to the cemetery. She'd learned the way here after that one visit. She had not had the heart to attend True's service. Three days had passed before she'd gathered the courage.

The wind howled behind her. She made several missteps as it pushed her awkwardly forward. The wind had raged all night long. She was certain it would continue to blow even after the sun rose. She knelt first at Walt's grave. She recited Psalm 121: "I will lift up mine eyes unto the hills. . . ." Though she wanted to, she refrained from throwing herself prone across the mounded sod. Walt couldn't reach for her through the soil, no matter how she wished it could be so. She pushed a stray strand of hair behind her ear. Her sunbonnet had long since fallen to her back. The knot of its strings tugged at her throat.

Placing her free hand on the grave, she whispered, "For Daniel, I will manage somehow. I don't know how, but I will do it. I must. And I will make sure he remembers you." Finally, her grief released itself in her tears. She bit her lip and tasted the salty drops.

She stood, allowing the wind to buffet her face and blow through her hair. She lifted her chin to its bluster. She stepped across six other graves and stood silently above the plot that held the body of True Malone. She knelt there, placing the broken fiddle string at the base of the wooden cross, knotting it around the cross and pushing it into to ground so that it would stay. She remained there for long moments.

The sun rose at her back. The wind stole its warmth, whirling around her and whistling through the tree branches and across the graves. She closed her eyes. Listening, she heard True's precious fiddle tunes. She trembled. She heard clearly the notes of "My Old Kentucky Home," the tune he loved because he hailed from Kentucky.

"True," she said, when the wind died down a bit. The music she heard faded with it. She smiled halfheartedly. "I didn't even know your given name was Ephraim until. . . ." Her voice creaked in her throat like the steel wheels of trains beginning to spin on railroad tracks. "Amybelle told me. She told me you'd been true to your wife's memory for ten years." Laura wiped the freezing tears from her cheeks. "That's why they called you True." She didn't say aloud the rest of what Amybelle had said, "True's been faithful to his dead wife all the time he's been here. Exceptin' you maybe."

Laura closed her eyes against the painful memory. "I brought back your fiddle string. It belongs to you." She turned away. Her face stung. She took a deep breath. "I must do what I came here to do," she said to the sky. "They said no one sang at your funeral. The only sound was the wind. You believed that wind was prairie music, I know. But it just didn't seem proper. A talented musician like you should not have been laid to rest without human music, too." She blinked tears from her eyes. "I am going to do today what I should have done at your funeral. I don't know all the words to your Kentucky song, but I'll sing you what I can."

In a hushed voice she sang, "The sun shines bright in the old Kentucky home." When her voice failed on a few of the words, her heart guided her on. She hummed most of the verse, but sang the chorus. "Weep no more, my lady, O weep no more today! We will sing one song for the old Kentucky home, for the old Kentucky home far away."*

Tears coursed down her cheeks. "I'll never forget you, True," she whispered. She clung to the horizontal bar of the cross marking his grave, the wind whipping her cheeks raw. She wept for what had been and what might have been and for what would never be.

As the sun lifted above the mountains, she stood and turned her back to the wind. She accepted its presence. She would not curse its existence again.

---

*The Gray Book of Favorite Songs, Hall & McCreary Company.

River Watch

THE WIDOW WALKED INTO THE RIVER IN WINTER, KNOWING NOT THAT such a deed had been performed before. She stood for a moment on the shore of the deceptively placid North Platte on a still December evening, emotions roiling inside her as the icy water flowed past, at once beckoning and repelling. She knew not that a century before she took these fated footsteps another had broken the trail. She shook her head, letting fall a curtain of auburn hair, releasing it from its fancy braid, the likes of which I might have tried with my own locks had I taken a notion.

She stands, contemplating her fate, unaware of my presence. She considered all that had been and all that might yet come to be, as I myself had once done. I wanted to scream at her. I wanted to warn her of the numbing frigid river, to push her back as sudden gusts of wind might force her to retreat. But such behavior is not my place.

Instead, I turn to my own memories, see myself in her image on the snow-quilted bank. As she moves forward, I turn back. Emmett Stoner, my dear beloved Emmett, stands alone near the saloon door. He pushes open the intricately carved wooden half-doors. They creak, swinging back and forth like a broken metronome. The bartender has not yet seen fit to oil their hinges.

"I'll kill the man who did this," Emmett says. His voice, just a notch above a whisper, vibrates with terse anger. "She deserved better."

The happy hum of the saloon-goers faded into cold silence. Emmett brushed a stray lock of thick black hair from his forehead. I had once thought it an endearing gesture, but that day after Christmas 1895 in the saloon it looked ominous.

"Ah, Emmett," the bartender said, smiling, imparting a jovial tone into his words. "Come, sit and have a drink with us. I'll pour your favorite whisky."

But Emmett shook his head. "I'll not drink again with such ruffians."

"Come, come now. Your mind is a-grieving, friend. Twas indeed a tragedy." Already the bartender was filling a glass with amber liquid. "Was of no fault but the girl's own."

Emmett's eyes narrowed. "You're wrong, Duff. Someone drove her to it. And when I find out who, that man's dead."

Duff moved the drink forward. "Here you are. Sip it up, now. You can't go on living in the past, Emmett."

Emmett took the drink, downed it in a lengthy swallow. He licked his lips. "I must, Duff," he said. "There is no future now."

☾

Tears sting my already frozen cheeks. Emmett was my best friend. He told no one my secret, but held it in his heart like a living thing that needed nurturing and tender care. To watch him destroy himself on my account is almost too much for me to bear. A chill breeze beats waves into the darkness of the Platte's blue waters. The widow steps forward, stops. She teeters on the edge.

Indecision is a mighty coward. Her life has, to this moment, overflowed with the fulfillment of the wishes of others—children, grandchildren, and husband, who, until his recent sudden heart seizure, lay invalid for three years in their marriage bed. Her life has been much different from my own. Mine had not yet begun to blossom except for the dangerous love I felt for Amos Abernathy. In that, I was decisive. How very clear to me was the fact that we would share our lives together, that I would bear his children, and tell stories to our grandchildren in my old age like this widow walker has done. But my indecision on other matters sped me to my destiny.

I expected to burn in hell for that single night of shared desire. Instead, this icy river burned me, cauterized my very soul and catapulted me here. I live in a state in between the certain magnificence of heaven and the sure horridness of hell, but damned just the same. I chose. My decision overstepped the invisible boundary line and violated universal law.

On that sweet September night so long ago, I chose life. I chose to be with Amos Abernathy, to walk beneath the canopy of the cotton-woods, and dared to speak of love. Amos was tall, slender, with sun-blond hair and sky blue eyes and a thick mustache hiding his upper lip. He had come to Saratoga (he said) daring to risk all his money on a dream. A freighter, Amos dreamed of making his fortune by staking gold claims in the mountains.

"It will work, Lucy, I know it will," he told me, squeezing my hand as we traversed the bumpy knolls along the river.

"I've not heard of gold mines in these parts before," I replied.

Amos turned and rewarded my remark with a brilliant smile. "Exactly! That is the very reason that my idea will work. I'll be the first to find gold here. Let all those gold-diggers continue to starve in South Pass. Since sixty-eight they've looked, and they've been fools. I'm staking my claim here and now in the mountains near Saratoga."

"I can see that this idea excites you," I said, thrilled by his exuberance. "But perhaps a little restraint will save you money in the long run?"

Amos shook his head. "Ah, Lucy. A minister's daughter to the core. Have you no sense of adventure?"

We stopped to lean against a sturdy cottonwood as the sun set, blazing an even deeper golden hue into the autumn-changed leaves. Amos reached down for a blade of green grass. Chewing it, he looked askance at me. "Perhaps your father would be interested. He could be my first investor." Amos paused for a moment as I thought about this. "Those who jump in at the beginning reap greater benefits at the end," he said.

I watched the sun set, reveling in the array of colors—several shades of mauve and peach. "No, Amos. My father would not agree. To him, this investment idea would sound greedy."

"I suppose, then, I am lucky that he allowed me to visit with his beautiful daughter."

I did not answer. My father did not know my whereabouts that evening. After supper dishes were washed and put away, I snuck out of the house, leaving him to watch over my younger brother and sister.

I had met Amos just a few days before. I hurried along Bridge Street, anxious to attend the meeting of the literary club. We met weekly in the ladies' parlor of Frederick Wolf's elegant hotel. Mrs. Wolf, hostess extraordinaire, baked delicious pastries for us to enjoy as we discussed new books and sipped hot tea in her sumptuous second-story room.

In my haste, I dropped my copy of *The Adventures of Sherlock Holmes*. As I bent to retrieve it, a suntanned hand reached down and picked it up for me.

He took off his hat, holding it to his chest as he read the cover. "Sounds fascinating," he remarked, handing the fortunately undamaged book to me.

"Yes, thank you, sir," I replied.

"Miss, I find it always a pleasure to help a young lady in need. My name is Amos Abernathy. If I may ever be of further assistance, I would hope you would allow me to do so."

His formality struck me as quite sincere, so I said, "Thank you, Mr. Abernathy. My name is Lucy Willoughby, and I am pleased to make your acquaintance."

Then I picked up my skirts, hurrying forward so as to not be late to the book discussion. But I turned back for just a moment. And in that moment, Amos had turned back as well, looking at me intently with his blue eyes. Heat sparked in my body. I felt my cheeks grow hot. "Goodbye, sir," I said.

Amos again tipped his hat. We met again at the piano recital given by my young students that Saturday. Inside the church, where my father had allowed this exhibition of musical excellence to take place, Amos was quite the gentleman. But my father whispered, "Lucy, I do not like that young man. I believe he is quite smitten with you. You must watch your step."

I nodded, but secretly found Amos wondrously attractive. When he found a private moment with me, after the students and their parents had gone and my father had retreated into the sacristy to prepare for church the next morning, he asked me to come for an evening walk.

"The North Platte is beautiful at sunset, Lucy," he said. "I'll wait for you to join me this evening, then." With a smile and a flourish, he stepped from the church into the brightness of the afternoon. I stacked the remaining sheets of music I had been sorting, my heart filled with excitement.

"Lucy?"

His voice startled me from my memories. I looked up into his face, and swiftly, he caught my chin with his forefinger and thumb and stole a kiss. My body melted against the rough bark of the cottonwood as the river swallowed the final flames of the sun.

☾

I watch the widow. She takes a deep breath of wintry air. She steps back—one step, then two. She watches the river. She begins to pace—two steps left, three steps right. Back and forth, back and forth, her movements mimic the subtle swiftness of the undercurrent tugging at my ankles.

She turns toward me, seeing only her own life. I see she has painted her face, wearing what must be her favorite shade of lipstick and rouge. I reach up and feel Grandmother's pin holding my own hair securely in place. I selected it for wear on special occasions with my burgundy brocade dress. I wanted to look pretty, as the widow surely does, though she wears men's trousers and a coat that also appears to have belonged to a man.

I run my fingers through the icy water. Their sudden sting reminds me of another jacket, similar in color, that Amos wore the September evening we stood beneath the gnarled cottonwood. He removed his dark jacket in one smooth stroke, placing it on the ground.

"Please sit down, dear," he said, patting the fabric as he himself sat on the grass.

"Thank you," I said, still trembling with delight from the touch of his soft lips against my own. Again he reached for me and again I complied.

We consummated our love right here beside this very river in the cool evening air as the stars began blooming in a lavender sky. *Consummated.* A good word—for the flames of desire consumed us with greed. I had thought—wrongly—that such a tender man would love not just my flesh but my mind, too.

The water carries a broken twig past me. I look up and see the widow wading into the water. As it caresses her ankles, she stops, wincing. I watch, remembering the feel of Amos's hands caressing my body, delighting my skin with touch in places no man had seen before.

Full moonlight shone that night, and I feared discovery. But Amos reassured me that no one would see, as we were shadowed by the tall figure of the tree. The whisper of leaves above reinforced his words. As he held me, I gazed up into their delicate growth, imagining black lace like mourners wore.

"Sweet, sweet Lucy," my lover murmured between kisses. He placed a warm hand against my cheek. I shivered beneath him, partly from the thrill of the deed and partly from the chilling air. He hugged me to him, warming my flesh and sending my spirit soaring.

"Tomorrow, under this very cottonwood, my love," he whispered in my ear. "We'll meet again. But for now I must depart."

Quickly then, he dressed himself and helped me on with my dress. And I sat beneath the cottonwood for a few moments watching him walk away toward his dreams of striking the mother lode. I followed, my heart filled with dreams of a rather different nature.

The widow braces herself. She takes three more steps into the deepness of the water. I feel gooseflesh rise on my arms. The price that love exacted of me was too high to bear. The widow feels the same. I see it in her weary eyes and in the resolute set of her delicate chin.

The crescent moon barely lights this dark, oily river. Starlight is obscured by scudding clouds. The widow waited until the darkness would hide her. She chose a spot near the island where her husband fly-fished for years.

Her place is not so far from the cottonwood looming over me. I feel her temptation. She yearns for the cold water to envelop her and carry her to oblivion where one feels no pain and does not need to think.

Amos did not return the next evening near sunset, nor the next. I worried that some terrible accident had befallen him, but I dared not show my curiosity. As September melded into October, the price of my desire grew in my belly. Amos's child took over my body. By Thanksgiving, I found myself letting out my shirtwaists and adding hidden strips of cloth to the waistbands of my skirts. My father could never know of my incredible sin.

And it was then that Emmett Stoner earned my undying affection. He began to court me, sweetly, that fall. Unlike Amos, Emmett was dark haired and clean-shaven with dark brown eyes. His kindnesses over-whelmed me. A simple squeeze of his hand after I played particularly well for church. A single sprig of sage plucked from the plants growing on his ranch.

"I will become known as one of the cattle barons, Lucy," Emmett confessed one evening as we sat sipping tea on my father's medallion-back sofa. "I know that I can make my cattle ranch profitable and comfortable."

I sipped tea from the rose-covered porcelain my mother had received from her mother as a wedding gift, just months before my birth and her death. The china trembled slightly in my hand, making a musical sound against its companion saucer. "Many such ranchers have had sim-ilar dreams, Emmett. What makes you think you will succeed where others have failed?"

"A genuine love of the land, a fondness for the animals themselves, and a healthy portion of dogged determination," he replied. We laughed.

I set my tea cup and saucer on the table. Silence descended upon us.

I looked at Emmett and found him looking at me. Shy, he blushed furiously and looked away.

"Emmett, what's the matter?" Emmett had been my friend since we had moved to Saratoga five years before. We had both been just coming into our teens at that time. My father had encouraged Emmett, who had a strong tenor voice, to sing in church. As a result, Emmett and I had spent countless hours together rehearsing hymns and sometimes playing secular tunes like "Buffalo Gals" and "Oh, Susanna" when we thought no one was listening. "Have I embarrassed you?"

Emmett shook his head. A lock of black hair fell across his forehead, making him look like the young boy he had been when we first met. He swept the hair back into place. "Lucy, you could never embarrass me."

"I'm glad," I said, and turned the talk to Sunday's hymns and the upcoming Christmas celebration.

"My home is almost complete at the ranch," Emmett blurted.

"Oh, how wonderful, Emmett." I replied, puzzled at his sudden change of subject. "I would love to see it one day."

"I would hope you would see it every day," he said.

I looked at him for a long moment. He cleared his throat. "What I am trying to say, Lucy, is that I would like for you to live there."

I did not know what to say, for his words unnerved me. He was not asking for my hand in marriage. I placed my hand on my stomach. Holding my secret close to me, I waited. Was it possible he knew of my indiscretion with Amos?

The silence lingered.

Emmett's face reddened again. "As my wife, Lucy."

I let the words fall into the quietness. I stood up and walked to the window.

"Oh, Emmett," I whispered, for I knew my next words would hurt him. In speaking, I felt my own heart ache. "I cannot."

He had come to stand beside me. He placed a gentle hand on my shoulder and turned me to face him. "I care for you deeply, Lucy. I would take good care of you, provide a good home for you and our children."

I nodded. "I know."

"We could marry on New Year's Day. Begin the new year with love and laughter and happiness."

I felt tears sting my eyes. Emmett wiped away the single stinging tear that rolled down my cheek.

"Is this happiness that makes you cry, Lucy?"

I shook my head no. He waited. When I could speak, I took his hand and led him back to the sofa. We sat, and I told him everything that had happened to me in the past few months. Emmett held my hand through the whole tale. Only when I had finished did he rise. He raked his hands through his thick dark hair. Frowning, he paced the room and stopped at the window.

"Whose child do you carry?"

"I'll not tell."

"You must, Lucy."

"No. It is my cross to bear, and mine alone."

He whirled, unable to contain his anger. "What kind of a man would leave a woman with child and not marry her and make a decent woman of her?"

I bit my lip. I looked at my hands, folded discreetly in my lap. I did not answer.

Emmett came and kneeled beside me. He reached for my hand. "I am sorry, Lucy. I did not mean to imply that you are not a decent woman. I want to kill the coward who has done this to you."

"Then that would make you as cowardly as he."

Emmett considered my words. After a few moments, he nodded.

"Lucy," he said. "I would be most honored to father your child." He took my chin in his fingers and raised my eyes to his. When I started to protest, he put a finger to my lips. "Think on it some first, before you answer."

Then he left me to ponder his kindness. But all I could think about was the stricken look that creased his face like lightning cracking the sky when I told him I carried the child of another man.

☾

On Christmas Eve, I played my best. Emmett's strong tenor voice filled our small church with hope and love and joy. He shared our evening meal with us, complimenting my skill as a cook and helping me wash dishes afterwards. Before he left, he took both my hands in his, whispered, "I look forward to your decision," and kissed my cheek. "Merry Christmas."

"What a kind and decent gentleman," my father said, having noticed Emmett's affectionate gesture. "I hope that you and Emmett are getting along well."

"Yes, Father. Emmett is a dear friend."

Father smiled. "I'll be in my room. I need to work on tomorrow's sermon some. Sleep well." He handed me the newspaper. "Gertrude's doing well as an editor," he remarked.

He referred to Reverend Huntington's daughter, who had for some years published the *Platte Valley Lyre*. Although Father was careful not to let his voice reveal it, he allowed an unspoken competition to seep into my mind. He couldn't have known that at that moment I felt inadequate when compared to Gertrude. She was a smart woman. During book discussions she always brought up points I would never have considered on my own. And she had always been kind to compliment me on my music and had printed news of my students' achievements and recitals. "Don't stay up too late, Lucy. Tomorrow is a busy day."

He didn't know I had already read the news. He didn't know I had already seen the front page wedding announcement. Amos Abernathy planned to marry Holly Whitmore on January 1, 1896. The couple planned to make their home in nearby Grand Encampment.

"I want to sit up and admire the tree for a while more," I lied. I felt sick inside.

"Very well, Lucy. Do as you please."

When he was gone, I took a candle from the branches of the Christmas tree. As quietly as I could, I stole into the night. The candle lit my path to the river and across the bridge to the tiny island and the cottonwood. My hopes that Amos would join me here had long since faded. The news report confirmed my worst fears, for Amos's marriage hurt me worse than his death could have.

I stepped into the cold water. I wore my burgundy dress, the finest I had. I did not want my father to fuss over my attire if they found me.

I waded into the river, quickly, so I would not lose my nerve. The cloth billowed around me. My petticoats dampened first. The cold water set me to trembling violently. Every muscle, every bone, every sinew in my body cried for release. The urge to run was great but I resisted. Years of being taught obedience to my parents and the heavenly Father did their work. Discipline conquered desire this time.

Teeth chattering, I tossed my candle into the water. The flame hissed as the water extinguished it.

I prayed. "Lord, I just want to rest in the arms of this mighty river. I have already disobeyed your commandments and I am mightily sorry. I know You will understand."

When the widow walked further in, she was praying, too. "Lord," she said, "grant me peace within the waters of this river. My life has been unsatisfactory in your sight, I know. Please forgive me."

I shook my head. Why she sought solace in the river was beyond my understanding. She'd done plenty of good, righteous and godly things during her forty years of life. She had raised a family, cared for her invalid husband, baked meals for those who were sick or dying. She had not attended church every Sunday as I had done, but her beliefs shimmered through her deeds.

Emmett cried when he heard the news on Christmas Day. He was the only one who ever knew I'd carried a child into the river with me as well. He found the note I'd left him in his hymnal. I'd placed it by the hymn, "Shall We Gather at the River," knowing he would seek solace in those tried and true words. My note said only, "Emmett, I'll not shame you, too."

☾

A willow branch hidden beneath the water snagged the widow's trousers. Shivering, she struggled against it but could not pull away. She did not scream but her frustrated, "Oh!" carried to the banks.

Riley Stoner, the newspaper reporter, walked alongside the banks that night as he was wont to do almost every evening. Gertrude's *Platte Valley Lyre* had long since faded into the *Saratoga Sun*. Wedding announcements no longer made the front page but drownings and suicides did. Clouds parted, revealing the tiny moon. Its light shone on a bit of ice purling the water into a whirlpool near my skirt. Riley stopped.

Cupping his hands to his mouth, he yelled, "Who's out there?"

He was tall, and slender from riding horses during his spare time. At forty-three, he had not yet married, but several of the women in Saratoga had set their caps for him. He always wore a cowboy hat, perhaps a reminder of his days as a bronc rider. The light moved again. His face shadowed beneath his hat. Moonlight guided his eyes to the disappearing form of the widow.

"Oh my God!" Frantic, he searched the bank for a stick. "Hang on! Hang on! I'm coming." Riley scampered toward the houses near the river bank. He yelled and raised a ruckus until newfangled electrical lights shone out from their windows.

Riley raced to the river. Dazed, the widow floated among the waves, her foot dangling near the submerged willow. "I'm caught, I'm caught," she said.

"I'll help. Hang on, there. I'm coming." Riley crept down the bank as far as he dared. He anchored himself as best he could on the slippery slope. If he slid in, chances were good they would both die. Holding one end of the sturdiest cottonwood branch he could find, he reached toward her. "Grab the branch. Grab it."

As the cottonwood branch floated toward her, the widow reached for life again. The fabric of her trousers tore. She floated free of the willow's snare. Riley pulled her toward him. When the moonlight illuminated her face, he said, "Oh, Dr. Willoughby. You slipped into the river."

She came toward him, grateful for his strong arms around her as he pulled her onto the bank. A crowd had gathered. Whispers from the back echoed along the shore. "The veterinarian fell into the river. Riley saved her."

"You're from the paper," she said. He grabbed a blanket that a house owner tossed his way and put it around her shoulders.

"Yes," he said. "I'm Riley Stoner. You're lucky I came along when I did." Her suicide attempt was unimaginable to Riley, a broken rodeo rider with unquenchable spirit. A woman dedicated to the health of animals would surely be dedicated to preserving her own health, he thought. The word suicide never crossed his mind.

But when he told his fellow reporter the story of that December evening in 1995, a frown crossed his face. "She only told me that she slipped," he said.

The reporter nodded. "Lucky for her. This river had a suicide once a hundred years ago, practically in the same place."

"Really?"

"Yes. A woman named Lucy Willoughby drowned there on Christmas Eve in 1895."

"Lucy Willoughby? Are they related?"

"Lucy Willoughby is Dr. Anna Willoughby's great-great-aunt. Anna never took her husband's name, you know."

"Yes, I knew that." Riley sat down on the desk. "Lucy Willoughby?" he repeated. "They say my great-great-grandfather courted her before he married."

"Can I use that in my article?"

Riley nodded. "I'm going for a walk. Be back shortly."

He left the newspaper office and walked to the bridge. He stood in the center of the bridge's arch, gazing at the island named now for veterans. In the gray December light, with two weeks to Christmas, Riley Stoner watched me from the river bridge. He could not see my form as I saw his. But our spirits recognized each other.

I was punished for loving someone—the highest gift the earth provides. And I, in return, punished someone who loved me, a debt I could never repay. I held the tangled willow branch in my hands, the piece of torn trouser fabric still clinging to it. Riley walked back toward the newspaper office, hands in his pockets, deep in thought.

I walked the river, grateful for the merciful softness of waters that no longer sting me but cradle me. I turn south, watching the river.

The Diamond Ring Fling

I FIRST MET WILLIS AT AN EXECUTION. I RECALL THE EVENT CLEARLY, for this murder occurred not on the gallows as one might expect of such a grisly deed but inside the raucous environs of the Cottonwood Saloon in Cheyenne, Wyoming. Providence decreed that the murder was not my own nor was it my doing. But the blood remains on my hands. I played a part whether I like to admit it was so or not. Willis saved my life.

Cheyenne had earned a reputation as the "Magic City of the Plains." The nickname attached itself because the town had sprung up with great alacrity on the barren plains penetrated by the steel rods of the railroad. I found this city to be anything but magical—through my own folly entirely.

On that particular October evening in 1895, four men surrounded a table in the center of the smoky room, intent on winning money through the luck of the draw. Among them, confident and assured, sat Marcus Dalton. I sat at Marcus's side, gaily watching the proceedings. Other girls seduced younger men slick with liquor up the back stairs to Miss Ruthie's special rooms.

Marcus and I had no need of such diversions on this night. He gambled with funds he'd saved from his work on the railroad, planning to increase his holdings and then purchase land. Land! Every man's savior. Any man who ventured West and found himself on this humble open space filled with winter winds and harsh lessons desired to own property, as if he could take it over and make the lonely acres entirely his own. But land—and the passion for its ownership—is a demanding mistress. Land led astray many more men than it ever gave sterling living and well-bred respect to, or so I believed.

I pulled my frills tighter around my neck. Marcus did not appreciate my wiles being displayed even modestly when other men were present. The other *nymphs du prairie* had noticed my special feelings for Marcus. They had helped me with Miss Ruthie by taking care of the slack when Marcus came to visit me. And he paid extra, most of which I presented to Miss Ruthie, thus satisfying her greed and assuaging any anger she might have felt at my near-exclusive status.

I took pains to please Marcus Dalton most especially. Marcus was tall and slender, muscular with a dark, thick mustache, and dark hair. He had the bluest eyes. They were a bit pale, like the sky on the coldest of winter's mornings. Marcus was unfailingly kind to me. He alone knew of my past indiscretions and he had pledged to help me find a better life. His large, rough, workingman's hands dwarfed the money he left on the dresser after our dalliances. In my own delicate hands, the bills appeared larger and more numerous.

"I'm going to buy land, Charlotte," he announced early one morning as we cuddled beneath the covers. "I want to own my own piece of land, to have the pleasure of being my own man, my own. The landowner. And then I will build a cabin and purchase beef cattle and become a rancher. And marry and have children."

"Grand dreams," I said, snuggling closer, and luxuriating in the warmth of his skin next to my own. "But do you not have pleasure here?"

He smiled at me. He stroked my hair. "Ah, Charlotte. Yes, my darling. I am pleasured here for certain. But land. Now that's something that lasts forever. All wealth comes from land."

I kissed the vee of his collarbone, placed my hands on his hairy chest and rolled on top of him. "I don't feel like talking any longer, Marcus," I said.

"You have insatiable appetites for a woman," he answered, swallowing any reply I might have made with his lips.

Before the earliest morning light warmed the windows, Marcus dressed and left down the back stairs. He must not be late to his work on the railroad crew. Enough men had come through Cheyenne in recent years that the slightest infraction could throw them out of a job. And Marcus needed a bit more before he could afford to buy his land. I stood at the door and blew him a kiss, a gesture not missed by one of my coworkers, Lily. Lily did not like me. I knew from the look in her eyes she would find a way to use Marcus's overnight stay against me. I shuddered to consider how. Lily's door had opened at nearly the same time as my own. I supposed she was contemplating a chilly journey to the outhouse. A smile found her lips, the sideways grin that meant she had thought of something titillating to do. She was the only one of the girls who did not help me in my quest for Marcus. Jealousy beamed from her like the heat in a kerosene lamp piped toward the ceiling. She would do something. What, I did not know.

☾

The next evening, as Marcus enjoyed his card game, a smoky haze from the burning of cigars filled the room. The piano player delighted the sparse crowd with a variety of tunes. I recognized old favorites like "I'll Take You Home Again, Kathleen"; "Oh My Darling Clementine"; and "Oh, Dem Golden Slippers" and sang the words I could remember. Marcus placed his elbow on the arm of his wooden chair, moving nearer to me as I sang. I laid my hand on his starched sleeve.

Cold air rushed in, swirling the heavy cloud of smoke, when the saloon doors swung open to reveal Hank Terwilliger. He was tall, blond, more lithe than I remembered.

I stood, grateful that I had covered myself somewhat demurely.

"Hank," I said. "Hank Terwilliger."

His eyes searched the barroom. When they at last rested on me, he shook his head.

"Oh, Charlotte." His voice broke, as if he'd returned to adolescence again and could not speak a sentence without an unplanned and somewhat musical lilting. He took steps forward but I remained at Marcus's side. "They told me you'd been here. Oh, Charlotte. How did you ever go so wrong?"

The "they" he mentioned most certainly included darling Lily. My hand touched the ruffles covering my throat. "You're not Hank. Hank is dead."

"Oh, but I am Hank, dear Charlotte. I've returned for you, my dear." Marcus tensed beside me. I kept my eyes on Hank.

I shook my head. "No. Hank died in a railroad accident two years ago. Had he not, he would have found me before now."

The man smiled. "Charlotte, it was a terrible mistake. Another man died in my stead. Did you not receive my telegraph letter?"

"You know I did not," I said sharply. "For if I had I would have returned to my fiancé and my home with him."

"You have defiled yourself, woman, under the eyes of God." His hazel eyes narrowed, judging me.

"The frontier has not been as I thought it would be," I replied more calmly than I believed possible as I felt the heat of anger course through my blood. I had not meant to use my body as a tool to make money. I possessed few skills that would have allowed me to eat. I could not cook. I had not learned to sew for my mother had been ill for most of my childhood. "I arrived in this Godforsaken city to discover the fiancé who sent for me was dead. I never would have come here but for you, Hank," I retorted. With both my parents dead, I found no reason to return East and could not have managed the train fare on my own when the brief opportunity existed. "I accepted my fate and have done the best I could with my circumstances."

Lily laughed out loud, then covered her mouth with her hand to muffle her hiccupping giggles.

"You did not have the courtesy to let me know you were alive," I continued, ignoring her outburst. "When I arrived here, your employer told me you'd been killed in an accident. Why did you not come for me yourself?"

Hank dropped his eyes and his chin fell to his neck. He did not answer me immediately. Instead, he took a deep breath. When he raised his face again, I saw more shame. This time, though, I sensed his shame was for his own misdeeds rather than my own. "I was a fool, Charlotte. The thought of caring for a wife and a family in this rugged country—" He stopped, swallowing hard. "I could not see myself doing that. I did not feel that I could live up to such an obligation. When the other man was killed, I let them believe it was me. I only wanted to get my feet under me again. I needed time to get used to the idea."

"And why did you return now?"

"I found out you were here. I could not believe it. And now that I've seen you—" He shook his head. "Charlotte, I must ask for the return of my grandmother's diamond ring."

Marcus looked startled. "This is true?"

"Of course," I replied. Walking as proudly as I could, I mounted the stairs to my room. The barroom had become strangely silent during the conversation, except for Lily's snorting. She had found Hank and brought him here, hoping no doubt to discredit me in some manner. Biting back tears, I retrieved the ring from its hiding place within my dresser. I felt the cold gold band between my fingers. Though I had not confided in Marcus, I too had hoped to purchase a new life through saving what funds I could. The diamond had been the bulk of my savings. Miss Ruthie took more than she allowed her girls to retain, thus ensuring her work force remained on the premises.

Hank's return had never occurred to me. Had I been of more sterling character, I suppose I could have returned the ring to his family when I had thought him dead. However, he'd given it to me. I had kept it at first as a remembrance. I did not want such an ugly reminder now. I returned to the saloon.

The card players had not returned to their game. Activity ceased for those brief moments. No one talked. The piano player sat with his hands in his lap. Men at the bar had turned away from the bar to face the card game at the table in the center of the room.

I returned to my place near Marcus. I held the ring between my thumb and index finger and raised it to eye level. The diamond caught the light and sparkled like a star fallen from the sky.

"Do not give it back, Charlotte," Marcus said in a low tone. "He does not deserve to have it returned. Any man who would treat a woman in this disrespectful manner should be grateful that she would deign to speak to him."

Hank pressed his lips together in a line. He raked his eyes over Marcus, who remained seated at the card table. Hank's right hand lingered near his belt. His gun holster was near. He reached for the ring with his left hand. "I'll thank you not to enter into business which does not concern you, mister," he said in a menacing tone.

"Perhaps it does, Hank," I said. "I'll say here and now that I'll not remain betrothed to a coward."

I flung the ring toward him. It landed on the wood floor and made a tinkling sound like a dainty bell. It rolled to a stop near his feet. He kept his gaze riveted on me. His eyes narrowed.

"Shut pan, woman, I'll show you who's cowardly," he said, his face red with rage. His right hand lowered.

I closed my eyes and fell to my knees. A shot rang out. When I opened my eyes again, Hank lay dead on the floor.

Marcus's chair made a scraping noise as he stood. He unbuckled his holster and laid it on the table, gun still in place. I hadn't seen him produce it before. He must have pulled the trigger from beneath the table. But surely not my Marcus! An underhanded shot branded him as much a coward as Hank. I looked up at Marcus and he lifted his chin. A man I did not know had come to stand beside him.

"I'll go with you to the sheriff," he said, and Marcus nodded.

I crawled on the floor toward Hank's body. I reached for my ring. A slender man's hand covered my own.

"No, Ma'am. That ring will be used as evidence in the trial."

I looked squarely into the kindly visage of Willis Van Devanter, one of the most famous lawyers in Cheyenne. He introduced himself as I relinquished the ring to his control. I couldn't fathom the reason he had been inside the Cottonwood and hadn't even noticed him until now. But I knew, as did most folks, that he had defended the cattle-men in the Johnson County War just a few years back and had done so right here in Cheyenne. He had defended their right to murder rustlers Nate Champion and Nick Ray. Mr. Van Devanter was also known and well respected in highfalutin political circles. I did not much like that about him.

He gave my hand a squeeze. "Come to my office in a half hour," he said.

I gazed in amazement as he left the saloon. He followed Marcus, who was being led away by the unknown man.

"Things will work out all right, Charlotte," Marcus assured me. He kissed my hand—a most gallant gesture and one not often offered to one of my kind. I was not convinced.

I believed that his unfortunate shot had cost me all hopes of hap-piness. And I puzzled about what Mr. Van Devanter had in mind.

Lily sat smug at the end of the bar. She said, "About time you got what's comin' to ya, Miss High-and-Mighty. I've always wondered. What makes you so special?" She sneered.

There was no reason to answer her question so I did not. Instead, I held her gaze until she looked away.

☾

Mr. Van Devanter was much nicer than I had expected, given his pen-chant for politics.

"I saw the whole thing, Charlotte," he said, tapping his hands on his shiny oak desk. His fine wood chair creaked slightly as he shifted his weight and leaned back. "I've discussed this case with Marcus. We will plead self-defense. I will, however, need your testimony."

His office—in the interior of the building used by the increasingly famous law firm of Lacey and Van Devanter—smelled musty, the result of papers stacked from floor to ceiling near bookshelves filled to capacity, both gilded with a fine layer of dust.

"I didn't see anything until the whole thing was over," I responded.

"You are the reason for the argument that ensued between the two men, are you not?"

I nodded. Then I took a deep breath and said, "If you don't mind my asking, sir, why would an attorney of your stature consider taking on a case of such low magnitude?"

He peered at me. An unbidden image of butterflies stabbed to a collector's board filled my mind. "Why," he said and stopped, holding me in suspension for an uncomfortable moment. "For the principle of the matter, Miss—?"

"Oliver. Charlotte Oliver."

A small smile lifted his lips. "You see, Miss Oliver, Mr. Dalton shot to defend himself from a startling and unexpected attack. The fact that he fired through his holster and that the other man had not yet—" He paused and cleared his throat, then continued. "Supposedly, had not yet drawn his weapon is immaterial."

"If that is so, why do you need my word, then?" I folded my shaking hands demurely in my lap, held them tightly together, and stared at them. "Most people won't believe a woman such as myself."

"Miss Oliver, do not sell yourself short. Your occupation is not on trial in this case. Some people will believe you. Some will not." He stood up and walked around his chair. "A jury will be called first. This could take some weeks. Mr. Dalton will, of course, remain in jail until this trial is decided."

"He'll lose his job," I said.

He turned to me. "That is unfortunate but true. However, I am confident that he will find other employment after this blows over."

"I will do what is in my power to help Marcus go free," I said. "But I do not have the proper funds at my disposal for a person of your abilities."

Willis Van Devanter bit his lip. "I see. Perhaps we can manage something." He didn't offer any further comments. Instead, he remained standing. He lifted his right eyebrow slightly. His conversation with me was completed.

I stood and stepped toward the door. "Mr. Van Devanter," I said, stopping and turning to face him again. "What is so important about this principle that you would argue the case of a common gambler accused of murder without proper payment?" I could not understand how a man could murder another in front of witnesses and then not be punished for the crime but this thought I did not speak aloud.

He shook his head, waved an index finger in the air. "I must, Miss Oliver. I must defend those principles I believe in with all my human ability to protect them. For if I don't, then I lower myself and all of us by virtue of cowardice."

"But Marcus—"

Mr. Van Devanter walked to the front of his desk, nearer to me. "Marcus made a decision he will live with every remaining day of his life." He walked past me. A breeze scented with bay rum cologne tickled my nose. "I have done the same." Mr. Van Devanter placed his hand on the doorknob. "No, I cannot say that murder is ever justified. That is not for me to say. But I am a man of principles. And principles, Miss Oliver, deserve a strong defense."

He opened the door and ushered me into the narrow corridor. "I will let you know when you are to appear at the trial, Ma'am."

☾

I sit, fidgeting with the sturdy midnight blue brocade of the dress I made myself for this day of judgment. The fabric is smooth and comforting beneath my calloused fingers. My thumb feels numb after days of pushing the needle through fabric and my index and third fingers have roughened with numerous needle and pin pricks.

After I visited with Mr. Van Devanter in his office, I returned to Miss Ruthie's. Not long after that, Elise the dressmaker came to ask for my assistance in her shop.

"The Governor is hosting a ball at Christmas," she explained. Elise, a short, stout woman, never failed to look neat and freshly groomed. A virtue of her trade, perhaps? "You have learned the basics of hems through your frequent visits to me, Charlotte. I would appreciate your coming to the shop these next few weeks and helping us with the increased orders." She watched me for a moment, sizing me up in some way. Then she added, "I will, of course, pay you for your work. We can start you at fifty cents per day. As you progress in skill, perhaps we can increase that amount."

I stared, bewildered, at the tiny woman who'd taken precious moments of her time when I begged her to teach me to wield a needle during my own stolen hours. "Elise," I surprised myself by being able to speak. "I would love to work with you at your shop."

"Good." She nodded. "And I will speak to Miss Ruthie. Surely she can provide you room and board for the next few weeks until we find something more—" She cleared her throat and touched the stiff collar around her neck. "Suitable."

Somehow Elise had done as she promised. I was now employed properly at a dressmaking shop. I had even progressed to sewing straight seams upon the sewing machine. With Elise's help, I had made this dress I wore now in the lonely foyer of the courthouse. Elise was kind and encouraging. That provided me some comfort as I pondered the tumultuous events of the previous weeks of my life. A decision came to me as I sat waiting on a chilly polished wooden bench to testify on behalf of Marcus, who had murdered my fiancé.

The large wooden doors to my right creaked open. Lily stepped out and saw me. Her eyes narrowed. She undoubtedly felt jealous of my new dress, my new life unfolding before her eyes. In my mind, I saw my new life as a wondrous and pleasant blessing. Lily probably did as well. The fact of my improvement in social standing in the midst of such devastating circumstances caused her consternation, I feel sure.

She said, "He'll be in jail forever. I saw the whole thing and told them all I knew."

The guard touched her elbow and reminded her she was free to go now. She threw a final haughty look my direction and strode away. "Ma'am?" The guard said, nodding at me.

I stood, took a deep breath, and smoothed my skirt yet again. I refused to let Lily's venomous attitude shake me.

Inside the courtroom, I saw Marcus and then the firm countenance of Mr. Van Devanter. The attorney representing Hank Terwilliger's family reminded me of a weasel. His eyes were much too large for his face, and his neck too long for his body. I had seen such an animal once near a barn. I felt an involuntary shiver shake me. I took another deep breath and resolved to remain strong until the questions were finished. I did not look at the jury, nor at the people gathered in the room to listen to the proceedings.

The event passed in a blur. Hank's attorney made much of my previous profession, explaining that I had done my fiancé wrong by not waiting for him, and by that decision had perhaps instigated the entire incident.

Mr. Van Devanter argued in my behalf by asking me about Hank and learning that I had thought him dead and had done what I must to survive. "I'll remind you also, sir, that Miss Oliver is not on trial in this matter," he said, his voice resounding throughout the room like a chord played on a church organ.

We finished more quickly than I had thought, and I waited outside on the same bench for the news of the decision. The jury deliberated for less than two hours. Marcus was set free. They ruled that he had pulled the trigger in self-defense. Mr. Van Devanter looked pleased with himself. Marcus rushed from the courtroom and hugged me tightly and kissed me on the cheek.

I endured his attentions for a moment and then gently pushed him away.

"We'll marry, Charlotte. I can buy land now, we'll marry and . . ." My lack of enthusiasm stopped him. He frowned. "Charlotte?"

I shook my head. "No, Marcus. I'm sorry. I cannot marry you."

"Why not, Charlotte?"

"I cannot marry a murderer."

"But I wasn't convicted."

I allowed him a small smile. "That makes little difference to me, Marcus. You murdered someone almost before my eyes. I cannot reconcile myself to that fact."

"Charlotte," he said quietly. "Now's a fine time for you, of all people, to seek the high ground."

Mr. Van Devanter cleared his throat and excused himself to the courtroom.

"I cannot help it, Marcus. I would never fully trust you. I will not marry a man I cannot trust."

He blinked. "I see." He took a deep breath. "I believe you are making a tragic mistake."

I held my hand toward him. "Good luck, Marcus."

He took my hand in his own and then lifted it to his lips and kissed it. He held my eyes with his own for a long moment, and then turned on his heel and left the courthouse. I watched him go.

Mr. Van Devanter returned. "This belongs to you, I believe."

He handed me a small package, which contained the diamond ring I'd flung onto the barroom floor that fateful October day.

"I thought Hank's family would want it," I said.

"No. They want to be finished with the whole sad thing. His mother wants no reminders of her son's premature death." He squeezed my hands. "She said Hank gave it to you and it is yours to keep."

"Thank you, Mr. Van Devanter," I said. "I was hoping to purchase a sewing machine. I think I might be able to use this ring as a portion of the payment."

He motioned toward the doors, and escorted me into the deceitful November sunshine, which promised warmth but delivered only light.

"I must say I was hoping you might," he responded, smiling. "And please, call me Willis, Miss Oliver." He left me standing on the steps as he trotted down them and strode purposefully toward his office. I felt no need to explain that the next dress Elise had assigned to me at the special request of the customer was the elegant gown Dellice Van Devanter would wear to the Governor's Christmas Ball.

Grave Dancer

THE PRISONER STEPPED ONTO THE PLATFORM. HIS COWBOY BOOTS made dull thuds against the wood. All time stopped. A stifling silence overcame the spectators. Perhaps we all held our breath.

Tom Horn had, a full year before, been convicted of murdering young Willie Nickell. In a few short moments, he'd pay for the crime with his own life. He'd been a stock detective, someone ranchers paid to eliminate cattle rustlers. His could have been an upright profession, but Horn's sinister action had reduced it to a despicable business.

On this late November morning of 1903, I stood near the gallows at the Laramie County Jail with my friend, J. P. Julien, one of Cheyenne's fine architects. He had designed the special trap door mechanism for the gallows that would prevent another man from touching Horn. A perfect absolution of guilt for those about to commit a murder themselves, and an improvement over the usual method of several men standing in a circle and all pulling ropes at the same instant. With that method, no one knew whose tug sent the condemned to his death because all had the same opportunity. Julien's design eliminated the need for human contact. Death, when it came, would be as much of a surprise for the hangmen as for the hanged.

Horn took another step forward. This time his boot struck wood and rang hollow. Another sound, the sound of water dripping in precise increments, rose from beneath the platform. Julien took a deep breath. We waited.

Horn's death would ease the fears running rampant in the city about his possible escape from jail. Indeed, he had tried it once before and failed. Human helpers, it appeared, assisted even the damned. Suddenly Horn turned, shifting his accusing gaze to me.

I shivered and awoke with a start, soaked in sweat. My nightmare would come true today. Horn would die. Julien's mechanism would trigger the platform's release, dropping the condemned man to hell. And I would attend the execution, watching and waiting beside Julien. What had I gotten myself into?

❨

I first met James Julien at the recent Halloween masquerade ball at Cheyenne's Keefe Hall. Laughter and the thrum of conversation filled the ballroom that evening. Many of the conversations revolved around the fate of prisoner Tom Horn, languishing in the county jail, and most of them were most uncomplimentary to the condemned man.

"Horn did it. He himself said so. Hang him and get 'er done," said one man, pouring himself a glass of punch.

"There's talk the governor will decide," said another. "Silly to involve Chatterton, if you ask me."

"Damn legal folderol," said the first man. "What a waste! The fellow's been put up all high and mighty by the county jail for a whole year. They should have hung him right after the trial and been done with it."

"Think he'll escape?"

"Well, there's a damn fine chance, ain't there? He tried it once. He's probably got some patsy on the inside who'll manage it for him. And we know he's got friends on the outside, that's for darn sure."

I moved closer, hoping to enter the conversation. But the men stopped talking, as if they suddenly realized no one here appeared as he was. They might have said too much in front of a costumed man— someone who could be anyone—who could turn against them. Someone who might be a Horn ally. That my costume disguised me as writer Edgar Allan Poe undoubtedly contributed to their uneasiness.

I turned from the punch bowl, intending to take a glass to my wife, Amy. Instead, I found myself face-to-face with William Shakespeare.

"Hello," I said. Shakespeare gruffly returned the greeting. From behind him, Amy, dressed as Poe's child love, Annabel Lee, spoke.

"Samuel, I'd like you to meet Mr. Julien. He's an architect. He tells me he has need of an assistant."

"Mr. Julien," I said, extending my hand. He extended his own. "Mr. Richards. Your wife tells me you've recently attended university."

"Please, call me Samuel." I explained my meager qualifications. Hiring on with an architect was a position I had dreamed of obtaining, and Julien's reputation preceded him. He had designed many of the Union Pacific Railroad depot buildings, and to my mind, Cheyenne's was exquisite. I had a feeling I could learn much from this man. "If I may inquire, what project are you working on?"

Julien's voice was deep but not loud. I strained to listen.

"Your timing could not be better, young man," he said. "I've embarked on a project of the utmost importance, and would need your help to continue with other projects while I'm preoccupied. Those projects involve some drafting work, and perhaps after a time, you could be moved more into designing. Would you be interested?"

I could not see his face, as he wore the mask of the Bard. But his tone sounded genuine.

"Yes, Mr. Julien. I'd be quite interested."

"Come tomorrow morning, promptly at eight. We'll talk about your duties then."

"Thank you, Mr. Julien."

He lifted his mask. "My name is James," he said, smiling, and revealing a thin, hollow-cheeked, square-jawed countenance and bright blue eyes. "But most people call me Julien. Suit yourself."

I revealed my own face, certain my enthusiasm shone through my skin. My face was rounder, and I hoped my brown eyes conveyed as much intelligence as his did.

"A pleasure meeting you, Samuel," he said, departing and mixing in again with the other partygoers. He walked with a slight limp.

"Oh, Sam," Amy said. She had come to stand close to me and we embraced. "What a magical evening. I'm thrilled for you. Mama will be so pleased." She had not removed her youthful mask, but in the mystical green depths of her eyes I saw her delight.

"Thank you, darling," I said, returning her hug and then handing her a glassful of punch. Her mother, Mrs. Albert Alexander, known to friends as Elizabeth, and to me—her son-in-law—as Mrs. Alexander, would indeed be happy to learn I had finally found employment. Perhaps Amy and I could soon move into a home of our own and release her mother from the burden of keeping us. "Would you permit me this dance to celebrate?" I asked.

We swirled with the other dancers, moving to the lilting music of Cheyenne's mandolin club members. I held my delicate wife in my arms, happiness coursing through my body. We waltzed amidst other cloaked couples—a knight in shining armor held a damsel in distress and Marie Antoinette bowed to a skeleton. Assorted ghosts and goblins and others dressed in costumes from the simple to the ornate filled the floor.

Some of the dancers revealed their faces, seeking air and relief from their hot coverings and from what someone called "this tiresome charade." Some I recognized from their laughter and others from overheard snippets of conversation. Amidst the frivolity, I noticed another costume. The Grim Reaper, carrying his scythe, stood near the refreshments table. He played his part magnificently. He stood at his post for most of the evening. He never revealed his identity. He did not dance.

☾

The next morning I walked to Julien's residence. I passed a livery stable. The reeking odor of burning flesh assaulted me. I ventured a peek inside the dark depths of the stable. The farrier fitted a shoe to a horse. Though I knew he'd dipped the heated metal into a bucket of water to cool it down before fitting it, the iron remained hot enough to burn the hoof. By the burn mark, the farrier could ensure the shoe would fit prop-erly before he nailed it in place. The bay horse appeared undisturbed by the process. I could not say the same for myself. The bitter stench from the smoke made my eyes water. My lungs cried for clear air.

The farrier stood, waving the hot horseshoe in the air. "Mornin' to you," he said. I returned the wave and walked on, ever more appreciative of the opportunity to do work I enjoyed. I hoped that the acrid scent would dissipate before I entered Julien's office and that the costumes I carried in a box to return to Mrs. Clark, the costumer, would not be sul-lied by the odor. I planned to return them to her in the evening.

Once inside his comfortable home on the corner of Seventeenth and Reed Streets, I relaxed. Julien greeted me warmly, and introduced me to another Cheyenne architect, William Dubois, who had dropped by to invite Julien to a luncheon.

Julien's wife, Sarah, served us coffee in the dining room. After she departed, he explained my tasks. Sketching buildings was one of the most enjoyable assignments I'd had at the university, and Julien could put me to work promptly with similarly pleasing duties.

"And you? If I may, what is the project that you are working on?"

"Oh, Julien's gallows," said Mr. Dubois.

Julien winced. He stood with difficulty and held out his hand. "Thanks, Bill. We'll talk later. I'll plan on that luncheon Saturday." Thus curtly dismissed, Mr. Dubois excused himself and left.

I looked into my employer's eyes, confused. My inquisitive glance expressed my question with no need for words. Julien returned to his seat.

"I am to work on the gallows upon which Tom Horn will hang," he said, steadily.

"Did you design them?"

"The gallows? No." He sat across the table from me. "Frankly, the idea came from another prisoner. A man incarcerated in the Colorado State Penitentiary in Cañon City," he said. Julien tapped the fingers of his right hand against the table. The slow rhythmical movement regu-lated his words. "This is not the first time the design has been used here." The galloping sound of his fingers filled the silence.

"I see," I responded. "But what does this have to do with you, then?"

He resumed his unhurried explanation. "The Cañon City man told Sheriff Kelly of the workings of the gallows prior to the execution of Charlie Miller here a decade or so ago. I merely refined the design with trap doors by making a trigger mechanism."

I grimaced at his choice of words. In effect, he was telling me he'd refined a mechanism to "pull the trigger" and kill condemned men.

"Then why did Mr. Dubois refer to it as your gallows?"

Julien cleared his throat. He explained that he had assisted Sheriff Kelly with erecting the gallows prior to Miller's execution. Because of that, some people had referred to the instrument of death as "Julien's gallows."

"A nasty, mistaken term. Should the mechanism operate properly, as in the past, there would be no need for my name to be associated with the gallows at all."

"But an architect designing a gallows?"

"You say that as if it's an unpleasant thing," he answered somewhat gruffly. Our conversation caused my stomach to quiver. "It is a design like any other."

I disagreed but could not bring myself to say the words aloud to my new employer. A gallows was not like any other thing. A gallows was a weapon. Shocked that a fine architect such as Julien would take it upon himself to design any part of a weapon, when in my mind, he was a builder, a creator of gathering places for people to live in and dance in and admire, I again spoke.

"You didn't build the whole thing?"

"No," he said. "I hope, by the use of the mechanism, to eliminate the need for any of the hangmen to touch the condemned. That way, no one man needs feel responsible for killing another under such dire circumstances."

I stared at him. He stopped tapping the table with his fingers. How could he turn an object used for a morbid purpose into a good thing?

"Did it work?"

"For Miller?"

"Yes."

He pursed his lips. "Reasonably well."

I did not inquire as to his meaning. My imagination supplied numerous distasteful possibilities of its own.

"You are disappointed," he said, quietly.

"Yes," I admitted.

"The sheriff has requested my assistance," he said. "I'll not go back on my word."

"I respect that," I said.

He nodded. "Samuel, I would not ask you to take upon yourself any duties you would find distasteful. Should you decide to work for me, I will not give you any task that I myself would not do. The decision is yours."

"I would be working on building designs?"

"Yes."

I took a deep breath. I needed the job. "Then I will stay." A relieved look swept his face of the taut lines that had covered it moments earlier. The rest of the day passed quickly and I accomplished the tasks set before me with ease. But our conversation haunted me.

Had it not been for that strange discussion, I would not have ventured into the realm of Carrie Caspar, spiritualist. But because she was located next door to Mrs. Clark's costume shop, I chanced a visit. Carrie Caspar's sign announced she appeared in Cheyenne for only a brief time, encouraging customers to take advantage of the "once-in-a-lifetime opportunity."

My savaged spirit needed comfort and though I looked upon her field as nothing more than trickery, curiosity impelled me to enter the room she'd rented. At the very least, I might gain a laugh from the experience. And I felt in dire need of laughter this afternoon.

As soon as I entered the darkened room, Carrie appeared. She was a beautiful woman, dark haired and dark eyed, with skin the color of sanded oak. She was nothing like the hag I'd pictured in my mind. Her eyes bored into my own. I felt as if she knew all about me.

"What is it you have come to see Carrie about, dear sir?"

Her voice had a bell-like quality.

"Tell me my future," I said, keeping my words brisk. She nodded, motioning for me to sit across from her at a table covered with a heavy black cloth. At the center of the table was a clear glass ball resting on a stand. *Here we go,* I thought, wondering what unearthly topics she'd choose.

Her eyes narrowed. She reached across the table for my hand. She took it in her own and held it. My hand had cooled from the outside temperature. She held it for an uncomfortably long time. I found this woman extraordinarily beautiful. *I should be home with Amy,* I thought. *For goodness sake, what brought me here?*

Carrie's eyes popped open. She looked directly at me. "You will assist in the achievement of another's dream. I see dancing, a waltz, perhaps?" I smiled, recalling the masquerade ball. That wasn't difficult for her to discern. The ball was held last night, a fact she might have gleaned from the costumer next door. She closed her eyes again.

"I see bricks and stones and wood. A stream? And something tumbling, crashing. . . ." When she opened her eyes, she retained her hold on my hand. We peered at one another across the table. I feared pulling my gaze from hers. Gooseflesh tingled across my arms. She shivered.

She abruptly released my hand. "Do you feel that?"

I nodded, afraid to speak.

"You sparked something very deep. I feel chilled. Please go." She closed her eyes.

I left a small sum on the table and walked outside, trying to shrug off the strange feeling of dread that overcame me. I didn't succeed. It served me right for dabbling in fantasy.

When I arrived at the Alexander mansion, though, my young wife greeted me affectionately and dispelled my anxiety. At dinner, she recounted her day.

As we prepared to eat dessert, an apple pie, she brought me a brandy snifter. "You might enjoy this, dear Sam," she said.

"What's the occasion? My new position?"

Mrs. Alexander, dressed in her customary lace and finery, held her own brandy snifter aloft. "That is indeed worthy of honor," she said with asperity. I could tell from her tone she doubted I would ever make anything of myself.

Amy frowned. "Yes, it is, Mother, but I have even better news."

"What is it, Amy?"

She practically squealed with delight. "I've seen Dr. Johnston this morning."

"And he pronounced you in good health?"

Suddenly shy, she kneaded the tablecloth with long, slender fingers. "Yes," she said, "and—" She hesitated.

"Well, tell us," her mother urged.

"Samuel, you and I, well, we—" She stopped and looked at me. "We're to have a baby. I'm with child."

I placed my snifter on the table and rushed to hold her in my arms. I pulled her to me and kissed her full on the lips. "That's wonderful news, my darling."

Mrs. Alexander sipped her brandy. "Wonderful," she said in a clipped tone, indicating she herself was uncertain.

☾

The days passed quickly. Julien found my sketches pleasing and I had even gathered enough courage to show him a few of my original designs. His comments were encouraging. Despite myself, I had grown interested in his trigger mechanism. Governor Chatterton had not excused Horn. The execution was less than a week away. The townspeople talked of nothing else but Horn, his villainous deed, and his upcoming punishment.

The condemned man's fate and Julien's tool even entered conversations that occurred between my wife and me in the privacy of our bedroom. Amy and I often read aloud to each other before falling asleep. I liked to read the stories of Poe. Among my favorites of his works were "The Raven" and "Annabel Lee."

I began reciting "The Raven" from memory, arriving at the line, "Deep into the darkness peering," when Amy said, "Please stop, Samuel, stop."

"What is it, dear?"

She climbed into bed beside me and rolled to face the wall. "I do wish you were not so enamored of Mr. Poe. Could you read Shakespeare instead?"

"Certainly, Amy. I will read anything you like."

"Shakespeare didn't dally with death like Poe does," she said. "Poe finds the subject too impressive for my taste."

I picked up a volume of Shakespeare's work. Knowing she referred to the romances penned by the bard, I did not retort that Shakespeare consorted with death himself in works such as *Hamlet* and *MacBeth*. Even *Romeo and Juliet* flirted with death but the argument would have been lost on my pretty wife. I began to read a sonnet, the first I came upon. "To me, fair friend," I intoned, "you can never be old. For as you were when first your eye I ey'd, such seems your beauty still."

"Thank you, Samuel." She sighed heavily. "I suppose I'm not interested in reading tonight."

"What is the matter, love?"

She turned her face toward mine. "Oh, Samuel. I wish you'd leave this ghastly business with Mr. Julien behind."

Astonished, I said, "He pays me well, Amy. I thought you wanted me to have a job."

She frowned. "Yes, but I never dreamed you'd be involved in a man's death."

"I'm not."

"You are. Scarcely a moment passes when you don't mention something to do with Julien or his mechanism or the gallows. I rarely hear of your efforts with buildings."

I blinked. "I hadn't realized," I began, but again she interrupted.

"I fear your preoccupation with death is harmful. Not for yourself only but for our child as well."

I touched her cheek with my palm. "But I'm working for those who live," I said gently. "I have been working on office buildings and Julien likes my designs so the chances for future work appear bright." She covered my hand with her own. I continued, "Julien's mechanism is a force for good, Amy. It will help the hangmen. It removes the necessity of the hangmen touching the condemned. By not touching the prisoner, they will feel less like murderers themselves." I remembered Julien's argument for that same good—a position I had disagreed with on the first day of my employment.

"The condemned? The prisoner? You can't even bring yourself to discuss the man as a human. And hangmen are murderers. What has happened to you, Samuel?"

"Hangmen are not murderers, Amy," I retorted. "They are doing the job society set upon them. And I'm doing my job as well." I found it difficult to keep my voice low. If I raised my voice, Mrs. Alexander in her bedroom next door would surely hear our argument.

"Well, Samuel, I disagree. Anyone who has any part in another's death is, to me, a murderer."

"And myself, then?"

She stared at me. "Decide for yourself."

"It's useless to argue. You'll never understand," I said, pulling the bedcovers tighter.

"Samuel, I pray daily for understanding. And I've been praying lately for God to understand you and not punish you for your part in this."

"You introduced me to Julien yourself."

"Yes, I did, but . . ." She shook her head. "Oooh," she said, for she could not argue with my logic. "Samuel, I cannot stand your erratic behavior."

Angered by her own unusual outburst, I said, "Perhaps you'd prefer I stay at a hotel. I could obtain lodging at the Inter Ocean until this business is concluded."

She did not speak for long moments.

"Amy?" I asked.

I heard her sigh deeply. "Yes, perhaps you should."

A gray overcast sky covered the city the next morning. Stunned by our disagreement, I had taken a room at the Inter Ocean before walking to work. The weather apparently dispirited Julien as well.

When I arrived, he said, "What if it doesn't work?"

"The mechanism will work," I assured him, surprised by his unexpected lack of confidence. The hairs prickled on the back of my neck at providing reassurance about an instrument of death.

"It's been pointless," he ranted. "A pointless effort that's cost me time and money and perhaps my career."

"No, Julien. Your work has not been pointless," I argued. "At the very least, the hangmen will feel better about their unpleasant duty. And perhaps this will better the city in some way." I paused. I did not know how. "Thank God the whole sordid affair will be finished tomorrow."

He looked at me as if I'd lost my senses. "Samuel," he said, "it will never be finished." The light of his blue eyes dimmed. He turned back to the window, watching the wind pluck brown leaves from the lone cottonwood as gray clouds obscured the sky.

We lunched at the Inter Ocean. The whistle of the noon train jarred me. Travelers scurrying to eat and return for the train's departure crowded the dining room. Conversation proved difficult amidst the sounds of dishes clattering and the steady hum of others talking. We didn't find speaking necessary that day. The plan was in place. Julien would test the gallows that evening. I agreed to assist.

I had vowed to find another job, to steer my mind away from death as Amy wished. I had intended to tell him of my decision to find other employment while we ate, but I did not. I was drawn to Julien and his queer task like steel seeks a magnet. I could not bear to tell him on this day when he appeared so distraught.

A waiter dropped a plate. The white disk slid to the floor and then spun and bounced back and forth like a child's top. To the waiter's amazement—and our own—the plate did not break. He stooped to retrieve it and dropped another. That plate shattered. The waiter whispered a curse.

☾

Julien tested his device through macabre rehearsal. For this final experiment, the sheriff and deputies at the jailhouse lent assistance. They used three fifty-pound bags of flour to approximate the weight of the condemned man. The noose was attached to the flour sacks. Two deputies, careful not to touch the trap doors themselves, placed the sacks there, on the spot where Horn would meet his fate tomorrow. The wood creaked under the weight.

I heard the lonely sound of dripping water. Could Horn hear it, too? His cell was located on the second floor of the jailhouse, near the place where we congregated. A canvas curtain masked our presence, but surely even the muffled sounds of human activity carried to the prisoner.

Julien, though he knew his mechanism would function properly through the commencement of the annoying noise, appeared anxious. He would not be satisfied until the trap sprung and the flour sacks fell.

The weight of the filled sacks had released the plug on the water can located across a board from a counter-balance in the room beneath us. When the can dispersed enough water to make it weigh less than the counter-balance, the counterweight would drop, causing a rope to run through a pulley. The opposite end of the rope was attached to a hinged four-by-four beam supporting the trap doors. When the counterweight dropped, the rope would tug the hinge, opening the trap doors.

If the gallows malfunctioned, the only harm would be a little extra misery extended to the condemned. Since he was a killer himself, some folks argued that that didn't matter. He'd get what he deserved for murdering that fourteen-year-old boy.

Yet I knew it would matter to Julien. He'd feel remorse. Although his attention settled upon the hangmen, Julien didn't want to cause the prisoner extra pain.

We jumped when the trap doors sprang. Flour dust rose from the dangling flour sacks. The squeaking sound of the doors swinging on their hinges accompanied the grainy white mist accumulating in the air. We did not speak but set to cleaning up our mess. I felt keenly aware of the living, breathing man doubtless considering his fate in the nearby cell. Horn had been trapped between life and death for the past many months. Tomorrow, the doors between would finally swing.

☾

Execution day dawned gray and dreary. A howling wind added to my unease. A few moments before eleven o'clock in the morning, Tom Horn's muffled footsteps sounded on the platform. Already the proceedings differed from my nightmare. Horn's hands and feet were bound. One of the men who had assisted with our test the night before placed the noose about his neck and covered his face with a black hood.

Julien stood beside me. His expression was unreadable. Numerous spectators filled the room. I recognized the farrier and a few others.

Charlie and Frank Irwin, friends of Horn's, launched into a loud rendition of "Life's Railway to Heaven," at the doomed man's request. Following the musical interlude, stifling silence ensued.

Despite Julien's good intentions, despite his worry over the feelings of the hangmen, a human factor interceded that day. Horn, with feet bound and head cloaked, could not step onto the trap doors himself. Two men, Sheriff Ed Smalley and T. Joe Cahill, lifted the prisoner to his proper position, then stepped back abruptly.

"What's the matter," Horn said, "getting nervous I might tip over?"

Julien bit his lip. His skin drew taut against his face like the canvas of a tent sucked inside-out by the wind. His plan had failed. He had not intended men to intervene.

Water dripped for thirty-one seconds. Everyone started when the trap doors sprang. Horn fell. His head and shoulders dangled within our view. His body turned away from spectators as if taking this death journey was a private matter. Seventeen minutes later, the killer was pronounced dead of strangulation.

Julien whispered, "Deep into that darkness peering, long I stood there wondering, fearing. . . ." His voice cracked.

I finished Poe's verse, saying softly, "Doubting, dreaming dreams no mortal ever dared to dream before."

☾

"It is done," Sheriff Smalley proclaimed to the noisy crowd gathered outside the jail. Julien and I stood among them, having left the building together. Reporters clamored for more details. To my mind, the sheriff had said all that was necessary, but he patiently answered their questions, providing all the grisly particulars.

"On Julien's gallows?" one shouted.

The sheriff nodded, sealing Julien's fate. This single incident was so morbid that his connection with it would doom his magnificent building designs to obscurity.

I saw the pained look appear before Julien could reset his face into a more pleasant expression. What he had most hoped to avoid had come to pass. His name would be forever linked with executioner's tools.

"I have failed," he said to me, a somber expression casting an ashen color over his face. "I have done no more than dance on the grave of a condemned man, a fact for which I will always be remembered."

"Julien," I said, touching his arm. He pulled away from me and disappeared into the crowd. Despondent, I pushed through the crowd and emerged in the street. Julien was nowhere to be seen.

A touch on my own arm startled me. I whirled, discovering the tearful visage of my wife.

"Amy! What are you doing here? You'll catch a chill."

"Waiting for you, of course, Samuel. I couldn't let you suffer through this alone."

I took her elbow and steered her through the dispersing crowd. Echoing the sheriff's words spoken only moments before, I said quietly, "It is done."

Amy pressed her lips together and nodded. She did not speak. We walked together in silence, the flat sound of our footsteps marking time. By unspoken agreement we turned toward Ferguson Street, where her mother lived. Amy put her arm in my own. We walked the rest of the way alone. The sun had broken through the clouds with enough warmth to heat the wrought iron gate and melt an icicle clinging to its spikes. The icicle dripped with measured precision, methodically elongating its own form and saturating a pile of dirty snow below.

☽

AUTHOR'S NOTE

Speak the name "Julien" in Wyoming, and it's likely listeners will first remember him in connection with the gallows. But Julien, a Civil War veteran, arrived in Cheyenne, Wyoming following the war, and for a few years was the only architect and contractor in the city. He built Cheyenne's first Union Pacific station and others along the railroad route east to Omaha and served as a consulting architect on the Wyoming State Capitol. Julien's version of the gallows was used for the Laramie County executions of Charlie Miller and Tom Horn, and for nine other male inmates at the Wyoming State Penitentiary during the years 1912 through 1933.

Julien, his wife Sarah, Horn (who was hanged for the murder of Willie Nickell), and architect William Dubois, as well as Dr. George Johnston, the Irwin Brothers, Governor Fenimore Chatterton, Sheriff Ed Smalley, and T. Joe Cahill, were all real persons living in Cheyenne during the time of this fictional story. Other characters, with the exception of Poe and Shakespeare, are fictional.

Readers interested in a detailed description of the gallows should read Larry K. Brown's "Just Ice," in *True West*, June 1997. For more information on Tom Horn, consult Chip Carlson's book, *Tom Horn: 'Killing men is my specialty . . .'* (Cheyenne: Beartooth Corral, 1991). The Wyoming State Archives also houses some information on both Horn and Julien.

Creek's Edge

THE LITTLE GIRL'S FUNERAL WAS THE FIRST IN SARATOGA'S NEWLY BUILT Church of the Heavenly Rest. The pine scent of the freshly sanded pews hung in the air of the nave like smoke on that ungodly hot July morning in 1889. The cloying odor made the church feel uncomfortably cramped. So many people came to pay their respects to the family that the little church was filled beyond its capacity. Some mourners stood outside.

"What can we know from such a tragic event?" Reverend Huntington asked, his voice choked by grief. Evelyn MacNeil, not quite four years old, had drowned in Downer Creek west of town not two days before the service. "What can we know?" He asked again, looking not at the faces of the congregation but out the window as if to find the answer for himself first. "That God's love is forever with us. Surely He must feel the depth of our sorrow and the longing we will forever carry for the wonder of tiny Evelyn."

When he said the child's name, he returned his attention to the interior of the little church building and focused upon the plain wooden casket that held her body.

Evelyn's family sat in the front pew. Her brother, Toby, a slight, blond boy of seven, sat a bit apart from his parents. Wrapped up in their own mourning, they were. From my vantage point in the front pew opposite them, I ventured a sideways peek. Rachel, the toddler's mother, sat straight as a rod, tears streaming down her face. Douglas MacNeil, a man much larger than his wife, and of fairer hair and complexion, stared ahead. No tears fell upon his cheeks. He pressed his lips together and his tight jaw worked as the minister spoke.

Reverend Huntington said, "But with the painful knowledge that the longing will not cease in this lifetime, we are granted the surety of knowing that Evelyn rests safely in the arms of our Lord and that her loved ones will see her again."

The organist played "The Old Rugged Cross" on the organ that had been special-freighted all the way from Vermont to Wyoming Territory for this new frontier church. The congregation filed out of the church. People stood single file on either side of the steps to the entrance, and so many had attended the service that the line extended well past the wagon that would carry the child's body to the cemetery.

The family members were the last to leave. Rachel's tears fell afresh at the sight of the community providing such a hallmark of respect. Her eyes had the vacant expression of someone gone far away. Douglas merely nodded, a dismal expression darkening his blue eyes. He remained handsome, but Douglas had aged much in the years since I had last seen him. This tragedy no doubt had greatly contributed. Age had merely etched his strong features more deeply into his skin.

Heavy sighs and a few sniffles interrupted the somber silence. Evelyn's casket was ceremoniously loaded into the back of the wagon, making a wretched scraping sound as her coffin rubbed against the wagon wood. Douglas placed a bouquet of sprigs of sage tied with a bit of white lace upon the tiny wooden box. Flowers were scarce this time of year. The wild iris and roses had long since bloomed and faded. A few limp ribbons of silvery sage were all he had to pay tribute to his fallen daughter.

Douglas helped his wife climb into the wagon. He climbed into the driver's seat, shook the reins, and his fine Percherons began their steady gait, hoofbeats sounding a hollow requiem. The creaking wood of the wagon surely echoed the sound of his heart breaking. I wiped away my own tears as they departed. Those who would accompany the MacNeils to the graveyard followed.

I did not go. They needed time to say their farewells. Such moments are meant to be private. Especially such between parents and child. I returned to my work at the home of the Hawthornes. The bread I'd started earlier had risen. I punched it down with my fist. The very motion of kneading brought me some comfort. I wished hurt could be so easily massaged away but life was not like that. I gathered the sticky dough in my hands and held it as if I could hold onto life itself by cradling the yeasty ball in my palms. Fresh tears fell. Some pains hurt worse than others.

☾

I took my freshly baked bread to the MacNeils at dusk. A late afternoon hailstorm transformed the heat of the day into cold. Though I'd taken care to wear my finest wool shawl, the chill air raised gooseflesh on my arms.

Douglas himself opened the door. Recognition filled his puffy eyes. "Lorna." He blinked. "How kind of you to come." His blond wavy hair fell across his forehead. A growth of stubble strawed his chin.

I held out the bread. "From the Hawthornes. I baked it for you and Mrs. MacNeil and Toby. I'm working there now," I said unnecessarily. Douglas nodded but did not speak. "And this I brought for you. As I recall, you liked scones."

I handed him my best currant scones. I had also placed chokecherry jelly and butter in the basket. A flicker of light shone in his eyes. A wan smile brightened his face.

"My favorites," he said. But as quickly as the light had come, his eyes dulled again with unfaded grief. "I thought my breath would cease as well." He spoke of his lost daughter. Staring at some far-off mystery known only to him, he said, "It did not. My body continued to take breath after hers faltered and . . ." His voice broke.

I touched his hand. Our eyes met and held.

"You must go forward now," I said.

He closed his eyes for the briefest instant. When he opened them again, I felt something kindled within me. Something deeper than friendship sparked between us.

"Your voice comforts me, Lorna."

Surprised, I said, "You felt that way on the ship."

He forced a smile. "Yes. Your voice has a fine quality, soft but with a bit of salt to it." He rubbed the stubble on his chin. "The kind of sound that helps a man hold on."

"You've many memories to hold onto, Douglas," I said. "We were fortunate to have some pleasant times on our journey to America."

Another flicker of light shimmered in his eyes and was gone.

"You sang like an angel."

"Thank you," I said, feeling my cheeks grow hot. I remembered Douglas standing near me as we attended a Sunday morning service. As we were singing hymns, I had caught him watching me but not singing himself.

The far-off stare captured his eyes once again. "Without you and Mother's locket I might not have completed that journey."

He'd been seasick and homesick for the greater part of that frightful, stormy trip. His mother had passed on just before we sailed. I, with my similar Scottish heritage, had been drawn to him, and similar age bonded us. We'd both been in our teens.

We'd gone our separate ways when we arrived in America. By odd twist of fate, we'd both come on to Wyoming Territory, he with a new wife and I to work as the Hawthornes' domestic.

"And yet you did. You've made a grand life in this new country, Douglas."

He winced. I regretted speaking harmful words that I had meant to be comforting. "I should not have—"

"No," he said. "It has been good for the most part."

I swallowed hard.

He said, "You are well then?" His eyes, the color of creek water at twilight, again held mine, and this time in a way that negated the need for physical touch.

Heat billowed through my own body. This was not the right time, but I could not deny the longing. My cheeks burned. My emotions raged inside me. The man before me had experienced the worst sorrow a human can face. I was only someone who brought care to him on this day. Someone he knew before these tragic circumstances brought us together once again. But I wanted more.

I nodded. "I must be on my way," I said. I had not realized until that moment that I still cared—and intensely—for Douglas MacNeil. The depth of my emotion frightened me. That my feelings erupted at this time of mourning shocked me more. I trudged home. Douglas was married. I had no business letting my inappropriate feelings stand in the way of that.

☾

Rachel MacNeil's grief did not wane in the days following the funeral. Instead, sorrow overcame her. She remained cognizant of her surroundings but grew childlike in her behavior. She clung to her husband, crying when he had to leave to do his work. On some days she would not leave her room. She did not sleep. When she did allow herself slumber, she screamed herself awake from her frightening dreams.

So Mrs. Hawthorne told me. She had gone for tea one afternoon, feeling it her duty as a neighbor to pay a call. Douglas had not confided in her, but young Toby, starved for adult attention, explained his mother's condition when he walked Mrs. Hawthorne part of the way home.

"It is the child I feel sorriest for," Mrs. Hawthorne admitted. She compensated for her sorrow by sending me to cook and clean for the MacNeils every other day. This, she said, would do her heart good. "To know that young Toby is getting at least a few good meals to grow on," she said.

Just days after Evelyn's funeral, Douglas moved the MacNeils' log cabin from the creek bank, hauling it on skids pulled by his sturdy Percherons to a hill about a mile from the water. He dug a well and built a windmill to bring the water up to the house so Rachel would never again need to venture to the creek to fetch it.

Rachel began spending her days at the windmill. She sat on the lowest wooden rung and clung to the tower. When anyone approached her, she said, "My heart remembers her. The wind carries her laughter to me." Her porcelain face roughened from exposure. The wind dried her once graceful hands. Still she sat as if waiting for Evelyn to return, or perhaps praying God would take her, too.

Douglas walked as though in a fog those first weeks following his daughter's death. He forgot having done things, left tools scattered about and couldn't remember where he'd put them, so distraught with grief was he. Neighbors helped him put up the hay crop. Douglas chatted with them as if he were fine. But knowing looks between the hired ranch hands and tilting of heads following their conversations showed the truth of his upheaval.

With the blessing of my employer, whose heart was large and sympathetic, I baked extra pies and cakes and bread and took meat and cheese to the MacNeils. I paid for some with my own wages and stocked their pantry as best I could. I, too, grieved for the living. For Douglas, who walked the earth as a lost soul. And for Toby, who struggled with his own feelings of loss and did not understand the changes grief wrought in his parents.

Toby yearned for companionship. I stole time from my cleaning chores to read with him. With his father distraught over his mother and his mother yearning for a daughter never to return, Toby whiled away unending lonesome hours. The MacNeil family became disparate loved ones gathered around the festering wound that submerged Rachel. Her life became not unlike the wailing wind that rustled her dusty skirt.

☾

At one point, Douglas tried to pay me because I had been helping with the laundry and chores. I replaced the gold coin in his hand and curled his fingers around them. "No," I said, "that is not why I am here."

Douglas gazed at me for the longest moment. His eloquent eyes expressed gratefulness and then darkened with an unasked question. Again I felt heat course through my body, warming even the tips of my toes. Again I felt the profound agony of knowing that my strong feelings must be suppressed. I dared not follow my heart down such a dangerous path.

Any thoughts on my part that Douglas would leave Rachel, that he could place her under someone else's care and release his own soul from its misery, I dismissed as fanciful. My imagination was strong, and I could not hold back my dreams. I dreamed of our union. But I knew better. I knew in my heart that Douglas MacNeil was not such a man. He would not turn his back on a wife he'd promised to cherish. I felt infuriated and pleased at the same time over his choice and saddened by my own.

I walked each evening along Downer Creek. The twilight sojourns eased my heartaches. Dusk was a good time to seek wildlife. Sometimes a muskrat swam alongside, coyly acting as if he took no notice of me, but I knew he watched. Every so often, my footsteps startled ducks from their place. Their anxious *quack-quack-quack*, like sudden retorts from a hidden rifle, made me jump with fright as well.

One August evening, I stayed much later than usual. I gathered my shawl closer to me in the brisk air. Nighthawks chanted to one another. An owl whispered its low-toned *who-who-who*. A single coyote moaned in the distance. I lingered by the water.

I stood by the lone alder tree that grew in a bend past the bridge. I saw Douglas standing across the creek. The sterling moonlight softened his weary features. He stood on the bank, listening to the water. He did not notice me. He was lost in his own thoughts. I knew I should leave the man to grieve privately, but I could not move.

I looked at the dark water tickling the stones beneath its frothy surface. The creek's magnetism drew me closer. For a child, such a pull would have been irresistible. Evelyn would surely have wanted to be in this stream. The water was indeed attractive.

I allowed myself one last glimpse of Douglas. His body was partially hidden now by clumps of lacy willows at the creek's edge. I imagined seeing again the boy he had been. I remembered standing on the deck of the great ship, seeing the ocean stretch all around and beyond us. Scotland lay behind us. America and new opportunities stood before us. Douglas had shown me his mother's locket. She'd given it to him before she died.

"Someday you'll give this locket to your bride," I told him. But Douglas shook his head and grasped the golden oval in his palm.

"No. This I will keep for my own, for always." The set of his chin and the determination glinting like steel in his eyes that night made me believe him.

Now, he stood at the site where his home had once been, a similar tilt to his chin. I tore myself away from this vision and returned to my cabin.

☾

I began to walk later in the evenings, so I was certain to be there when he was. Douglas's destination was always the same—his old homestead. I felt compelled to watch. I tried to excuse my erratic behavior by telling myself that he might jump in, try to follow his child. If I remained near, I could at least save him.

However futile my reasoning, in my deepest heart, I feared Douglas might end his own life. I did not want Douglas to let go of life. I wished him, willed him, prayed to God to help him embrace life again. Every evening, he stood at the former site of his home, as if trying to understand the incomprehensible. Perhaps he pined for the incomplete life of his beautiful little girl or wondered how her death had washed away the happy home he'd meant to build in this new country.

On the third night, Douglas glanced up suddenly and saw me. Our eyes met across the rollicking water. Neither of us spoke. I barely breathed. I longed to speak words of comfort but none came. Instead, we watched each other. Two lonely people gazing at each other across an abyss of what had been and could never be. I broke the spell first. I turned and walked away, my footsteps snapping fallen willow branches in counterpoint to singing frogs' tunes.

☾

If Rachel were aware of the growing bond between her husband and myself, she did not show it. Her heart deadened as mine awoke. Douglas and I built an uneasy trust between us. Our bond grew over bits of conversation shared at the dining table, as I washed dishes after dinner, as I ironed shirts. But even stolen pieces of conversation—those as casual as inquiring about the weather—charged the air between us with the fire of lightning strikes.

I prepared a tea tray for Rachel each afternoon. One rainy day, as I placed shortbreads becomingly on a lacy doily, Douglas startled me by coming into the kitchen.

"I need a drink of water," he said.

"Help yourself," I replied and finished my task. "I'm ready to take this to Rachel now. Would you like to join us?"

He swallowed hard. "No, thank you, Lorna."

"Douglas," I said sternly as I could manage, "I can no longer hold my tongue. It pains me greatly to see you in such a miserable state." I picked up the tray. "You need to cling to the living when someone dies. Hold onto life that way. The reassurance of knowing others continue to live and breathe on this earth and under the same sky and the same stars as your beloved—" I sensed his eyes upon me. I stopped.

Douglas's expression was unreadable.

"I know that," he said. And that was all.

Fearing I'd ruined whatever fragile bond existed between us, and clinging to that slender thread even while I sensed the harm it might cause, I redoubled my efforts to encourage Douglas to embrace life. I sensed in him a reluctance to face the future. I could not let him give up on life itself. I had sheltered him on one rough journey. I could not let him travel alone now.

With Rachel sitting at the windmill seeing only the past, Douglas loosened his own hold on life. He lost interest in the haying. He spent hours alone, often in the barn. The neighbors looked after the chores. Some made sure the MacNeils' fences were kept in good repair and visited frequently to see to it the horses were fed and watered and that the cattle hadn't gone astray.

☾

One evening as I served roast beef, Rachel looked at Toby and inquired sweetly, "And who are you, child? Why have you come to eat with us?"

Toby's eyes teared up. His lip wobbled as he fought unwelcome emotion. "Mama," he said, his voice a hoarse whisper.

"Why, Rachel," I said, spooning gravy across her meat with trembling hand. She didn't notice. "This is your own son, Toby. You've just sat out in the sun too long this day."

She sat silent for a moment, eyeing the child. "No. You are mistaken, ma'am," she said. "I have no children now."

Toby bolted from the table. His movement shook the water glasses. They rocked precariously. Douglas's spilled across the table but did not break.

"Damn it all, woman!" he shouted.

Rachel turned to him wide-eyed, not understanding the chaos she herself had created.

I cringed. I'd never heard Douglas yell before. I placed the gravy boat on the table on a dry spot.

"I'll see to Toby," I said.

What happened between Rachel and Douglas that evening I do not know. I held Toby in my arms and stroked his wind-tangled blond hair until his tears changed into jolting hiccoughs.

"Your mama is not herself these days, darling," I said, lifting his chin so I could look into his innocent blue eyes, so like his father's. "She loves you still, but her memories are locked someplace deep in her heart. She didn't mean to hurt you so, Toby."

He hugged me tight. I bit my lip to quench the flow of my own tears. "Remember always, Toby. She didn't mean to hurt you. Her own heart is hurting and the pain has changed her."

I stayed with him until he fell asleep. I kissed his forehead before I left the room. I met Douglas in the hall.

"Toby is asleep," I whispered. "And Rachel?"

Douglas took my elbow. "Come," he commanded. I followed him outside. A quarter moon spread a soothing light over the buildings. When we arrived at the barn, the smells of fresh hay and manure mingled not unpleasantly with the tangy scent of saddle leather. Douglas set the kerosene lamp he'd needlessly carried to light our way onto a wooden divider of the horse stalls. One of the Percherons whinnied, then quieted.

"Rachel sleeps," he said.

Alone in his presence, I felt tongue-tied and shy. The kerosene lamp flickered, throwing undulating shadows across the stalls. Douglas turned to me and smiled. In the stall where we stopped stood something large and rectangular under a brown burlap sack.

"You're a good cook, a kind woman. You deserve more than you have here. I can'na pay ya." I opened my mouth to protest, but he held up his hand. "You wouldn't let me, I know it."

He tugged on the burlap sack, revealing a shining, polished pine three-drawer dresser. The brass handles on the drawers gleamed in the lamplight.

"It's beautiful," I admitted.

"It is yours."

"Oh, I could not."

"You misunderstand, Lorna. I made this for you."

I put my hand to my throat. The lacy ruffles of my shirtwaist scratched my fingers. Touched by his intimate kindness, "thank you" was all I could think to say.

I walked to the dresser and ran my hand over its smooth top. "Douglas, it is beautiful and a treasure indeed, but you have given me too grand a gift. I am not able to repay you."

"I will bring it to your cabin at the first opportunity." We stood at opposite ends of the bureau. He came toward me and took my hands in his own calloused palms. "This I have done for you. You are a shaft of welcome sunlight in this house, Lorna."

He pulled me to him and kissed me on the mouth. I accepted his kiss and returned it. I knew that I would never love another man to the depth and intensity with which I had fallen for this one. In my mind, I knew my action was wrong. But my heart knew otherwise. The will to live is fierce. I tried to share my will for life with Douglas, to give him some of the vibrancy of my own soul in the hopes that it could heal him.

His arms encircled me and I felt completely made of spirit, as if my flesh had melted away. An instant of blinding heat forged a strong bond between us just as a moment of intense pain had frozen Rachel's heart and locked her into a prison of memories. The rise and fall of his chest comforted me. His heart beat rapidly as did my own, like the pounding of horse's hooves when the horse ran frightened from an impending storm.

At that single moment, I wanted more than anything to give myself to him, if for nothing else to ensure that he would continue to hold on to life through holding on to me. I sensed to the deepest points of my bones that he had not held a woman for the longest time. And holding on to him, my own body reveled in the rapturous feeling of a man's embrace, a luxury I myself had not experienced for too long a time. We parted. I could not read Douglas's eyes.

"Lorna, I still love my wife," he admitted.

"You'll always love her. She bore your children," I said. I laid my hand against his stubble-roughened cheek. "Love lasts, but people fear what they do not understand. And how could anyone ever understand this?"

"I'll not apologize for kissing you," he said. "I only hope you won't think less of me for it." He paused, cleared his throat. I felt no need to speak. Shame might have overcome me, but for Douglas's kindness. He touched my arm. He said, "Were things different, Lorna—" and his voice faded.

"Kindred spirits know one another always," I said. I shared his despair.

Love is God's great gift to humankind. If there were two human beings in greater need of love at that time I knew them not. The giving of the pleasures of the flesh makes us most alive. And yet, the sweetness, the tenderness of our love, was tempered by deplorable sadness. I knew I must leave. All that was left for us was to pretend this kiss had never occurred or to steal guilty moments in seclusion. I could not bear that. Difficult as it was to have lived in such proximity with a man whom I cared so deeply for and watched suffering so, staying with a forbidden lover would have been even harder.

I wished for him to come to me with respect. Had I let our affair progress any further, Douglas would not have been able to keep respect for me. I needed to respect myself as well. If I stayed, I would feel diminished rather than nurtured by love, as would he.

I did not tell Douglas of my plan. I left the next morning. I first stopped in the Church of the Heavenly Rest and sought comfort kneeling before its altar. I could not bring myself to pray for Rachel's death as some within the town had said they did. God should let her go, they said. She only sought release from a circumstance too hard in this life. But perhaps God would see her pain and release her from it in time to enjoy her son's growth into manhood and to realize the gift she had in Douglas. I prayed for the child, Toby. For it was he who would understand the least. I had not intended to harm him. Yet, by my own selfish actions, I had already done so.

☾

I moved across the mountains and settled in Laramie, a small town with a charming atmosphere and filled with the youthful exuberance of college students hungry for knowledge and the vibrancy of life. Twenty years later, Toby found me.

I opened my door to his soft knock.

"Douglas," I said, daring still to hope our love could be rekindled after such a lengthy absence.

Toby shook his head and removed his hat. "No, Ma'am. I'm Toby."

"Oh, Toby," I cried, and hugged him. "Please come inside. Can you stay for tea?" I settled him in the parlor and served tea and scones. Toby displayed the same fondness for my currant scones as his father had.

Between bites, Toby said, "We missed you, Lorna."

"And I you, Toby." I looked him up and down, raising my chin. "You have grown into a handsome young man." He resembled more the rugged handsomeness of his father than the fine features of his mother. But his voice retained the same airy quality of tone that resonated in Rachel's.

He blushed. "Thank you. It is in part due to your care," he said. To his credit, he did not ask why I had departed his life so quickly. Had his father told him?

"No." I shook my head. "It is yourself. I merely reminded you that living after another's death was not sinful but necessary."

His eyes held mine. I shivered. I suddenly felt as if I looked into Rachel's vacant eyes. "As you must have done for Father," he said.

My china teacup rattled against its saucer. My mind searched for a satisfactory reply but found none. We sat, suspended in time. Toby said, "He was never the same after you left." His words stabbed my heart. I looked away. "Father continued as before, but it was like the light had gone from the day."

I held the arm of my sofa, transfixed. Had I destroyed his father with our one-time dalliance? In my effort to give love needed so deeply, had I erred by giving it? Perhaps holding back those strong emotions would instead have given us both something to hold on to. By satisfying my own longing, had I created an even deeper yearning in Douglas?

Toby noticed my confusion and touched my arm. "He told me once that you had given him hope to hang on to life, and that I should be grateful you came into our lives at the time we needed you most. That you left was unimportant. What you gave us was."

I closed my eyes. Tears fell. I had never forgiven Rachel for imprisoning not only herself but her family in a maelstrom of her own making. And I saw now that in my guilt I held myself apart from life as she had done.

"Life is best lived," I whispered. Toby leaned forward to hear me. A look of concern clouded his face.

"And have you applied such reasoning to yourself?"

I smiled as best I could. "I remained among the living," I replied. "And that is all any of us can do." He nodded, then took something from his trouser pocket.

"Father asked that I give this to you." He handed me the locket that had belonged to Douglas's mother. The locket he had kept himself rather than giving it to his wife. I knew because Rachel would have worn such a sentimental token. To my knowledge, she had not done so. And now the precious necklace was to be mine.

Douglas had loved me. I curled my fingers around the cold gold oval. I hesitated to ask the next question. I dreaded the reply. By what I held in my hand, I already knew the answer.

"Is your father ill, Toby?"

The child had become man enough to answer directly. "No, Lorna, he is dead."

I clutched the necklace tighter and pressed my lips together. I had left Douglas when his need for me was greatest. The locket showed me he had not forgotten. I knew that by this gift, Douglas communicated not only his love but forgiveness. He was a stronger human than I.

Toby's voice broke into my thoughts. "I am sorry that I had to be the one to tell you. He did not suffer. A heart malady. He passed a little over a month ago."

The time delay in telling me occurred because Toby had had difficulty locating me. He had finally found me through another former employee of Mrs. Hawthorne's.

"And your mother?" I asked.

"My mother died many years ago. Lightning struck the windmill, burned it down, and caught the house afire in the night," he explained, his voice faltering. "After you left, Father had taken to sleeping in the barn, in the hay loft. By the time the smoke awakened him, all was lost."

I cried for Toby's loss, and for Douglas.

"Father wanted to see you again before he died," Toby continued. "But he could not find you, Lorna."

When I did not break the silence, Toby said, "And I have brought you something else that belongs to you now. My father said you were to have it." He stood and held out his hand. "Come," he commanded. I followed him outdoors to his wagon. In the box stood a large rectangular object covered with a brown burlap sack.

"The bureau," I said.

Toby gave me a sideways glance. "Yes, how did you—?"

I squeezed his hand. Douglas had not told Toby of our indiscretion, although he must have guessed. "Your father and I shared a special bond." I smiled. "Please bring it inside."

He did so. I embraced him a last time, dreading his leave-taking. Then he was off, as quickly as he came, someone with a gift to bring and a life of his own to live.

I returned to my bedroom, where I stood alone, still grasping Douglas's locket in the palm of my hand, clinging to the forsaken dreams that lingered in my soul and allowed my heart little rest. I laid the locket on the dresser Douglas had made for me so long ago. I touched the firm, smooth dresser top with both hands. I wept.

❨

AUTHOR'S NOTE

The first worship services in Saratoga's Church of the Heavenly Rest were held in early 1889 and Reverend R. E. G. Huntington was the minister. The church later became St. Barnabas's Episcopal Church, which is still in use today in Saratoga, Wyoming. The rest of this story is fiction.

The Apology Tree

ON THE NIGHT AUNT IRIS DIED, A BITTER SPRING FROST KILLED THE crabapple tree in my front yard. I had not even thought to take a photograph of it, so the tree was lost forever, except in my memory. The tree's demise disturbed me. In my mind and heart, the tree and Aunt Iris were bound together. She had loved that tree. That the tree gave up its life on the night she lost hers wrenched my already aching heart.

Not a full three days before, my fiancé had broken our engagement while we stood under that very same tree. He had discovered, he said, that the tie of love would be too confining. He wanted more from life than I did. He wanted to travel and see the world. His final words still rang in my ears. "And you, Claire, you're a homebody. You cling to this spot as if it's sacred." He rubbed his hand across a low branch of the tree. "And this tree. You have that crazy attachment to this tree. As if it had a spirit or something. It's just a plant." He was wrong. I loved the tree, too, and felt as if in some mystical, unexplainable way, its roots and branches and leaves and blooms connected me spiritually to my aunt. Most certainly, the tree represented a valued part of my heritage. Aunt Iris had made sure I prized the tree because she had always treated it with respect and perhaps a bit of awe herself.

Our last conversation had been unusual. Aunt Iris's voice sounded weak. I had called the hospital at an inopportune time. Separated by five hundred miles and this icy and unexpected snowstorm, we found the telephone helped us stay connected to one another, yet the lines offered a poor substitute for being there in person. Aunt Iris had to ring off quickly. We didn't even say goodbye. I hadn't even thought to say, "I'll call you later." There hadn't been time for niceties. A sudden heart attack squeezed the life from her. I ached for the squandered privilege of telling her one last time how much I loved her.

I lived in the house where Aunt Iris had grown up. The tree she loved so had belonged to her aunt, Madeline Brandt. Madeline had planted this tree especially for her niece, as a "connection to the past," Aunt Iris once told me. As she grew up under its summery canopy of pale pink blossoms, Aunt Iris learned about Madeline's history. She never talked about it with me. "Too much water under the bridge," she'd say, and then hastily change the subject, asking, "Say, did you notice that the quilters are going to have another raffle?" Aunt Iris had been adept at telling me what she wanted me to know but not necessarily satisfying my curiosity.

I walked outside on the cold May morning after Aunt Iris's death. The tree's leaves hung limp and black like tiny mourning wreaths scattered among the branches. There would be no more beautiful pink blossoms, no more crabapple picking, no more jelly-making sessions. I touched a branch. Though it felt surprisingly firm, I knew the tree was dead. All contact with Aunt Iris and my curious "connection to the past" had disappeared. I must have stood there for a long time. My neighbor, Susan, jolted me from my memories.

"Claire," she said, opening the metal gate to come into the yard, "you'll catch your death, dear. Come inside, it's too cold for you to stay outdoors today." She clucked over my not having worn a coat, ushered me into my own house, made me a cup of coffee and heated a slice of her sinful streusel coffee cake in the microwave. Once she satisfied herself that she'd gotten me comfortably settled, she sank into a chair and took a bite of her sweet concoction.

"I'm so sorry about your Aunt Iris, dear," she said. "Is there anything I can do to help you?"

I shook my head. "Thank you, Susan."

"She was a dear person, a truly dear person." Susan took a sip of coffee, then sat back and looked out the picture window at the tree. "And the tree. Well, if it's any consolation, I lost my lilacs for this year. They look awful, and they were just budded, too."

"They'll come back," I offered, taking a bite of cake.

She smiled, and reached over and patted my hand. "So will your tree. So will your tree." When I started shaking my head, she said, "I know it looks bad today, but sometimes trees are more resilient than we give them credit for, and this is a special tree."

I tried to smile. "Susan, you always know the right thing to say."

She laughed. "Practice." At age seventy, Susan possessed remarkable energy. She exhibited the most positive outlook of anyone I knew. Aunt Iris and Susan had been childhood playmates and lifelong friends. Susan grieved, too.

"I feel like everything is gone, Susan. Aunt Iris, the only living thing connected with her—" My voice broke and my lower lip wobbled.

"I know," she answered. "I know. It's not the same, but I'm a living thing, and I'm connected with Iris. She had many friends and so do you. You'll get through this. And if the tree doesn't come back, you can plant another."

"But her aunt planted this tree for her. I can't replace that."

"No, you can't." She took a sip of coffee, thinking for a minute. "But then this is not the only crabapple tree that's grown in the yard. Madeline planted this one to replace another."

I sat my fork down with a loud clank against the plate. "Aunt Iris never told me that."

"She wouldn't have. Didn't talk much about Madeline, did she?"

"No."

"I thought as much. Oh, Claire, Madeline was a fine woman. She'd gone through a lot in her life. She doted on Iris. And Iris returned the feeling. There was something different about those two. Something special. A wonderful bond. That doesn't happen often and when it does, the experience is so extraordinary." She paused, then bit her lip. "Sort of like the relationship you shared with your aunt. In a way, the love she and Madeline felt for each other was passed on to you."

I nodded, dabbing fresh tears. "I knew they were close, but all Aunt Iris ever told me was that she didn't want to talk about Madeline because she didn't want to disrupt all the pretty memories she had."

Susan smiled. "I suspect she didn't want you to know all the problems Madeline faced." She stood up and went and rummaged in her purse. "She wanted me to give this to you when she died. You'll understand why she didn't talk of Madeline much. I think she wanted you to get to know Madeline yourself."

She handed me a package wrapped with brown paper. Aunt Iris had scribbled a note, "For Claire, from one niece to another, so you'll always know the story of your tree—and how very special you are to me. With love and affection, Aunt Iris."

Tears blurred my vision. Susan patted my shoulder. "She knew I loved history and the stories of the pioneers," I blurted. "When I was in the fourth grade, she sewed my long pioneer woman dress and sunbonnet for the Pageant of the West festival we had at school."

Susan smiled. "She wanted you to read this when the time was right, Claire. I think that's now."

❨

I curled up on the couch near the fireplace and began reading Madeline's diary. Madeline had been a strong writer. Soon the walls of my room fell away and I lived on the edge of Madeline's life, traveling through time and peering into her life from my vantage point one hundred years distant. I imagined buggies moving along the street as horses' hooves tapped the ground.

Madeline's first entry, written on a separate piece of paper and folded to fit inside the leather-bound journal, was dated March 21, 1900. She wrote, "I've mapped the terrain of my soul and found it barren. Not the oasis I hoped it would be. The man who broke my heart came into my life for a short time. Edward. But strong bonds can be forged in a moment, or a series of single moments. Length of time has nothing much to do with love's sweet deepening."

Madeline's words startled me. Aunt Iris always spoke of her as a happy person and she certainly never mentioned a man in connection with Madeline. Intrigued, I read further. "Edward and I met under strange circumstances two years ago," she explained.

> *I had gone to my favorite place near Willow Creek. I rarely had the time to walk by the creek in the afternoons but on this day my stepmother had ridden into town leaving me with a spare hour or two. I couldn't resist the opportunity. As I stood there, thinking of everything and nothing in the way the wandering of the creek followed its channel, I became aware of the soughing sound of the water, the last of winter's ice breaking and creaking, and the calls of the crows as they flew overhead. I grasped the branch of the lone alder tree which grew at creek's edge. I relied upon its strength to sustain me.*
>
> *A foreign noise startled me. I gasped, and stepping back from the tree, my ankle gave way beneath me. I tripped on a willow branch.*
>
> *"Oh, I've frightened you," said the man who had interrupted my solitude. He sat on a clump of grass, shaded and half hidden by the willows lining the bank.*
>
> *I reached for a branch of the alder tree and steadied myself. "I had not expected to see anyone here," I said.*
>
> *"I don't suppose so." He held up the stick he'd been whittling, turning it this way and that, examining his work. Then he wiped his hands on his trousers and stood. "You all right?"*
>
> *"Yes, thank you," I replied. I bent to rub my sore ankle. I stepped forward, but it would not hold my weight.*
>
> *He winced. "I'd better help you home."*
>
> *As unseemly as it was to allow a strange man to walk me home, I had to do so for I would not have managed it under my own power. Edward— we had introduced ourselves by that point—even carried me part of the way.*

*He was a tall, dark-haired and strong man. Edward appeared clean and
neat. His moustache was well-groomed. Still, I couldn't help but wonder
what kind of a man had a life which allowed him time to sit and whittle
in the afternoon.*

The letter melded into the actual diary entries. Apparently,
Madeline had wanted to make sense of her experiences through writing
about them. As this was something I often taught my students, I felt
pleased to realize one of my ancestors had believed in that method as
well. Her beginning letter read like a summary. Scattered diary entries
followed.

MARCH 11, 1898: *Rose scolded me handily for my clumsiness when
I returned from Willow Creek the other day. I'm glad that Edward had
gone by the time she returned from town. I might have suffered worse
than a scolding for allowing a strange man inside the house when I was
all alone. I dared not tell her about him. My ankle has healed some, but it
still causes me pain at times when I walk. I have finished the chores Rose
set before me. She found many items for me to mend and kept me busy
while my ankle healed. I had no time to write and missed it dearly. I wish
she would praise me. She finds many words of praise for her son—whether
or not he's done what she asks of him—but only reprimands me, no matter
how hard I try.*

The next entry reaffirmed Aunt Iris's insistence that Madeline loved
moonlight, another interest we shared.

MARCH 19, 1898: *I'm well enough now to return to my evening walks
along Willow Creek. I love the moonlight. It soothes me, softens all the world
as if making a different kind of daylight. The moon is gentle, like a loving
mother's caress or a long-haired cat rubbing against your leg or settling down
to purr in your lap. I needed the moonlight tonight. On these moonlight
evenings, I sit by the alder tree, careful not to bump my head on its low
branches, and let the moon cleanse my emotions.*

> *Rose is on the rampage again. I cannot do anything to suit her it*
> *seems. I'd like to believe that I could someday. I think my blood frightens*
> *her. I am not of her blood and yet, being that of the man she married, she*
> *cannot rid herself of me. My father saw to it that she would keep me when*
> *he died. Rose is a tough woman but she will not break her promise to Father.*
> *She will not let me search for work until I am older. I might try to fit myself*
> *to be a teacher. I think I could pass the test. Rose, though, believes women*
> *should marry and leave the working to the men. I wonder if Edward feels*
> *differently.*

I stood up and stretched. Madeline's story touched me. I searched
my bookshelf for the family Bible and found her birth date. In 1898, she
had been sixteen years old. Her stepmother, Rose, had obviously been
tough with her. Still, nothing in the diary so far pointed to any great
catastrophe. What could have been so bad that Aunt Iris didn't want to
talk about Madeline's life but expected me to learn about it on my own?
And what happened to Edward? I read further, hoping to find the
answers to my questions.

> MARCH 21, 1898: *I cannot get Edward out of my mind. He meets me*
> *often now by the creek in the evenings. Rose does not know, nor does Danny.*
> *If he found out, he would surely tell his mother and make my life miserable.*
> *Edward treats me so kindly. He is a wonderful listener. Tonight, I noticed*
> *his feet. They are large for a man of his height, and I suppose they appear*
> *even larger in his shoes. He is several inches taller than me. His laughter*
> *delights me. We often laugh. He does not say much about his own situation.*
> *I wish I could learn more about him.*

Then, about a week later, Madeline explained how deeply she had
fallen for this man with large feet and a penchant for whittling.

> MARCH 26, 1898: *I gave too much of myself too soon. I couldn't have*
> *stopped. I felt so lonely, and Edward was so gentle. Tender. Our first kiss*
> *was tender. We stood watching a mink glide down the creek. Though the*

*animal acted unaware of his surroundings, we knew he watched us as we
gazed at him. In the same way, I suppose, there was an awareness between
Edward and I.*

*I had gone to the creek at dawn to fetch water. Edward had never met
me here in the mornings, and I asked if something troubled him. He replied
that he had no troubles on this day. He reached to steady me as I lifted
the water bucket. I looked up into his brown eyes and saw there the desire
expressed in my own. Slowly, he placed a hand upon my cheek. His calloused
hand felt warm and its roughness did not harm my skin. His lips claimed
my own. Our kiss ended much too quickly.*

*"Madeline," he said, his voice husky, and making my name sound
like an expertly-fingered piano arpeggio. I'd not heard him use that
particular tone before.*

*"I must go, Edward," I said firmly. He ran his hand over my hair.
"I'll wait," he told me. When our bodies united a few days later, beneath
the moon and beside the creek, I wanted more. This delighted him. He
laughed with joy. So did I. Rose did not know of my dalliances but I
felt certain Edward would come forward to tell her of our growing love
one day soon.*

*I began rising earlier in the mornings and meeting Edward by the alder
tree at dawn. The chill air proved most invigorating. When I inquired one
morning if he did not think it more prudent that we meet in his home,
Edward said only that this place was much more enjoyable. He wanted us to
have a special place all our own. We had found a secluded area sheltered with
willows and a soft, grassy place to lie upon and there we shared our love.*

The next two entries were much shorter. I had thought perhaps,
that Madeline had married Edward and then been widowed or abandoned, as sometimes happened in her time. That would account for
Aunt Iris's complete omission of Edward's name in connection with
Madeline over the years. I read further, discovering how wrong I was.

MARCH 27, 1898: *Edward did not meet me at creekside this morning.
I waited. When the sun rose to the place it usually occupies when we part,*

*I returned home. Perhaps he plans to come to the house soon and tell
Rose of our intentions to marry. This day has felt longer than any other.*

MARCH 28, 1898: *Two days now and my love has not appeared. I am
desperate with worry but must not show my feelings. I dare not spend all
my time at the creek waiting, for that would cause trouble with Rose.*

MARCH 31, 1898: *This morning we awoke to find a small sapling decorated
with a blue satin ribbon planted in front of the house. Rose said, "That looks
like an ugly dead stick," and she would have had Danny uproot it and burn
it with the willows, but I stopped her. "Marking it with a ribbon?" she said.
"One would think it was a gift." I believed perhaps it was a gift. But Rose
said she hadn't found any one else who had been the receiver of such a strange
kindness, and she didn't believe it was proper to let it grow. I called it the
Miracle Mystery Tree, and for some reason, she allowed it to remain. Before
she returned to me she said, "Well, the likes of that won't grow here." I told
the tiny tree I felt differently than she did. "You'll grow," I told it. "My
love will make you grow." Edward at last has contacted me.*

The contact Madeline yearned for was not meant to be. Edward
hadn't come to see her at her home, neither to formalize their courtship
nor to ask Rose for Madeline's hand in marriage.

APRIL 1, 1898: *I puzzled over the gift of the tree all day but today all is
clear to me. Edward sent me a letter. He had given me the tree as a reminder
of our beautiful love, he said. I could look upon it as a type of apology since
he was not good with words but found wood to be more lasting. He could
not stay and I could not come with him. He found the traveling life too
enthralling. "My life is no life for a woman," he wrote. Then he dealt me the
final blow by revealing he already had a wife. "She did not long cotton to my
traveling ways but continues to welcome me when I return to her." She lived
in another town far away, he explained. But he would never forget me.
"Madeline, you were the only one," he said. "I never loved another except for
you." I threw the letter into the fire and watched it burn to bits. In my anger,*

I hastened to rip the tree out of the ground. I was not fast enough. Rose stood
there pouring water on it. She said, "Well, if somebody's kind enough to
give us a tree, I guess we ought to try to take care of it, hadn't we?"
 "What changed your mind?" I asked her.
 "The gesture, Madeline. No one has ever been so kind to me before."
So the tree would remain with us.

The tree remained, and with it undoubtedly Madeline's bitter memories of Edward and his betrayal. What a scoundrel he had been. Now
I knew why Aunt Iris had never spoken of him.

JANUARY 3, 1899: *I suppose it was destiny that I lost the child by the creek.*
No one heard my moans of pain that early December day just weeks ago
now. I picked up the filled water bucket, but it was too heavy for the young
life inside me to bear. I had risen early. Rose had gotten used to my early
morning absences. I still walked by the creek and hoped Edward would
return and tell me he had made a terrible mistake. I sat by the alder tree for
a time. Washed the blood away with creek water as best I could and when
I returned home, clothes damp and myself chilled from the wintry air and the
loss, I lied and told my stepmother I slipped in the snow and fell into the
creek. I took my chores more slowly the next few days and let my body heal.
But my heart held deep sorrow. I had loved Edward, given all I had of
myself and my heart to him, and lost. I pined for him but dared not show it.
 At dinner, Danny commented on how I looked older and wiser and he
didn't know why. Like it had happened overnight. I had caught him watching
me several times. I felt he knew by something in my countenance that must
have been subtly changed. Maybe an appearance of women that is known
only to men—for it is by virtue of loving them that such a change occurs.
He never spoke to me about it if he did know. Rose said I'd merely matured
as all young ladies do.

I could read no further. Tears fell down my cheeks. Poor Madeline.
I flipped to the back page of the diary and found an envelope, marked
with Aunt Iris's handwriting and addressed to me. She had written me

a letter before she had fallen ill. In it, she explained more about Madeline, saying, "I found Aunt Maddy's diary too sad to share with you, Claire. Please forgive me. She was so dear to me and I could not bear to think of her hurting so. Also, her words are intensely personal. I'm trusting you to keep her secrets.

"As you must realize, the tree has remained with us over the years, although it is not the one Edward planted. That tree died in a willow fire gone out of control. The neighbors had been burning willows along their irrigation ditches, and the wind changed suddenly. Why they had decided to burn during a drought is beyond me, but the fire destroyed the tree and stopped there. The house was not harmed. Thankfully, the town had not grown around us at that time as it is now. I was just a youngster then, and I believed the tree possessed magical powers and saved the house from the fire. I was distraught over the loss of the tree, so Aunt Maddy purchased another and planted it for me. I've always wondered if perhaps she might have liked to have just forgotten it, and left the yard treeless, but she wanted me to be happy. That was just her personality. She tried to make others happy. When Rose suffered a stroke, Aunt Maddy stayed and took care of her until she died.

"The tree gained a reputation outside of our family. Because Rose had considered it a gift of mystery, she spread the tale that the tree had healing powers. Why people believed this, I don't know! But they did. Rose didn't know that the reason the tree was planted was in apology for a betrayal. Even so, people began to believe that the tree could heal their arguments and problems, that if they would stop and chat for a while under its branches, things would work out for them and their lives would be happier. So, like Aunt Maddy said, love made the tree grow, and I believe love keeps it alive still.

"If I believed in such things, I'd think this second tree was magical. As if Aunt Maddy's misfortune were drawn from the ground by the first like a leech sucks poison from the blood. But then, that's a fanciful notion, isn't it? Still, there is something special about this tree and more positive than I've made it sound. I've made a list of all the happy things that occurred under this tree. I hope the tree never has to be destroyed."

❨

Outside my window, the withered tree looked barren and sad. I couldn't grant Aunt Iris's last wish. Nature had taken its course and the crabapple tree was gone. Her letter, her handwriting, stirred such deep emotions within me that I believed I heard her voice. But I had to face facts. Aunt Iris was gone, too. If she were here in person, she'd probably also mention the pretty shape the tree grew into—and all on its own without pruning—as if by being beautiful it could beckon people to sit beneath its branches and thus perform its magical deeds of healing. Of course, that's silly. Plants don't have minds or human characteristics.

But Aunt Iris—practical, down-to-earth Aunt Iris—kept records of the romances the tree inspired and the apologies she knew had occurred under its sheltering canopy. She listed fifty-three couples who had gotten engaged or courted under the tree. There might have been fifty-four if my own romance had lasted. The apologies ranged from drastically altered business deals to simpler fare, like one man's broken promise to bring his wife a rose everyday. I smiled as I read that one, for the resolution of the problem—roses had become too expensive for their financial circumstances—was clever. Rather than bring her a flower, he promised to compliment her sincerely each day before he left for work.

Instead of destroying the tree—and Madeline had two chances to do so—she let it grow. She never married. Apparently, she never loved a man again. She never forgot the anguish Edward had caused her. Toward the end of her diary, Madeline expressed her hurt feelings. "Other men came courting," she wrote, "but I had lost heart in the ways of romance. With the child who died, I lost also my desire to conceive others. Love teaches us about ourselves. We don't always like what we learn. I followed my heart and found only pain." The plant she tended over the years became a living reminder of her single transgression. The crabapple tree bore fruit. Madeline never had. But she'd left a legacy just the same.

I owed a great debt to Madeline—an ancestor whom I had not known—and whose story had not been told because of the societal taboos of the time and Aunt Iris's wish to provide her own aunt with a modicum of privacy. Now that I knew the story Aunt Iris had been reluctant to share, I felt relief. I vowed to plant another tree in Madeline's honor. The new tree would not share the magical qualities of the one that she had planted, but the seedling would grow, symbolizing the love she showered on Aunt Iris and the resulting love she passed on to me. Madeline hadn't experienced the kind of love she had dreamed of in her lifetime, but she had given love that outlasted her life. What better kind of courage existed?

☽

The withered leaves of the tree showed signs of life again in mid-June. One day, returning from the post office, I thought the fruit tree looked fringed with green as it had before the severe frost. I could not believe my eyes. I held one firm branch in my hand and sighed with relief, tickling the tender green buds with my fingers.

Delighted with the new growth, I went inside. In the mail, I discovered a letter in familiar handwriting. Richard, an old college flame, had written to me. We'd shared several dates and dinners and even had gone dancing at the Volunteer Fireman's Ball. I'd believed our romance had been progressing, but he didn't call again after the dance. His sudden silence hurt. We lost touch. I had found myself longing for his company and then feeling bitterness and finally accepting things as they stood. Perhaps, I realized, the emotions I experienced had been similar to those feelings Madeline confronted in her life.

Wondering why Richard had chosen to write to me now, I slit the plain white envelope and pulled out his letter. He explained why he'd ended contact abruptly. He had moved to Missouri when an opportunity for a better job came along, and he didn't believe I'd ever want to leave my home and my job as I appeared happy and stable. He admitted he'd been afraid to tell me he was leaving. He had taken the coward's way out, he said, and hoped I'd forgive him and that we could renew our friendship. He'd written to me rather than telephoning because that seemed more appropriate. But if I wished I could call him.

Richard also mentioned he planned to return for the summer Arts Festival. Would I care to join him for lunch when he arrived?

I gazed at Madeline's remarkable tree. I would indeed join Richard for lunch. Maybe I'd even take along a jar of crabapple jelly.

The Upholsterer's Apprentice

BEVERLY STOOD BACK TO ADMIRE HER HANDIWORK. SHE WHISKED THE stray fabric fibers from her hands. "Every chair has a story, Irene," she said. "Remember that."

"And you have a way with chairs," I said, smiling. I liked my new boss, and I loved making old furniture new. I'd wanted to learn how to upholster furniture since high school when my parents took a class and redid our lumpy sofa. Both of them were dead now but I still had the sofa.

She laughed. "I guess I do, now that you say so." Beverly was a dainty woman with short dark hair. I helped her remove the chair from the special spinning tabletop her son had built. "Lots of practice," she said, as we placed it on the floor. Even there, in the middle of the shop, with chairs and sofas in all manner of disarray, the made-over wingback chair looked elegant.

Beverly rubbed the fabric on the chair's back. She fell in love with each piece after she'd transformed it from something headed for the dump into a beautiful, usable item. Because it was so difficult for her to let go of her craftsmanship, she took photos of each finished piece. Before and after photos, kind of like those make-over pictures of women featured in the glossy women's magazines. For Beverly, this was necessary vanity.

"I wouldn't even do this," she said, as she reached for the Polaroid camera. "But it does help other people see what we can do to ratty furniture."

I swept the scraps away from the chair's legs and she took the photo. When it developed and we placed it next to its "before" shot, I saw how complete the transformation had been.

"This chair belongs to Father Bob, the new Episcopal minister," Beverly told me. "His grandfather owned it before him. His grandfather was a minister, too, and gave him the chair when he was ordained. Isn't that a sweet story?"

"Yes, he'll treasure it." Prior to its being redone, the chair had been covered in gold velvet fabric. The color picked up the color of the wood exposed in the legs, but because the chair had obviously been well loved, the fabric looked brownish and shabby. Beverly's and my work changed the chair into pale blue brocade with strips of gold running through it. The gold strips picked up the chair leg colors, and the blue gave it a handsome appearance. We couldn't take all the credit. Father Bob had chosen the fabric, so really the transformation came from him. We just performed the handiwork.

"I'm sure. Admire your work here for a minute while I write out the receipt. Then would you deliver this to him and pick up Nola Wagner's chair at the Smith House?"

"Sure." I cleaned up our mess as best I could. Fabric swatches, from velvet to chintz, hung from the log walls in plastic binders looking like wall-hangings and decorations themselves. The diversity of colors stood out against the whitewashed logs. The industrial sewing machine stood in the corner, and I swept around its base and replaced the scissors on the counter beside it for Beverly's convenience. While I was in town, she'd start cutting fabric for another article.

"I wonder if this chair will perform the miracles that the other two you've worked on have?" Beverly asked me.

"What miracles?"

"Well, it's like you 'fix up' more than the chairs. It's weird, but the last two have led to love affairs."

"What?"

"That first one, remember, the red rocker-recliner that we put floral chintz on?" She continued when I nodded. "Well, it belonged to Mrs. Andrews. She'd been widowed for twenty years or more. But she'd gone to high school with Harvey Carter, a widower, who just happened to be there when you delivered the re-upholstered chair. They rekindled their high school relationship."

I knew the rest. "And she and Harvey got married after that."

"Yes," she said. She finished the receipt and handed it to me. "And the second one, that was a sofa. We redid it from a plain gingham into a blue velvet, for the bank's new lobby. And the young loan officer there helped you carry it inside and bumped into a girl from a tourist family who was coming back out. She tripped, and he helped her. They got married soon after. Remember?"

"Yes, I remember. We're lucky she only bruised her leg. I thought she might have broken it. But Beverly, you surprise me. You are so practical and logical when it comes to work. Then you find these romantic notions and all that logic flies out the window."

Beverly smiled at me. "Romance is magical," she said. "You'll find out one day yourself."

☾

To save time, I picked up Nola Wagner's chair first. I felt disappointed. Not by the chair, for it was a lovely wood and would be a fairly quick fixer-upper. It was round-backed with a tapestry seat. Unlike most clients, who told me the stories behind the chairs and then gave their chairs a love pat before they entrusted them to my care, Nola said simply, "I don't know much about this chair. I believe it's old, but I really don't know."

"You might find out someday."

"I suppose," she said, distracted. "I thought it would be a nice piece to place in the lobby here."

I nodded. The lobby of the Smith House was welcoming, but Nola had eclectic tastes. The antique chair, if it truly was one, would stand out among the thick oak log pieces crafted by a local artisan.

As I was leaving, the newspaper publisher, Hunter Thomas, was entering. He held the door for me. Nola came to greet him.

"I'm having that chair redone," she said. "I'll put it in the lobby here. We wondered if it might be an antique."

Hunter pursed his lips and looked at the chair. "Might be. Lord knows I'm no expert at that kind of thing." He thought for a moment. "I know someone who is, though. Joy Anne Wilson might know. She knows everything about the history of this town."

He helped me lift the chair into the pickup. It stood next to Father Bob's, which was covered in black plastic garbage bags to protect it from wind and the erratic spring weather. I grabbed another bag to cover Nola's chair. "You might talk to Joy Anne," he said.

Nola, who did not have a lengthy attention span, said, "Thanks, Irene. I'll be interested to know what Joy Anne tells you." She held the door for Hunter. "I expect you've come to sell me advertising," she said. They disappeared inside.

I held my tongue from saying something like "It's your chair, Nola, don't you want to talk to Joy Anne?" because I decided Nola wouldn't have understood the remark and because I was intrigued by the chair's story, too.

Traffic downtown was heavy. It was nearly noon on an early summer Wednesday, and tourists crowded Bridge Street both on foot and in vehicles. I drove toward the Hotel Wolf. I stopped at the corner and switched on my right turn signal. I glanced toward the Episcopal manse. I hoped I wouldn't miss Father Bob because of the lunch hour.

The engine died. I tried to restart it, but nothing happened. Behind me, several vehicles formed a line. I heard horns honking. People stared. Traffic behind couldn't go around because they couldn't see over the top of the chairs I was hauling.

A young man I didn't know got out of his truck behind me. He came to my open window and said, "Can I help?"

He was tall, slender, with dark hair and a mustache. He wore dark green aviator sunglasses so I couldn't see his eyes. But he had a friendly smile.

"My engine quit," I said, unnecessarily.

"Okay," he said, "Put it in neutral, and open this door. You steer and I'll push you around the corner and out of the traffic."

The maneuver, awkward as it was, didn't take long. When we had me safely parked around the corner by The Flower Pot, he said, "I'd better move my car in behind you, so the traffic can pass."

When he did, traffic flow resumed. He said, "Let me give you a ride to the gas station. They'll help you with the engine there. My name's Andy, by the way."

"Irene," I said. "But no, thanks, I can walk over there. It's only a couple of blocks."

"Okay, well." He patted the door. "Hope things go better."

"Umm, Andy?"

"Yes?"

"Would you help me deliver this chair to the Episcopal manse? It's just down the street a ways," I pointed to it standing on the corner a block away. "I don't want to scratch it, and I see you have a pickup, too. I shouldn't ask. You've been kind enough already."

"No problem."

We loaded the chair into his pickup and arrived just as Father Bob and Ida Lou Cummins were coming outside.

"Ah," the minister said. "We were just going to lunch. Come on inside and let's have a look at that chair."

Andy and I carried the chair inside. When we unwrapped it, both Father Bob and Ida Lou oohed and aahed over its revitalized appearance. The gold striping in the fabric echoed the gold carpeting of the living room floor. I gave him the receipt and declined his offer to join them for lunch, as did Andy.

"I'm on my way to the gift shop to deliver some polished rocks for my grandfather," he said.

Father Bob, being new to the area, asked, "Who is your grandfather?"
Andy said, "Ben Wright."

"Ben Wright is your grandfather?" I asked. "He used to give me sticks of Beechnut gum when I went to the town hall with my father. Ben was the mayor when my dad was on the town council." I smiled. Andy did, too. He'd taken his sunglasses off and I saw that his eyes were warm brown.

"Sounds like Grandpa," he said. "Sure you don't need a lift to the gas station?"

I shook my head. "But may I use the telephone? I'm sure my boss would like to know why I'm going to be late."

☾

We all parted company on the lawn of the stately white-frame Episcopal manse. Its black shutters and colonial appearance made it one of the most beautiful buildings in Saratoga. I thanked Andy again for his help. He said, "See you around sometime."

While I waited for the engine to be repaired, I visited Joy Anne Wilson. She lived in a small, two-story red brick house, her inheritance from a maiden aunt, about two blocks from the gas station. Joy Anne was tall for a woman, and she had unusually large feet. She had a plain face framed by nearly white-blonde hair styled in a pageboy. Her hazel eyes were large and magnified further by heavy glasses. Probably a result of reading in dusty archives and museums and libraries. But Joy Anne was cheerful. She whisked me inside to her study.

The study was a large room painted ivory, with two walls fully lined with built-in bookshelves completely filled with books. A turquoise Victorian-style couch sat across from a cherry wood desk, both of them standing on a braided rug of ivory, rose, turquoise and pale green strips.

"My, this is an interesting task, isn't it?" she said, when I explained the reason for my visit. "Let me look through my files, here," she said. She turned and opened a large cabinet door beneath the counter that lined a third wall of her study. She pulled out a large D-ring notebook, and began flipping through plastic-covered pages. "Now, isn't that something," she said. She pointed a bright pink fingernail at the page and nodded at me to come look.

"You said the chair came from the Smith House, right?"

I nodded. She continued. "Well, I'd say that chair dates back to the time that the blacksmith had his shop there, oh, probably back about 1885 or so. This would have been in the real early days of Saratoga."

She tapped the page. "See this newspaper clipping? That was about the time the blacksmith's wife disappeared. Do you know that story?"

I shook my head.

"The blacksmith shop, as you know, was located on the same spot as the Smith House stands now. That's why we call it the Smith House, of course." She removed her reading glasses and rubbed her nose. "The blacksmith was rumored to have shot his wife, you see, because, she supposedly had an affair with the saloon keeper. But we don't know for sure. She was lost for several years—just disappeared into thin air." She bit her lip. "Her bones were found several years later, even after the blacksmith himself died. They were discovered in the mountains with a cameo brooch that was supposed to have belonged to her grandmother, so the searchers determined that the skeleton was the blacksmith's wife."

"And of course, the Smith House has changed ownership five or six times in the past hundred years. Nola probably wouldn't know, she hasn't been here long enough. But I'll bet that chair came from the blacksmith's things. The hotel owners saved them in a back room somewhere. One of the owners meant to decorate with them, but when she found out about this story, she changed her mind."

"Do you think this chair belonged to the blacksmith's wife?"

"Quite possibly," Joy Anne admitted. "Would you like to join me for a cup of tea?"

"Oh, no, thank you. I should be getting back, if my engine's repaired," I said. "Joy Anne, could you make me a copy of that newspaper story? I'd like to show it to Beverly. We always like to know a chair's history."

"Certainly," Joy Anne said.

❰

By the time I returned to Beverly's workshop, it was late afternoon. I apologized for being so late, but I showed her the clipping.

"It's like I said. Every chair has a story." She waved me off when I started to work on the sofa she'd almost completed. "I can handle this one," she said, her mouth filled with tiny brass tacks. Beverly liked to do her work the old-fashioned way. She had an electric stapler, but she preferred to use tacks. "Would you mind tearing down Nola's chair? That way we can get a head start on it and we won't fall behind."

I had just begun to pry off the worn tapestry fabric on the chair's seat when someone drove up. "I'm going to save this fabric, Beverly," I said, holding it up for her. "If that story is true, then this material is old. It could be valuable."

She agreed and went outside to greet our visitor. She re-entered the shop with Andy Wright. I blushed. "Oh, hi," I said.

"Hi," he said. "You made it back to work okay, I see."

"Yes, thanks to you." I told Beverly of the heroic rescue on Bridge Street.

"Geez, Irene, you probably owe the poor man lunch at least," she said, smiling broadly and embarrassing me without meaning to. At least, I'm sure she didn't mean to embarrass me that much. I disliked her attempt to play matchmaker.

"I do owe him for the favor," I said.

Andy said, "How about tomorrow?"

"What?"

"If you'd like to take me to lunch, I'm free tomorrow. Hotel Wolf?" He didn't appear to be embarrassed.

"Sure," I replied, trying not to laugh.

"Great," he said. "I'll pick you up. Say eleven-thirty?"

I looked at Beverly for confirmation. She said, "That's fine with me."

Andy said, "Good. I'll look forward to it. But I really came here as a customer." He explained that his grandfather's favorite chair was wearing out. "I'd like to have it redone for him as a gift before I leave at the end of the summer. But I don't know how we'll get him to sit anywhere else while you're working on it."

Beverly told him to bring it by any time and we'd do it as quickly as we could. She let him leaf through a book of fabric swatches, and then she showed him the portfolio of past chairs.

"These are the two love affair chairs," Beverly said, when he came upon the most recent of our endeavors.

"Beverly," I scolded.

Andy looked up at me. He had a kind face. His expression reminded me of the one displayed by his grandfather when he gave me the chewing gum treats.

"Irene's embarrassed about this, but she's worked on these two chairs and they've both resulted in love affairs."

"Coincidence," I said firmly. I busied myself on the padding in the blacksmith's chair. It was not foam rubber, but a packed material, like bunches of cotton balls wadded together to make a satisfactory pad. I knew the chair was old.

Beverly explained about the two chairs. Andy, being kind, said nothing. He chose a sturdy burgundy color with a jacquard design for his grandfather's chair, and thanked Beverly for taking on the project. "I'll see you tomorrow, Irene," he said and left.

As soon as he turned onto the highway, Beverly said, "Maybe this chair will be your fixer-upper."

"I doubt it," I answered, but she had awakened my curiosity. I thought of Father Bob and Ida Lou Cummins. Ida Lou had been widowed for about ten years. Her husband had died in a logging accident when she was in her twenties. Father Bob was a bachelor. I guessed them to be about the same age. She played the organ at church and served as the church secretary. Their work would cause them to spend quite a bit of time together, and they both had been present when I delivered the chair. I didn't speak my thoughts to Beverly but decided to wait and see what, if anything, developed through the wingback chair.

Instead, I said, "I should work late to repay you for all the lost time today. First my pickup quit and now this interruption."

"You don't have to do that," she said. "But if you really want to, I'd let you. Maybe then we could both take a couple of days off at the end of the week. We've been working pretty hard lately."

Beverly was fair. We worked hard, but she was surprisingly flexible. She and her husband, Jack, even invited me to share dinner. Jack made a chicken and rice casserole. Beverly and I decided to work until ten o'clock and then call it a day.

We finished the couch she was working on and moved on to Nola Wagner's chair.

"It's been broken," I said, showing Beverly the fracture line on one of the chair legs. "What would cause that? Maybe someone too heavy sat on it?"

Beverly ran her finger over the marred area. "Smoothly done," she said. "I don't know what would have caused that. This chair's pretty old, so maybe it arrived on a wagon and was dropped or something."

"Maybe someone got really angry and threw it."

Beverly didn't discount my theories. "Sometimes things got tough in the mining towns in these mountains," she said. We were deciding how to handle re-stuffing the seat when Jack burst into the workshop.

"Bev," he said, out of breath from running across the yard full speed. "There's been a shooting. I've got to go." He kissed her on the cheek. Jack served as an EMT for the town. He was on call today and so would sit in for the EMT in town who'd be dispatched with the ambulance. "I might be a while. Nola Wagner's been shot."

His words struck me like tacks pounded into the base of overstuffed sectionals. I looked at Beverly's horrified expression and dropped my scissors on the floor. The clatter startled us both.

I backed away from the blacksmith's wife's chair.

Beverly said, "We can call it a night, Irene. You worked hard today."

I agreed to meet her at nine in the morning and left. My home was just two miles away by the highway. I drove slowly, watching for the ambulance and prepared to get out of its path. The speeding rescue unit didn't come.

I felt on edge and too wound up to sleep, so I spent the rest of the night on my parents' sofa, my living room drapes opened to the starry sky. A full moon illuminated the landscape in a softer version of daylight. The Snowy Range Mountains rose in the east, jagged and filled with shadows.

I knew as soon as Jack told us that Nola Wagner had been shot. She was dead. I felt involved in a weird way. If Beverly's theory about the "love affair chairs" were true, then that magical mysticism most likely worked in reverse. Had I set something incomprehensible in motion by finding out the history of the blacksmith's wife and her chair? Maybe I was jinxed. I fell asleep just before the sun broke free of the mountain range the next morning.

❨

I arrived at Beverly's a few minutes before nine. She gave me a cup of coffee and poured one for herself before we entered the workshop.

"You didn't sleep well, did you?"

"No. Did you?"

She shook her head. "Jack didn't get home 'til after three A.M. He's still asleep."

We went inside. The Fergusons' sofa was nearly completed and sat against one wall. All that was left was stapling the covering on the bottom. Nola Wagner's chair stood on the spin-top table, seat and back devoid of padding and fabric. The sturdy pine wood skeleton mocked us.

"Let's put that away for a while," Beverly said. She sat her coffee on the counter and lifted the chair. It wasn't very heavy so I held the door for her. "I'm going to put this inside the shed for a few days," she told me.

When she returned, we lifted the sofa onto the spinning table and prepared to staple the filmy brown covering to its underside.

"So what happened to Nola?" I asked, dreading the answer.

Beverly pointed to the sewing machine. "Sit down," she commanded. When I had done so, she said, "Nola's dead."

"I thought as much," I said.

"Her husband shot her."

I groaned. "Oh, no."

Beverly nodded. "Jack says the story is Herb Wagner found her and Hunter Thomas in bed together. Herb aimed for Hunter but Nola stepped in front of him just as Herb pulled the trigger. I guess Herb was inconsolable. They've got him in jail on suicide watch."

"Beverly, this is awful. You know, they say history repeats itself. Do you think that's why this happened?"

"Do you mean is there a curse on the chair?"

I nodded.

"No. I don't believe that at all. Coincidence."

"But your idea on the 'love affair chairs' doesn't seem to have been coincidence."

She watched me for a long moment, then took a sip of coffee. "I shouldn't have said those things. Guess I was trying to help you adjust to the new job and feel happy here. I like having you here," she said.

"Thanks. I like working with you, too. But Beverly, maybe I shouldn't be. I mean, what if I do have a magic touch in upholstery? Obviously, it works both ways—good and evil. I don't want something like this to happen again. And it's so strange that what happened is so similar to that chair's history."

"I agree it's strange. Nola Wagner made her choices, and so, dang blast him, did Hunter Thomas. You didn't make them do it, and neither did that chair. They did it themselves." She sipped her coffee thoughtfully. "Besides, chairs are inanimate objects."

"But the wood in them lived once. Maybe it soaked up things. You know, like if the walls could talk?"

"That's creepy, Irene."

"I know. Maybe it's something we're not supposed to interfere with, something we're not supposed to know."

She took both my hands in hers and squeezed them. Her hands were rough and calloused from years of working with fabric and wood and tacks. "I don't know the answers. What I do know is you're a good worker, and I'm a firm believer in getting right back on the horse after you've fallen off. Let's finish this sofa. Then we can work on Andy's grandfather's chair. I told him to bring it by when he came to take you to lunch. I'm betting the fabric will arrive this afternoon and we can finish by tomorrow. Are you game?"

Her optimism was contagious. I didn't tell her I'd decided to finish the projects we were already working on and then I'd look for another job. The implications of this one frightened me too much. I couldn't bear to hurt her feelings.

By the time Andy arrived, we'd finished the Fergusons' sofa and managed to finish some paperwork she'd neglected for a few days.

He looked handsome in a pressed plaid cotton shirt and chinos. "I heard the news," he said. "Irene, if you'd rather not go today, we can make it another time."

Feeling tired and shaky from the events of the past day and my lack of sleep, I was about to agree when Beverly butted in. She said, "No. She'd love to go with you, Andy. You can talk about your grandpa's chair. Irene and I are going to work on it this afternoon."

"Great," he said. "I had to practically wrestle it away from him. He's sitting at the dining room table playing solitaire now."

"He could have come with us," I said.

Andy smiled. "I invited him, as a matter of fact, but he's not much on getting out these days. He'd rather people come see him. So he can sit in his chair." We laughed.

We lunched at the Hotel Wolf. The usual lunch crowd had gathered, along with several tourists. We waited in line for a few minutes for a table. People in the line were abuzz with the sad news.

"I'm sorry," Andy said, reaching for my hand and squeezing it. "I know this must be upsetting."

"You don't even know the whole story," I told him. The waitress came to seat us and we passed Father Bob and Ida Lou Cummins. Father Bob smiled at me. "Irene," he said, "I love my chair. Thank you."

"I'm glad," I said, and smiled back.

"Isn't that great?" Andy said. "Doesn't that make you feel good?"

"Yes, but I'm finding out that even the upholstery business has ups and downs."

After we ordered, I told Andy about my meeting with Nola and the chair. "So Beverly put it in the shed today. We couldn't stand to work on it."

He sipped his soda. "I don't blame you."

"Do you still trust me to work on your grandfather's chair?"

The waitress brought our meals. Andy's was a huge taco salad. I ordered my usual French cuisine—a French dip sandwich and French fries. I munched on a fry. "You haven't answered me, Andy."

Fork poised over his salad, he said, "I prefer the 'love affair chairs' theory." He took a bite, glancing over at the minister and Mrs. Cummins. Then he explained his version of events to me. "See, even this chair sparked a love affair, an ill-fated one, of course, but it did inspire romance." He wiggled his eyebrows and tilted his head toward their table.

"Maybe you're right. It's easier to look at it in that light." Feeling better, I finished a bite of sandwich.

"Besides," he said, "I'm kind of partial to that chair. I believe it brought you to me."

I blushed. "Thank you," I said, feeling much better indeed.

☾

Andy returned me to Beverly's workshop promptly. Despite my protests, he paid for lunch. "I asked you out, remember?"

"But I'll still be indebted to you," I protested.

"Not at all," he insisted. "The pleasure was all mine. I do expect good things for Grandpa's chair, though. I'll be back tomorrow to check on it."

Once inside, I asked Beverly if I could do the work on Andy's chair.

"I would love to have you do it," she said. "The material's right here. Came just like I thought it would. If you have questions, just ask. I'll work on the museum's rocker." She handed me a pair of scissors.

We worked until past five. Once again, Jack fixed dinner. We ate a quick meal of heated frozen pizza, and, with assurances that I wouldn't

disturb them if I stayed, I returned to work. I put my heart into Ben
Wright's chair. This chair's story was that it had been a beloved family
object for many years. Andy remembered his grandfather rocking him
to sleep in it when he was a child. I liked them both, and I was determined to focus on the positive. No one would ever know, of course, that
as I tore it apart and repaired the broken springs and re-stuffed and
shaped the padding, I was trying to pour my love into the chair. As I
worked, I consciously turned my mind to caring thoughts. I decided my
strategy was not much different from that of pregnant women who cro-
chet afghans for their babies. Every stitch contains a loving thought
bursting with pleasant expectations. And, when the babies come, they
are embraced with a blanket of love. If nothing else, Ben Wright would
feel loved when he sat in his favorite chair.

I finished at dawn. I displayed the chair on the spin-top table. I
rubbed my hands across the wine-colored fabric, delighting in its firm
feel. I snapped a Polaroid and laid it on the counter next to the "before"
photo. I wrote a note to Beverly, explaining I was going home to sleep
for a few hours and that I'd return after lunch. I asked her to contact
Andy. If the chair earned her blessing, I'd deliver it that afternoon.

☾

Ben Wright was not at all frail as I'd expected from Andy's descriptions.
Instead, I recognized him immediately as the jolly mayor from my
childhood.

"Grandpa, this is Irene. She works for Beverly at the upholstery shop."

He reached out to shake my hand. As he did so, he placed his other
hand on top of mine and squeezed. "Sure, I know this one. This one's Bud
Runner's daughter, the little blonde-haired tyke who liked chewing gum."

I squeezed his hands and blinked tears from my eyes. "You remember
me," I said, pleased. We let go.

"Of course I do. Bud was a good friend, a good man. I was sorry
when he died. Looks like he raised you right, though."

"I hope so."

"Well, let's get that chair back in here. I've missed it."

"You won't recognize it, Grandpa," Andy said. "Irene did a good job. She worked on it all night so you could have it back today."

"Did you do this one by yourself, Missy?"

Andy rolled his eyes at his grandfather's term of endearment, but I kind of liked it. "Yes, I did. And I'll tell you what, Mr. Wright. If you don't like it, I'll do it again until you do."

He raised a bushy eyebrow. "I'd expect so after all those sticks of chewing gum you bilked me for."

We placed the chair in its spot. I could tell it had sat there for years. Even with their attempt to vacuum the charcoal gray carpet, two mashed sections showed where the chair should be placed. Andy and I unwrapped the chair. It was a rocker, and wood sides flared at the head. The back had a padded area, like a pillow, for Ben Wright's head. The wooden arms each had a band of padded upholstery secured with brass tacks. The chair looked much different than it had the day before. The old blue fabric had been shiny from use at the head and the seat and worn in some places, especially the arms. The padding had peeked through there.

Ben didn't say anything. He stared at his "new" rocker.

I looked at Andy. He looked at his grandfather. We heard the hum of the refrigerator motor from the kitchen.

"My," Ben said, almost in a whisper. "Irene, this is a lovely chair. It's too fancy for the likes of me now."

"No. You should have something beautiful, shouldn't you? Sit in it. That's the true test," I said. "If I didn't get it padded just right, you won't like it."

"Go ahead, Grandpa," Andy said.

Ben sat in the chair. He closed his eyes and ran his hands up and down the arms.

I held my breath.

"It'll do," he said. "It'll do."

I leaned forward. I didn't know if that meant he liked it or was being polite. When he began rocking and winked at me, I knew he would not part with his chair again for a long time.

Andy exhaled. He'd been holding his breath, too. We laughed with relief.

"I think you've got a real talent for this upholstery deal," Ben said. "Better let my grandson take you back to work before you get fired for spending too much time on a delivery."

"Actually, Grandpa, if you'll be all right alone for a while, I planned to take Irene on a drive in the mountains. Beverly gave her the afternoon off because she worked all night."

"I didn't ask——" I began, but Andy shushed me.

"If you're not too tired?"

"No, I'm not tired," I said. "I'm glad you like the chair, Mr. Wright."

"You'd better start calling me Ben, young lady," he said. He waved us away. "Go on. My game show will come on in a few minutes. I'm going to just sit right here in this chair and watch it."

Andy and I walked outside. He caught my arm just as I was about to open the wooden gate. "Thank you, Irene," he said quietly. The afternoon was soft and warm. The heady scent of lilacs mingled with the sweet smell of a honeysuckle bush. Bees buzzed amidst the blooms.

"You're welcome. I'm glad I could do it." Maybe I'd keep my job after all.

"Me, too," he said. "I believe in that 'love affair chair' theory. Work your magic on me." Then he kissed me.

Natural Causes

Carl Walker's patience wore thin. The lost man cost him time. Lambing was a hell of a time for Johnny Shale to disappear. Frigid air stung Carl's nostrils, smelling like metal and burning his lungs. April in this valley at the base of the Wyoming Sierra Madres yielded blizzards more often than showers, and this year felt colder than most.

He'd already returned two ewes to the shed. He'd left them in Anna's care. Anna suggested he ride out to look for Johnny. He was addicted to her homemade biscuits and never missed breakfast, most especially when he knew she planned to whip up a batch. When he hadn't arrived by eight o'clock, Carl began his search.

"Maybe he's staying away because of—"

"No." She spat the word. They looked at each other for a long moment. Carl saw something he didn't recognize in his wife's eyes. Normally they shone as silvery blue as the water rippling down Kayley Creek. As she spoke, her eyes glinted like the steel of the butcher knife hanging in the rack by the window above the kitchen sink.

"Carl," she said, "something's wrong. Bad wrong. I can feel it."

He had drunk the last of his cup, walked to the sink to stand beside her, looked out the window. Viewing the sky, a man might mistake the season for spring. The sun shone in a docile blue sky, reflecting on the snow drifts piled by yesterday's raging blizzard. The brightness blinded him. "This storm was a bad one. Maybe he's holding the herd near the wagon."

Anna took the cup from him, and began filling the sink with hot water. She wiped her hands on her gingham apron, and said, "Let's hope so."

Carl dressed warmly, and Anna patted his heavy wool winter work coat when he pulled it on. He put on his hat, secured the woolen scarf she'd given him for Christmas around his neck, and bent to kiss her before facing the cold.

To her credit, Anna hadn't wavered when he brought the ewes in. She'd dropped her house chores, layered sweaters beneath her coat, and prepared to sit it out in the lambing shed. He hadn't even had to tell her what he was thinking. Since he'd returned alone, she knew that he hadn't found Johnny.

☾

The sheep wagon hadn't been used in the night. There'd been no tracks except the ones that his own horse, Scout, made as they approached. When Carl dismounted and shouted, no one answered. No smoke escaped from the chimney pipe of the little wagon, and when he pushed open the door, he saw messy quarters but no one inside. Johnny had eaten beans but hadn't cleaned up after his meal. A partially filled pan sat on the stove next to a dented enamel coffee pot containing a cup or so of the bitter brew. A few books lay scattered about near the rumpled bed. Carl smiled when he noticed Pearl Buck's *The Good Earth*. Anna had lent the book to Johnny when he'd admitted he liked to read. The gesture was a kind one; the book was Anna's favorite—a Christmas present from Carl.

Carl shut the door. Finding the vacated sheep wagon knotted his stomach. Johnny hadn't planned to leave, or had he? Maybe he just stayed the night in town and hadn't returned. And maybe Carl didn't know his hired man as well as he should. Nothing had been stolen, at least nothing that Carl knew about now. Johnny's sudden disappearance was plumb odd, that's all there was to it.

Carl remounted, patted Scout on the neck, and turned toward the west pasture. His sheep were scattered. Some had frozen during the blizzard yesterday when they'd lost their way. He'd have to do the best he could rounding up the remaining ewes. Damn, but he'd needed a good lamb crop this year. As he squinted across the white snow, breathing sharp air, he prayed that he'd save enough to meet the mortgage payment on the ranch. If not, well, he didn't want to think about it just now.

"Johnny, you damn fool! Where are you, man?" He shouted to the snow-covered hills. He received no answer. He expected none.

The rest of the morning was taken up by rounding up the survivors and penning them near the house. Even then, Carl's eyes watered from the exposure to the blinding sun and snow combination and he couldn't be certain he'd found all the sheep.

Anna proudly showed him the efforts of her morning—two healthy lambs produced by two healthy ewes.

Carl hugged her but could not smile. "We've lost more than we should have," he said.

Anna blinked back tears. She coaxed him into their house for a hot lunch of chicken and dumplings and an apple crisp. "You'll feel better after you've eaten," she said.

"I'll go to town after lunch and see if he's there. Maybe he stayed in town for the night."

Carl's words sounded hollow. Johnny Shale had worked for the Walkers since last October. He'd never missed a day. He'd been good help up till now, but Carl had dealt with hired hands who appeared to be good workers and left at the worst times before. Some spent most of their nights at the bar in town. Not Johnny. He only partook of the drinks once a month. At least that's what he'd told Carl. Odd that he hadn't collected his pay. Most hands who left insisted on being paid before leaving.

Carl considered their unusual argument of the previous day. He'd stopped at the bank in town, then had found Johnny in the bar. Carl didn't like that, but he couldn't stop the man from seeking his fun on a Friday evening.

"I expect you'll need your wages, Johnny," Carl said, sitting on a stool beside him.

"Why, hello, Carl." Johnny took a swig from a beer bottle. "I've been thinking about improvin' our arrangement."

"How so?"

Johnny suggested keeping the sheep near the wagon. "That way, they'll be in the lee of the hill if a storm comes up."

"And they'll be farther from the shed." In the corner of his eye, Carl noticed a young woman dressed in a ruffly dress and stockings and heels a few spaces away from them. Johnny paid no attention, but Carl wondered if she was the reason for Johnny's sudden bravado.

"Ah, Carl, sheep crowd together and keep themselves warm and cozy."

Carl shook his head. "No, Johnny. We ought to move them on down to the corral nearest the house. I don't want to take chances on some of them smothering. And a ewe giving birth—the herd might smother the lamb, too."

"Well, if you don't mind my askin', who's the sheepherder? Me or you?"

Carl managed to contain his anger but he felt his jaw tighten as he spoke. "Well, if you don't mind my askin', Johnny, who owns the sheep? Me or you?"

Johnny frowned. "You may as well pay me then."

Carl handed him an envelope filled with most of what he owed. He paid the amount he could. The banker kept pestering him about the ranch debt. He needed a successful lambing season to appease that man. And he needed Johnny to help with the lambs.

The argument had left a bitter taste in Carl's mouth. What a lame-brained idea the man had. He couldn't believe Johnny had left over their dispute. Yet the sheep wagon stood empty. Why would he leave so suddenly if he had earlier planned to keep the herd nearby? And without collecting the rest of his pay?

Anna said, "Do you want cream on your dessert, Carl?"

Carl shook his head. "No, thanks. Cream's too heavy for me today."

She smiled at him and dished up the apple crisp. Handing him his portion, she said, "I warmed it in the oven while we were eating."

He took a bite, letting the cinnamon caress his nose and savoring the soft warm apple slices and brown sugar's crunchier texture. The sweetness soothed him. He said, "Mm, Anna, this is good crisp."

She thanked him, said, "Better than bride's crisp?" They both laughed at the joke he'd made when they'd been newly married ten years before. Carl's way of complimenting her cooking was to tell her the meal was "better than bride's cooking." He had complimented her often for her tasty cooking since, especially her homemade biscuits. He never tired of eating them. Sometimes for breakfast, she'd fry up some ham and make gravy to go with them. He savored the taste of those light biscuits doused with thick, creamy ham gravy. For morning snacks, he usually covered a biscuit or two with a good helping of salty butter and a healthy dollop of Anna's sweet chokecherry jelly. A fresh, warm pan of Anna's golden, airy biscuits gave a man the strength to go on, especially when things looked bad.

She got up to pour him another cup of coffee. She stood beside the counter for a moment to pick up the coffee pot. She turned toward him, and he wondered again why Johnny would leave without his money, without even telling Carl he was going.

Unless it was the incident with Anna. Carl watched his wife. She continued eating her lunch, taking careful bites, blowing on the hot food before tasting each. Her hard work in the cold air had made her hungry.

Carl had walked into the house mid-morning one day last week. Johnny had been reaching around Anna's waist for a biscuit, and Carl had been on the same side of her, so he didn't see the man's face, just the shaggy cut of the dark hair on the back of his head. But Carl could see Anna's. Beads of sweat had formed on her forehead, dampening the blonde curls she worked so diligently to maintain. Tight lines cut the edges of her thin mouth. She faced Johnny, her right hand behind her gripped the counter. Her left hand was lifted behind her, its palm extended in an awkward position, out of Johnny's sight. Her hand halted in that distorted way within inches of the handle of the butcher knife. Viewing the scene, a man might have mistaken her movement. Maybe she was reaching for Johnny.

"Carl," she said and exhaled.

Johnny spun to face him.

"She makes mighty good biscuits, Carl. You're lucky to have her."

Carl said, "I believe I'll have one myself." He walked closer to Anna as Johnny walked away. "We'll plan to take a break in the mornings from now on," Carl said, careful to keep anger from his face and his words. "I'll bring the biscuits with me so you won't have to bother Anna in the house."

Anna's hand, still gripping the counter, trembled. She turned her gaze to her husband's. "Here, Carl, I'll get you one." She turned shakily toward him and lifted a biscuit from the pan, handing it to him. Unsteadily, she reached for a napkin. Carl was certain from her actions that Johnny had made an unwanted advance. He forced unwelcome thoughts of the even more disturbing possibility that they were together in the house for another reason from his ravaged mind.

He vowed he would not ask her. Anna would not have done anything to jeopardize the success of lambing season. They needed the money too badly.

Johnny remained silent through their exchange. He ate the biscuit, after spreading some spicy apple butter on it, and drank coffee as if nothing had happened. Anna never spoke of it again. Carl did not ask questions. He needed the hired man to help them get through the lambing. But the memory lingered in his mind.

☾

No one remembered seeing Johnny in Chalk Bluff the night before. Carl inquired at the post office, the Hotel Goldwin dining room, the bar, the grocery store, the newspaper, and finally found the deputy sheriff at the town police office and told him all he knew. Pat Branson shook his head. "I'm sorry, Carl. Rough time to lose a hand."

"Sure is. Know of anyone who'd care to help us with lambing on short notice?"

Pat shook his head. "If I run across someone, I'll send him your way."

"Thanks, Pat." Carl started to leave the office, then turned back. "And you'll tell me if you find Johnny?"

"Sure."

As Carl rode back to the ranch, the newspaper reporter jumped on the story, seeking out Pat Branson for the sensational details. He needed a story for the next week's issue, and this would be a good one. He could tie it in to the blizzard, too. Though Pat told him that Carl Walker was an upstanding citizen, a quiet sheep rancher who kept to himself with a wife who attended church regularly, the reporter also checked in at the bar. There, he heard the tale of a heated argument between the hot-tempered Carl and his hired hand, Johnny Shale. The bartender had seen money exchanged. The information provided the balance he needed to write the article fairly. He envisioned the story being carried in the 1933 yearly wrap-up, and the thought of a reporting award crossed his mind while he worked.

By Sunday, when Carl and Anna had lambing under control as best they could, and the cold air had abated some, Anna attended church. Carl watched the sheep while she went.

Instead of finding her singing in the kitchen, as was her usual way following church, Carl found her in tears at the table. He poured himself a cup of coffee and joined her.

"Carl, I overheard something at church today. I think you should know."

"What, Anna?"

"People were saying they thought you—" She muffled a sob in her handkerchief and started again. "That you got rid of Johnny so you wouldn't have to pay him."

Carl stood abruptly. He struck the oak table with his flat palm with such force that the dishes rattled.

"I'll be go to hell, Anna," he said. His quiet, rage-filled tone frightened her. She stood.

They looked at each other for a long moment across the round oak table that had belonged to her grandmother.

"Anna," he said, "what do you believe?"

"Oh, Carl," she said, turning away toward the stove.

"Anna?" His voice was soft now.

She turned to him. Silvery hair slipped down across his forehead. His face was burned by the wind and the snow and the sun, and the unanswered question trying to burst through his skin.

"Carl, you know better than to even ask me."

He blinked, pressed his chapped lips together.

☾

April and May finally melted into a spring-like June. Carl and Anna managed the lambing chores alone. No word came of Johnny Shale. Folks around town instead focused on Carl. He'd soon tired of suspicious glances and whispers behind his back. People he'd thought were his friends spread rumors that he'd killed the hired man to save money. The newspaper report let the story dangle in people's minds. The reporter couldn't decipher the true story, so in telling the tale, the open-endedness of it pointed to Carl. The report explained the facts—Shale turned up missing; lambing time was the worst time he could have gone missing; Carl and he had argued in public; Carl had handed Johnny money in the bar. Though the sheriff's comment had been to explain that Carl had reported the man missing and had cooperated with his efforts, the sensational aspects overshadowed the facts. The money, however, was not explained. A second report a week later had reiterated the story. Johnny Shale could not be located, and he had worked for Carl Walker at the time of his disappearance. Sheriff Branson admitted that Johnny had been a regular weekly customer of the local bar. That comment angered Carl. Johnny had told him otherwise. He'd once told Carl he'd rather read a book than gallivant around at the bar in town. Maybe they were better off rid of the man, even with the scandal he'd produced.

Carl knew of the nasty rumors because Woody Martell told him of them. Woody built houses and had helped Carl build his and Anna's. Woody and Carl had been friends since elementary school. Carl told Anna, "A true friend will tell you unpleasant things. Those who don't tell you the things you'd rather not hear are not your friends."

Anna searched his face with dull eyes. A long moment passed. "Some things are better left unsaid, Carl," she said.

The town talk wore on Anna's nerves. She jumped when Carl entered the house and called her name. She dropped plates as she washed dishes in the evenings and then had to clean up two messes. She picked at her food. She lost weight. Carl began to wonder if she had taken the butcher knife to the man. Out of guilt? Maybe she believed he had killed Johnny. If they'd been having an affair, she might have imagined the worst.

Carl thought it odd that she seemed so shaky in the house but she bore her lambing chores cheerfully, as if a weight had been lifted from her shoulders.

In mid-June, Carl rode around the ranch, fixing irrigation ditches as best he could and keeping tabs on his grazing sheep. He rode near the sheep wagon. He'd cleaned up the mess but left it sit where Johnny had last left it, thinking the man might return for his things. The wagon was parked in the lee of a rocky hill Carl started calling "Johnny's Knob." As he crested the hill, he could see the house. On the fence hung a white dishtowel—Anna's signal that she needed his help.

Carl returned home, greeted by Anna and a neighboring rancher, Ben Thompson. Carl took off his gray felt work hat, smoothed the locks of sweat-curled hair at the nape of his neck, twisted the length of leather that he used to hold his hat on his head, and stuffed the leather inside the crown, placing the worn Stetson upside down on the counter. He looked toward Anna, seeing first the bloody butcher knife on the counter. She moved toward him. Near the knife, pieces of chicken lay in disarray, pale skin pulled back to reveal white protuberances of bone where cuts had been made.

Ben stood, but Carl motioned him to sit.

"Ah, sit still, Ben." He shook the man's hand. Ben remained standing.

"We found Johnny," he said, voice quiet and somber.

The room was hushed as if covered by a heavy wet spring snow. The only noise was the bubbling sound of the coffee Anna poured into Carl's mug. The lid clanked against the porcelain-enameled pot. Anna held the knob, covered by a red gingham potholder, with her middle finger . The lid shook in her hand.

Carl stopped, midway through removing his winter overclothes. Though the calendar indicated late spring, the outdoors remained chill. One hand, still gloved, held the empty glove. He tapped it in his palm. "I'll be." He looked at Ben over the table for a moment. Carl sighed, pulled out a chair and sat down. "What happened?"

Ben followed suit. "We don't know. Found him out in the sagebrush flats—on my land. About four miles from here as the crow flies."

"Dead." Carl didn't ask. He stated the fact.

Ben nodded. "Not much left I'm afraid."

Anna gripped the counter top, and stood still, her back to the men.

Ben picked up his cup of coffee, and as if becoming aware of Anna again, said, "Sorry, Anna."

Carl's gaze rested on his wife. "You all right?"

"Yes," she answered. She turned to face them. Her pale face belied her words. Carl reached for her hand and held it in his own. To Ben, he said, "I expect you've gone to see Pat."

Ben finished another sip of coffee. "No, Carl. I came here first. I thought we should go together."

Carl squeezed Anna's hand. He blinked. Ben's kind treatment of him lifted a weight from his shoulders. Ben said, "I'll take you out to Johnny first if you'd like."

Carl said he should go and Ben explained how he and his son had stumbled across the body. They had been out riding fence, checking to see how much of it had held up through the winter. The horses caught the scent in the wind and shied.

"Raised quite a ruckus," Ben said. "We had to approach on foot. I wonder how he got way over there?"

"Guess we'll never know," Carl said.

"I bet he was out in the storm and got disoriented." Ben explained that the body was hidden in a draw. The wintry snows had buried the corpse and so it hadn't been easily visible.

Carl nodded. "Makes a crazy sort of sense, don't it?"

The three of them were each lost in their own thoughts for a moment. Carl broke the silence. "I expect we'd better go." He released Anna's hand, unaware he'd held it through the whole sorry tale. "Anna, you'll write his mother, then?"

She closed her eyes for a moment as if gathering strength. "Yes, Carl. I'll write Johnny's mother. She'll be anxious to know."

Ben said, "His mother?"

Carl explained, "We contacted her when he first went missing. I sent her the rest of his wages and such then. She lives in Nebraska. Maybe she'll want to come out or want a service or something." Carl paused to take a sip of coffee. "She's been ailing. She hadn't seen Johnny since he'd left as a teenager. He sent her money from time to time. I don't think they got along." He took another quick sip. "Still, it's right that she know." He rose from his chair and Ben did the same.

Anna said, "Yes. It's right that she know."

A draft of cold air made Anna shiver as the men left the house. She watched them drive Ben's red Dodge pickup down the muddy road toward town, past Johnny's Knob. She stood at the kitchen window looking at the knob. Suddenly, she realized that the earthly bulge was covered with the green grass of summertime. She turned back to the oven, wiping her hands on her apron, and began thinking about what she could cook for supper to go with a big, golden-crusted pan of Carl's favorite.

Twisted Reins

"Damn, Gussie! You didn't tell me you was married." Clint Parker grabbed a sheet and leapt from the bed, struggling to cover himself.

"I didn't think it mattered."

Across the bed, Augusta Ford donned her clothes in haste. Her husband, Homer, stood in the doorway, eyes narrowed in an expression of extreme disgust. She said, "You picked a mighty fine time to start wondrin' about me, Homer."

She stood between the two men like a contested dance hall girl. Clint, lean and hard-muscled, his thick brown hair mussed now from their dalliance between the sheets and falling across his perpetually sunburned forehead, watched her from the corner by the window. She could not read his blue eyes. Homer, by contrast, kept his blond hair trimmed close to his head, making him appear even pudgier than he was. His round face glowed red as a hot coal. A murderous rage surged from his black eyes.

"You're coming home with me," Homer insisted. His nasal voice sounded tight as a fiddle string about to bust.

Homer was a stinker. Always had been. He made Gussie wish that she'd listened to her Pa. Pa had never liked Homer. But in a fit of stubborn teenaged rebellion she'd married Homer and broke ties with her father in one fell swoop, easy as falling off a bronco. Now she couldn't even tell Pa he'd been right after all. He'd been dead for several years. Pulling on her fancy riding skirt, divided like a man's pair of pants to give her greater mobility in the saddle, she felt a sudden unbeckoned longing for a finer and more feminine woman's dress, of satin, with petticoats. The intense yearning took Gussie by surprise. Clint had awakened these womanly feelings within her toughened tomboy heart. Now she had to go home with Homer. She said, "And if I don't?"

Silence fell.

The lovers stared at Homer. He centered his gaze on Gussie. "Don't even give it a thought."

To Gussie's surprise, Homer didn't draw a gun and shoot Clint or her. She exchanged an anxious glance with Clint. He turned and grabbed his jeans.

Gussie remembered that a friend in the circuit once told her that men are very jealous creatures. No woman could fully understand what would set them off. Sometimes it was small things. Gussie gazed at Clint, his body taut from tension and his muscles firmed from his work breaking horses. He limped a bit from a recent knee injury. That's what had got him interested in her. He'd been forced to stay off the horses for a while and he'd turned naturally to his sketching talents and to his interest in photography. He'd wanted to take her photograph. In doing that, he'd claimed her heart.

Gussie's feelings for him were no small thing. She'd fallen in love with him. Clint understood her in a way no one else did. He had stayed with her on the circuit these past weeks. Clint didn't begrudge her the dream of being a cowgirl in a Wild West show. These past few weeks with the Irwin Brothers' Wild West Show had been grand indeed. Now, though, the fun was over.

"Hurry up," Homer hissed through clenched teeth. Gussie rushed to button her shirt. Homer grabbed her arm. She turned to look at Clint. His eyes met hers. He gave a slight nod.

"Come on," her husband said, pulling her out of the bedroom and through the parlor to the door. With her blouse half-open, her hair disheveled and her heart breaking, Gussie trudged outside. She wished Clint would have at least put up a fight for her.

Homer pushed her into his fancy phaeton. He said, "You will return home and stay there, Mrs. Ford." He took special pains to emphasize her title. Homer climbed into the buggy. He grabbed her wrist. She struggled to break free. Homer squeezed her wrist until she winced. "You will stay home with me or I will kill your paramour." He shook her. "Is that clear?"

Gussie nodded. Homer dropped her wrist. She rubbed it, trying to take the pain away, but the worst pain existed in her heart anyway. "I didn't know you cared," she said, in the sweetest voice she could muster but in a tone sharp enough to cut timber. Homer shook the reins, and the horses pulled the buggy forward. Gussie looked at Clint's log cabin, the place where she'd found such sweet happiness. She glimpsed him watching them from the bedroom window.

☾

Homer took her home to their frame house in the town of Sagebrush Junction, just below the hills where Clint's cabin was located. Homer expected fine meals and fastidious housekeeping. He kept Gussie busy, fussing at the least sign of dust or suggesting she make a pie when she had just sat down to rest after breakfast dishes were done. Gussie detested her enforced chores. She worked as hard as she could because she didn't want Clint harmed. Even though Homer said he'd kill Clint if she didn't do as she was told, she had no guarantee that her husband wouldn't hurt her lover anyway. Gussie tried not to think about that. Gussie believed in her heart if he would have hurt Clint she would have killed Homer herself.

Homer had not yet made her fix meals or wash linens for any of the women he bedded. When Gussie had left several weeks ago to tour with the Irwin Brothers' Wild West Show, Homer hadn't even been around. He'd been spending time with another woman, one of several with whom he'd kept company since marrying Gussie.

Once Charlie Irwin, owner of the show, had teased Homer about his flirtatious attitude. He said, "I saw you flirting with that young woman at the Mercantile."

Homer blushed furiously. "I don't even know her name."

"The way you were carrying on, I'd have sworn you were fast friends." Charlie cast a warning glance at Gussie. He apparently believed he was imparting important news to her, trying to help her. He didn't realize she already knew about Homer's extramarital attachments.

Homer swore. "I don't even know her name," he protested.

"You were talking to her like you knew her pretty well," Charlie insisted.

Homer strode off in a huff. Charlie had simply shaken his head and gone on about his business. Because of Homer's wandering behavior, Gussie could not understand why he felt so upset at her seeing Clint.

Now, having elected to keep her tied to their house, Homer curbed his own appetites. He rarely left her. He wanted to ensure his wife stayed where he intended. In doing so, he shackled her with so many domestic chores that she rarely found time to ride her horse. This treatment was much rougher on her, he knew, than mere death or imprisonment would have been. He owned her body but not her soul. She became Homer Ford's slave for the protection of another man who owned her heart.

❨

When Charlie Irwin himself came to the Fords' home about a week later to see if Gussie would come along again and perform for the upcoming Cheyenne Frontier Days, Homer grew furious.

"I'd love to, but—" Gussie began.

Homer said, "Mr. Irwin. You are a family man yourself, and I know you will understand that my wife needs to attend to her duties at home. She's had her fun."

Gussie saw by Charlie's stunned sympathetic expression that she had a friend. If he caught the double meaning in Homer's phrase, he didn't acknowledge it. He had recognized her desire to perform and helped her cultivate it. Charlie was a good man. He wouldn't break up their marriage just to have her appear in a performance.

Charlie said, "I'd ask you to consider something, sir. Augusta is one of the best riders we have. She has a genuine talent for the saddle that few people—male or female—are granted. She would be well paid. We run a family outfit. My own daughters are part of our show. You yourself would be welcome to come along with us."

Homer had none of it. "I would expect her to be well paid, of course. However, our standards are quite different, Mr. Irwin. Good day." Homer opened the door. Gussie felt saddened that Charlie had come all this way from Cheyenne, all the way here to Sagebrush Junction to see her and gain nothing but trouble for his efforts.

She wrapped her arms around his thickening girth. Charlie patted her shoulders. "Sorry, honey," he whispered. "You'll always be the 'Jewel of the Rockies.'" She pulled away, forcing a smile at the stage name he'd tagged her with, and saw in his eyes the sincerity of his statement.

"Thanks, Charlie," she said, biting her lip so she wouldn't cry. "It means a lot to me, your comin' out here and all."

Charlie donned his hat and left. Augusta stood at the door and watched him go. She stared a Homer for a long moment. She felt sorely tempted to say the words but didn't. *You bastard. Falling off a horse never hurt this bad.* She returned to the kitchen and the chores she hated. Peeling apples for a pie provided some consolation at least. She imagined herself working out her frustrations on the fruit. As she worked she wondered how emotional pain could cause a spirit-wide almost physical ache, an ache that hurt much worse than physical ailments caused by enduring spills from a horse.

☾

By moonlight, Gussie struck out on her own. Buddy nickered at her. He was the one male being on this earth who loved her solely for herself. She hugged the horse. "C'mon, feller," she instructed the gelding. "We've got to make tracks before daylight."

Her plan was not well-conceived. She just wanted to escape. She headed to the first place Homer would look, but she figured she had some extra time on her side. Homer, having decided that Gussie would indeed remain at home, had sought a night on the town at the end of the first week of their required togetherness. She had no idea where he'd gone.

Buddy knew the way to Clint's cabin. The small structure stood in a clearing in the foothills of the Thunder Mountains. A lone pine grew near the house. Gussie felt grateful when she saw the light of a kerosene lamp glowing through the window and a wispy curl of smoke winding its way skyward from the chimney.

☾

Clint invited her inside. When she reached to embrace him, he did not reciprocate.

"You should have told me, Gussie."

She dropped her arms to her sides. "I know. I didn't think it mattered."

"So you said." He motioned her to sit at the table, which was strewn with dozens of sketches.

She glanced at them. "Hey, these are good." She held one up and examined it, then sorted through the rest of the stack. "They're all of me."

Clint nodded. "You're often on my mind."

She smiled and felt him warm toward her a little. "Thanks. You, too."

He pushed the stack aside. "I'd wanted to ask if you'd let me try something new at Frontier Days. Kirkland's trying to make a photograph of a bucking bronc in action. It's something that's never been done before. I'd like to try it. If I can do it, maybe he'll take me on full-time." C. D. Kirkland was one of Cheyenne's finest photographers. Apprenticing with him would certainly be a feather in Clint's cap.

"Oh, Clint, that would be grand. Then you wouldn't have to worry so about your knee." The doctor had told him that further horse riding would not only harm his knee but might hamper his ability to walk. Despite the medical warning, Clint had continued his work breaking colts for anyone who needed his services. He sometimes helped the

Irwins work their stock as well. He carried his sketch pad with him wherever he went, drawing during every spare moment. Moving to camera work seemed a logical progression to Gussie. "But why ask me?"

"Because I—" Looking at her, Clint suffered a sudden attack of timidity. "I wanted to practice by taking photographs of you. I was going to ask you the other day when—"

She raised a hand. "No need to explain. I'd love for you to. But Homer's forbidden me to participate."

Clint raised an eyebrow. "That hasn't stopped you before."

I didn't love you before now, she thought. Gussie chose her next words with care. She didn't want him to know that his life depended upon her actions.

"This time it's different."

"Because all of a sudden like he remembered he's married to you?"

She pressed her lips together and feigned intense interest in a sketch.

Clint reached out and took her hand. He remembered well Homer's tightly controlled anger. "Wouldn't have anything to do with me, now, would it?"

Gussie closed her eyes and then looked at the window. "I don't think anyone followed me."

"Look at me, honey," Clint whispered.

She broke under his encouraging gaze.

"He'll come after you, Clint. I'm taking an awful chance on your life just comin' here." She touched his cheek. Rough calluses on her fingers scraped against the stiff stubble of his nighttime beard. "I know he will. I—I just couldn't stand to stay there another minute." Tears clouded her eyes. She turned away so he would not see her distress.

"I know," Clint said, turning her towards him and stroking her hair. He loved her hair, a beautiful shade of brown glowing with red tints. She usually wore it braided and atop her head in elegant fashion. He'd sketched her that way many times. Tonight, her hair fell across her shoulders and caught the flickering light from the kerosene lamp. He drew her close to him. "Things will work out, Gussie."

"You put the bright side on everything." She raised her face toward his. "Oh, Clint. I've fallen in love with you. I want to be with you. I made a terrible mistake when I married Homer."

Clint hugged her tighter. "You make me very happy, Gussie. I've not felt this way about any other woman I've ever met." He thought for a moment. "Do you want to perform in the Frontier Days show?"

"Oh, yes, and Charlie even rode out and asked me himself."

Clint held her away from him. "Then you ought to do it. Maybe Charlie will help you. We'll have to figure a way to get you to Cheyenne. He'd protect you as long as you were part of the show. And there'd be people all around so Homer couldn't get to you."

"But what about you?"

Clint pinched her cheek with his thumb and forefinger. "Mustn't waste time worrying about me. It's getting you there. That will be the tricky part."

"If Homer doesn't come home for breakfast, I could catch the early train." She couldn't keep the excitement out of her voice, but then she said, "But he'll come here. He'll come after you. I can't let that happen."

Clint took her by the arms and shook her gently. "I'll watch after my own self. Do you think he'll come home tonight?"

"Not if whoever he's with has enough whiskey."

"It's a chance we'll take. I'll meet you in Cheyenne in a few days."

She didn't speak, but turned her wide eyes to his. They were the exact color of a mountain bluebird's wings. He kissed her.

"Best get movin' now. We don't want him to catch you here again."

"He'll come here, Clint."

"I know it, gal. I know it. Don't you worry now. I'll see you in Cheyenne."

"I'm always having to leave you, Clint," she said. "I don't like it at all."

They lingered over one last kiss. She let go of him with great reluctance, holding his arms as long as she could before breaking contact.

☾

Homer did not come home that night. Gussie figured he probably had satisfied his goal of having kept her under his thumb and believed that she'd remain there. She caught the morning train, boarding with deep anxiety. What if Homer had taken a notion to head to Cheyenne himself? Looking around the car, she glimpsed only a motley group of passengers. A few well-dressed women and some who were dressed in plain calico like she was. Some had men with them. Only two men she could see traveled alone. One was dressed in fine britches, ruffled shirt and coat and hat. She guessed him to be a banker or a lawyer. The other wore clothes more suitable for work. There were a few from nearby Springdale who'd come to Sagebrush Junction by stagecoach.

Gussie found an empty seat and relaxed and watched the scenery. The rolling hills of sagebrush ascended into the mountainous terrain of Summit Pass and then flattened again into the wide plains and soon Cheyenne came into view. She hired a buggy to take her to the rodeo grounds, grateful she'd stashed some of the cash from her first paychecks in a pair of moccasins underneath the bed. Had he known about her cash, Homer would have argued it was his.

At the rodeo grounds, Charlie Irwin's crew set up what was in effect a makeshift home for his family and employees. Tents abounded and there were special pens and a barn for the livestock. Nearby, a cook house stood, offering meals intended for Irwin's clan. Gussie smiled as she walked past and caught the scent of roasting beef. No one who came by at meal time was ever turned away.

Charlie greeted her warmly. "I'm so glad you decided to come after all. Talked Homer into it, did you?"

"No," she admitted. "I don't know where Homer is."

Charlie frowned. "Let's hope he keeps it that way. You're safe here with us, Gussie."

He seemed to have read her mind. She hoped her fear wasn't so plain on her face but she couldn't help it. "I don't want to make you any trouble, Charlie," she said. He took her bag and showed her a tent, explaining he'd have someone tend her trunk as well.

"You'll be a great help to the show." He made her feel like one of the family again. She loved being a part of it all. The sharp odors of sweating horses and fresh manure tickled her nose as she headed for the tack room. She wanted to practice the trick roping feat and fancy saddle work she'd planned with her friend, Marie Doland.

On the way, she met one of the Indians who performed tribal dances as part of Charlie's show. Jake squeezed her hands warmly and made her feel welcome. He'd never revealed his Indian name, so everyone just called him Indian Jake. He'd admired her skill with horses and had shown her a few tricks of his own on how to gentle a nervous mount. Now, he handed her an intricately beaded bag. "I made this for you," he said.

"Oh, it's lovely. And so fine. I can't accept such a fine gift," she said. "How did you know I'd be back anyway?"

"Jake just know." He laughed. "You couldn't stay away. Good horse-woman." He held her hand and closed it over the tiny leather bag. "Good fortune," he said. He insisted she take the bag.

"Thank you," she said. "I'll carry it with me always." She tied it to her belt then and there.

☾

Two days passed. Gussie had heard nothing from Homer and even more worrisome, nothing from Clint. Her nerves felt as jangly as the fancy show spurs she wore.

Marie said, "You're awfully fidgety, Gussie. Is it the show? We're doing great."

Gussie shook her head. "No, it's personal." She'd made an appointment with a divorce attorney and he'd assured her that she'd soon be free of Homer Ford. But his assurances couldn't keep Gussie's anxiety at bay. She missed Clint. Not knowing where he was or if he was all right was like to drive her crazy.

"Oh." Marie checked her saddle. She wasn't one to pry. She changed the subject. "This leather worries me. It's almost worn through. I need to get it repaired. Don't know if the saddle shop can get it done in time for the opener Friday night."

Gussie patted her own saddle. "Here. Use this one. I have another that I can handle. We'll practice with them at dress rehearsal tomorrow."

While they ate lunch in the cook house, a young boy came to find Gussie. He handed her a letter, then stood beside her. "For you, Augusta Ford."

She recognized the handwriting and ripped the letter open. Marie laughed. "Must be something real special."

Gussie read the note. "Kirkland's taken me on. Will you? Buggy waits. Plains Hotel, room thirty-seven, Love, Clint." She sighed with relief.

"Marie," she said, "I'm going to be gone this afternoon. I'll see you in the morning."

"What about practicing?"

Gussie grinned. "We're good enough now. Rest up. I'll see you tomorrow." She took the hand of the young messenger and guided him to the tent. "Wait outside," she instructed. She took off her dusty riding clothes, gave them a shake and laid them carefully on her cot. Then she poured some water in the basin and gave herself a quick washing. The young boy said, "Ain't got all day, Ma'am."

"I'll be along shortly," she hollered back. "You just wait a minute." She dabbed orange blossom cologne on her neck and wrists, then fetched the emerald green satin gown that had been her mother's from her trunk. The gown was her favorite because it reminded her of the color of the pine trees in the Thunder Mountains. Hurriedly, she donned the dress and matching petticoat and used the button hook to button her fancy kid boots as quickly as she could. Flustered from speed and excitement, she missed some of the buttons and had to try again. She swore.

"Are you coming?" The young man's impatience with her grew.

"Yes, I'm a-coming," she shouted. She freed her hair from its braids, gave it a quick brushing and secured it on the top of her head with her mother's tortoiseshell comb. She grabbed dangling silver earrings and attached them to her ear lobes, walking out of the tent as she did so. The young boy's mouth fell open. He'd escorted a dusty cowgirl to the tent and now an elegant lady appeared in her place.

"I'm ready now," she said. "Let's go find that buggy."

❰

The woman who stood at the door of room thirty-seven of the Plains Hotel appeared calm. Inside, her heart pounded against her chest, threatening to burst the seams on the elegant gown. Gussie had enjoyed the attentions of the men in the lobby of the hotel as she made her way to Clint's room. They smiled as she passed or raised eyebrows and smiled. But what would Clint think? She wanted to surprise him. She took a deep breath and knocked on the door.

Clint answered. His fascinated gaze told her she had indeed surprised him. He let out a low whistle. "Oh, my. Gussie."

Then he whisked her inside and whisked off the gown and fancy boots almost as quickly as she had donned them. Later, as they cuddled in bed, Clint asked Gussie, "I've never seen a woman look so fine as you. Homer doesn't deserve you. Why on earth did you marry him?"

Tears stung her eyes. "I wanted to show my father I was smarter than he was, that I knew how to run my life better than he did. I didn't."

Clint caressed her shoulder. "It's a mess, honey, but we'll work it out. I love you."

"I love you, too." She reached up and rested her hand against his cheek. She wrapped herself in the sheet and sat at the vanity table near the mirror. Gussie said, "There comes a moment when you feel like an animal caught in a trap. Strugglin' just makes you tired. You know in that moment it is useless to try. You are caught. You can't never escape it."

She took a brush and began to brush her hair. Looking at Clint was almost like looking into a mirror. Blue eyes, dark hair, charming smile. Their similarities ended there. She could see his reflection as he lay in the bed watching her. She was rambunctious. He was quiet, preferred sketching to showing off. Yet his talent brought him recognition, too. As the thoughts crossed her mind, he reached for his sketch pad and began drawing her.

Clint's heart fell at her words. "Love isn't supposed to be like that," he said. "I won't——" He cleared his throat. "Did you love each other at first?"

"I thought I did."

Clint frowned.

"It's complicated."

"Either you did or you didn't."

"He was so nice to me in the beginning. You wouldn't believe how much so. Then it changed. He started treating me like a thing, a servant, instead of a woman."

"I don't understand, Gussie."

"He expects too much. He told me I'll never make enough money to pay him back for all he's done for me."

"Just trying to tell you how much he's given you, I guess." He sensed in Gussie a soul mate but did she feel the same? He wanted to believe so. Small things, he realized, told him she did. She was shy as he was. The way she blushed and looked away when he caught her looking at him in a crowd. In public, she laughed more loudly when he was near and sometimes reseated herself so her vantage point allowed her to look at him.

All these things made his heart flutter and he had to concentrate harder on holding his pencil steady. All these things could have been fancies of his imagination. In her position, she was supposed to be outgoing. She most likely was nice to everyone. Why then did he feel so tingly? So special? It felt good. It felt good to let those feelings wash over him again.

"No. He said it in a mean way. I like to be independent. I want to make my own way, seeings how I can. I should keep what I earn."

"I can see that. And pay him a fee for managing your career or something?"

She nodded. "He wants it all." She slapped the table. "Dang it all, Clint. I can't live trapped like that."

"Some women do."

"They're the ones having babies and cookin' and cleaning and the like." She looked down. "I'm not that way. I'm not fit to be a mother."

"I think you'd make a good mother, Gussie."

A strange light brightened her eyes.

"Ah, Clint, you're my champion."

"Always."

She told Clint she had seen an attorney. Divorce would end her marriage, would free her to stay with Clint. But it wouldn't end her fears about Homer.

☾

Years of riding horses had taught Gussie to squelch her fears. She and Marie talked to a group of reporters before the dress rehearsal. Standing among them was Clint. He'd talked Kirkland, the photographer, into letting him have a go with a camera. Gussie said, "Horse wrecks teach you life. If your horse is a little fresh and drops you on your backside then you ache like hell and get back on. But you learn not to fear death. Trying and falling doesn't hurt nearly as much as not trying. Fear of falling stunts you." Marie nodded. Gussie continued, "You can't let yourself feel it or the horse will know. Horses sense when the rider's scared. So you've got to just get rid of fear."

With her marriage in such trouble and Clint's life and her own in danger, she realized as she spoke she exhibited this numbing of fear in her personal life, almost to a reckless degree. But she was never reckless on a horse even though it appeared so. The reporters asked to stay and watch. Marie agreed to that and the two women mounted their horses to show their fancy act. Reporters always hung around the women because they couldn't believe women could handle horses as well as men. Gussie saw Clint give her a good luck wink. She nodded to Marie.

They rode round the arena, gathering speed. Marie stood in the saddle as her horse galloped round the circle. Gussie did the same. They performed a few other saddle stunts. The reporters clapped, but Gussie and Marie concentrated on the tasks at hand. Marie rode ahead to pretend to fall off the saddle and ride sideways against the horse, always a crowd-pleaser.

But something went amiss.

Marie slid off to the side as she usually did, grasping the pommel horn and keeping her legs stretched out horizontally along the horse's side. The saddle lurched sideways with her.

Gussie cried out. She kicked Prancer forward, hoping to rescue her friend before she fell.

Marie hit the ground and bounced. Worse yet, she had gotten hung up some way in the slipping saddle. Her horse dragged her.

Gussie galloped ahead but too late. Prancer came close to Marie's now-frantic horse. Her horse bucked and ran and tried to get untangled from the precarious mess that dangled beneath him.

That made the tangle even worse. Prancer leaped to avoid being kicked. Gussie, unprepared for her horse's sudden movement, felt herself airborne.

When Gussie fell, she landed on her back in time to see Prancer's hooves sail over the top of her. She screamed.

Clint raced from the stands. Others followed behind him, running to stop Marie's horse.

Clint reached Gussie and gathered her in his arms. She opened her eyes. "I thought I'd be gone. That the blue sky would be the last thing I'd ever see. But it only knocked the wind out of me."

He held her close. "My sweet Gussie," he said.

"Marie?" She asked. "How's Marie?"

Clint pressed his lips together and shook his head.

"Oh, no." She clung to him. "Clint, she was using my saddle. Mine. Something went wrong with my saddle."

He stroked her forehead, but she jumped up and ran toward the group crowded around Marie and her horse.

Marie lay on the ground, a reporter's jacket covering her face. The horse remained flighty but stood nearby, with two men holding him. Gussie stopped there, examining her saddle. Clint caught up just as she found the cause for the wreck. A slit in the cinch leather. She showed him but did not speak. Clint hugged her to him. "Homer," he whispered.

Gussie blamed herself. "I should have seen it coming," she said. "I should never have lent her my saddle. It was all right yesterday." She had gotten off easy with a bruise on her upper arm, caused by Prancer's squatting down to jump across her body. As he poised to spring, his back hoof had nicked her.

They couldn't prove Homer had tampered with her saddle. His whereabouts for that time were unknown. Marie's death had been ruled an accident.

Clint couldn't reconcile himself to letting things be as Gussie had asked. Her life was in danger. He found Homer through the private investigator he hired.

"You weren't difficult at all to find," Clint explained when he saw Homer at the South Street Saloon. "You have voracious appetites."

Homer, finishing a robust lunch, coughed and dabbed his ruddy cheeks. "You. I asked you once to leave my wife alone. That should have been sufficient."

"I love your wife. That's more than you can say."

Homer's tiny eyes seethed with fury. "I should have shot you the day I found you together."

"What's to stop you from shooting me now?" Clint asked.

Homer raised an eyebrow. "Nothing. Except too many questions would be raised. You're on borrowed time."

"Gussie's worth the risk." He pulled out a chair and sat across from the man he detested. "Why did you marry her, Homer?"

"I thought I could tame a wild thing. Being with her felt exciting, like the thrill of the hunt."

"But she's not one of those animals that your English nobility guests would enjoy shooting during their hunting expeditions. So you have to take it upon yourself to kill her in order to tame her, is that it?"

Homer did not respond. He merely stared at his accuser.

Clint continued. "I've stood back long enough. For too long. She wants to leave you. Can't you just let go?"

"I wondered how long it would take you."

Clint frowned. "I know about the saddle."

Homer shook his head. "What saddle?"

"Don't play games with me, Homer. Gussie's a fine woman. I don't take kindly to your attempt to kill her."

Homer laughed.

"You hurt Gussie and I'll kill you myself."

"Ah, yes. Lovers often make such passionate statements. Especially when they themselves are in the wrong."

"I mean it." Clint stood to leave.

Homer cleared his throat. His high-pitched nasal voice acquired an even haughtier tone. "I don't think it's men she craves," he said. "As much as the horses. She's crazy about horses. But there have been others, you do realize that, don't you?"

The phrase repeated itself in Clint's mind. He blinked. He leaned over the table, close to Homer's face. "I'll not believe your lies. If you hurt her—"

Homer merely smiled at Clint's menacing tone. "There is one way you can keep me from harming her and perhaps I could then—ahem—overlook her adultery."

"Shoot you?"

"There is another way. If you tell her goodbye and never see her again."

"What guarantee do I have that you'll keep your promise?"

"You have my word," Homer answered. "I ask you the same."

"It's not enough."

"It's all you're gonna get."

Clint straightened. After a moment he said, "And you'll let her continue riding and performing? She loves horses, you admitted that much yourself."

Homer nodded. "That's only reasonable. She'll provide me with much cash that way."

☾

With heavy heart, Clint headed to Gussie's tent near the rodeo arena. As he was certain he would, he found her riding. He hated himself for what he had to do but he loved her too much to risk her life.

She'd left her hair loose around her shoulders. She saw him and dismounted. Sunlight caught the red highlights in her thick brown locks. Her eyes sparkled with delight at seeing him. He swallowed. He had to do this quick. He must not allow her to hope, even for a minute, that things could be different. If he did, he would not be able to break off their relationship.

Clint said, "There haven't been others." He hesitated. "Have there?"

The light faded from Gussie's eyes as if he'd poured cold water on a campfire. Her jaw dropped. She swallowed hard. "You have to ask me that?"

Clint didn't believe for a moment that she'd been with other men. He knew of no other way to break clean. For her sake, he had to do it. He had to go. He'd have to rely on Homer's flimsy promise. He loved her too much.

Gussie's temper, true to her nature, flared. "You never even fought for me, Clint Parker." She winced when the sharp words were spoken.

His heart breaking, Clint took up the argument. "Is that what you wanted? Wanted me to fight and die for your honor, Gussie? There was a time I'd a' thought you were worth that." He stopped himself from saying, "Now I don't know."

Gussie looked as if he'd just slapped her face. Misery tore through him like a bullet. He came near to telling her about his pact with Homer. A deal with the devil. But he stopped himself. If Homer allowed her to continue performing, that was her dream. She did love her horses, that much Clint knew was true. The most important things were her life and her happiness. Painful as it was now for both of them, this was the best he could do.

Gussie bit her lip. "Get out!" She yelled. "Get out!" She threw the beaded bag Indian Jake had given her at him. Tears stained her cheeks.

Clint stood, watching her for a long moment. He memorized her hair, her body, her face. Even red and filled with tears, she was beautiful. He turned away and whispered, "I love you, Gussie," then he walked away.

☾

Homer confronted Gussie about the divorce action the next day. She had returned to Sagebrush Junction, intent on riding into the Thunder

Mountains to try to set things right with Clint. But Homer had been at home.

"Still going through with it, Gussie?"

Gussie thought it an odd question because he had first behaved as if the request had been a surprise. "Yes, Homer. I don't want to be married any more." She wanted Clint, but he was gone.

She saw the anger rise in his cheeks. He did not speak. She did not press further. Yesterday's argument with Clint had taken all the fight from her. She wanted only to be free.

She mounted Buddy, stretching her legs before placing her feet in the stirrups. She turned to ride away.

Homer said, "Don't leave me, Gussie. Please don't leave me." He pleaded like a child. It hurt her to a place deep inside to see a man humbled so—even Homer, who had treated her so badly. She did not turn back. She must move forward. She must seek a new life. She must find her way back to Clint.

Gussie heard the gunshot pop as if it came from a faraway place, felt the fabric of her shirt tighten and break, felt a burning sensation in her side before she realized what had happened. The pain in her side nearly knocked her from Buddy's back. She gripped the pommel horn and tried not to slouch. Let Homer think he missed. She'd not give him the satisfaction of turning round and showing him her fear and pain. There'd been enough of that.

Then another thought occurred to her. What if he meant to kill her? Then he'd follow, believing she wasn't dead. She urged Buddy faster and slid from the saddle. Gussie watched the horse's hooves sail over her face. They moved real graceful-like, too. Buddy jumped her. The animal hadn't wanted to hurt her, had maybe even been as surprised at the fall as she was. She'd had nightmares about this very same thing. Frightened by the smell of blood, he galloped away from her. She felt too weak to move.

From Homer's vantage point her fall had to look like death. She looked away. Buddy didn't run far. He escaped from his torment into the trees beyond them. The horse would turn around and come back to see about her. She gambled a bit but figured Homer would not. Now that she'd fooled him into believing she was dead, she had to concentrate on survival.

"You don't suppose I'm gonna die all alone out here in the middle of these damn Thunder Mountains, do ya?" She spoke to herself, knowing it at once to be a true statement and yet hoping to God that it wasn't.

Buddy came toward her. He gave a quiet nicker. Gussie spoke to him and touched his soft nose. Horses were much more loyal and dependable friends than humans. Thunder from the mountains signaled the imminent arrival of a storm. She grasped Buddy's reins and pulled herself to a standing position. He shied from the scent of blood, but she calmed him by talking. She put her nose to his and breathed into his nostrils so he'd recognize her and not the blood. She hoped Indian Jake's trick with horses would work. Buddy calmed. Gussie squeezed the beaded bag she wore on her belt. "Thanks, Jake," she whispered, "good fortune." Grasping the reins beneath Buddy's chin, she walked alongside the horse until they were sheltered by the branches of pines. This would be a cold, hard night. Thunderstorms terrified her. But Gussie had no choice. She'd rest here until the storm passed. Then she could ride somewhere in the morning. She couldn't go back now. And Clint's cabin was a mile up the hill. She could make a try for that come morning. Let Homer have his silly game anyway.

But after their argument, would Clint stop and wonder about her? She wanted to make things right with him. She eased herself next to a tree with wide, abundant branches. Exhausted, she lay down among the pine needles, the tree's branches overhanging and forming a makeshift shelter. She tried to fight her exhaustion, but sleep overcame her as the first drops of rain began falling.

❲

Clint didn't worry about Augusta until Buddy returned alone to his cabin. The horse was still saddled. He hadn't been ridden hard recently. Gussie was meticulous about her horse. She always removed his saddle and brushed him after a ride. "Treat your horse right and he'll treat you right." He'd heard her say the words so often that he turned to see if she said them now. But no one was there. Something was wrong.

Clint donned a slicker and set out to find her. The slanted rain pelted his cheeks and dripped from his hat. He called her name but only the wind answered. Thunder rumbled and lightning flashed, turning his own horse skittish. The lightning brightened things far too briefly for him to see anything but the outlines of trees and their shadows.

He found the beaded bag that Indian Jake had given her. Frantic, he scampered around from tree to tree, hollering her name. No one answered. He saw nothing. Shivering in the cold rain, he tore his ragged scarf from his neck and hung it in a tree to mark the spot. Clint remounted and headed toward Sagebrush Junction to fetch the sheriff.

The lawman formed a posse and they made plans to begin their search after the storm eased. The hour that had taken seemed like days to Clint. They searched for three days afterward. No sign of Gussie. Clint suspected her husband and told the sheriff of his concern. But the sheriff explained that Homer himself had paid for the posse.

"He did act rather surprised that we didn't find her," the sheriff admitted. "But that's not unusual in a case like this. I'm surprised we didn't find her."

Clint said, "Isn't there anything else we can do?"

"'Fraid not," the lawman replied. "You said you'd had a fight. Maybe she's up there in the mountains stewin' a bit and she's lettin' you stew some here. If she wanted us to find her, we would have found her."

"But not if she's been hurt."

"No way of knowin' that."

Clint argued for a few minutes more, but he wasted his breath. The sheriff wasn't going to search any further. Homer, he said, had gone on a business trip to another city. "You might take a break yourself, Clint."

Rage flamed through Clint's blood at the thought of Homer leaving when Gussie hadn't been found. But as soon as his anger engulfed him, it dissipated. He'd been putting off his own business trip to Denver himself. He couldn't believe Gussie was gone. Futile as it was, he'd have to believe the sheriff's theory. Maybe she had gone off to be by herself. Didn't explain why Buddy had come back to his cabin. She'd never have left her horse if she'd been all right.

Outside of the sheriff's office, Clint looked at the Thunder Mountains, ragged over the eastern horizon. He blinked back tears. "We were good together, Gussie," he said. "I'll miss you."

Clint traveled to Denver to view the camera techniques of an old friend of Kirkland's and a man who was becoming a renowned photographer throughout the country. While thrilled at his increasing skills with cameras, a piece of him felt empty and dismayed. He continued to hold hope that Gussie lived and would return to him. When he returned to Wyoming, Clint became a man with two souls. One learned the photography business, the other pined for Gussie. He thought he saw her on the street; he thought she rode by astride a horse; he saw light shining on someone's dark hair and his heart leapt. But it was never Gussie.

All Clint had left of her were his sketches, the beaded bag she had loved, the single photograph he'd taken on the day of the tragic dress rehearsal, and the memories of the harsh words he wished he'd never said. The photograph mocked him. Kirkland set it in the front window, hoping that anyone who had seen her would come forward. The smiling cowgirl, waving her hat high above her head, wearing trademark split skirt and fancy boots, clearly loved what she was doing. Viewers could feel her enthusiasm and often remarked on the vividness of the picture. To Clint, the picture became Gussie's last goodbye, eventually replacing the memory of her tear-stained face on that day of their bitter argument.

☾

Photographers from throughout the nation gathered in Cheyenne a century after Augusta Ford disappeared. They stood gazing at her in Clint's photograph, now part of a private museum collection. Near the photo, kept in a lighted display case, Gussie's beaded bag lay atop a clear plastic platform. An explanatory card nearby said, "Sioux Indian beadwork, circa 1890s, believed to have belonged to Augusta Ford."

"Augusta Ford is legendary in rodeo circles," the curator, Emily Howard, a distant relative of one of the friends of the Irwins, explained. "She didn't perform for long but was considered one of the best women trick riders in the country. She disappeared a few days after a freak accident when her riding partner, Marie Doland, was killed during a dress rehearsal for Charlie Irwin's Wild West Show. Most historians believe that the accident frightened Augusta and she left in an attempt to find other opportunities outside the rodeo circuit. The bag was found near the area where she is said to have disappeared, near the Thunder Mountains. This photograph, however, has come to symbolize that era of the rodeo cowgirl."

"And what happened to the photographer?" a member of the crowd asked.

"Not much is known about Clint Parker. He appears to have had as short a career as Augusta. He's said to have worked here in Cheyenne for Kirkland for a time after her disappearance. Then he moved to Denver. The Denver city directories have him listed as a photographer there for a few years. That's all we know." Emily pointed to a photograph taken by Kirkland. "Kirkland was one of Cheyenne's best photographers of the day. He always hoped to capture a bucking bronc in action but was never successful in that quest. He became known instead for fine portraits. This portrait is of Homer Ford, a well known Cheyenne philanthropist, shortly before he died. Homer was murdered, but his killer was never found. He was married to Augusta at the time she disappeared and had earlier conducted members of the English nobility through the area on hunting expeditions. He blamed Augusta's love of rodeo for her disappearance and never donated money to that cause, but he helped found and establish many other charitable activities in the region."

The group of photographers moved forward to the next exhibit. Emily held back. Something about the story of Augusta Ford haunted her but she couldn't pin down a specific reason. Though she had researched extensively, she found no answers to her many questions.

One of the photographers lingered at the display with her. He said, "Maybe it was difficult for a man with such notable connections to be married to a famous rodeo cowgirl in those times. She must have traveled a lot."

Emily replied, "I don't think it mattered." Chatting, they walked ahead to the next exhibit, a display of guns and rifles, one of them a Colt ivory-handled pistol owned by Homer Ford.

The Fiddle's Lament

I came to life in the hands of an unknown master but found fulfillment in the hands of a frightened young man. Grandpa Hampton showed me to his only granddaughter, Estelle, with much joy in his eyes and a smile on his lips that January day in 1880 when she turned six years old. With his large gnarled hands, he gave my body a gentle caress. Holding me up so the firelight danced against my recently dried varnish, he said, "My finest piece for my finest granddaughter."

Young Estelle laughed. "Grandpa, I'm your only granddaughter," she said. She reached for me, but Grandpa Hampton held me at bay.

Carrying me as if I were a precious newborn babe of his familial line, he reached for a bow. He said to Estelle, "I hope that someone will cherish this instrument one day as much as I do, Estelle. And I hope that someone is you. Listen."

Then he played a scale and a beautiful turn of "O Dem Golden Slippers" and then a few measures of "Silver Threads Among the Gold." My voice pleased me. A strong tone and yet the delicate sound of my strings vibrating made the music especially appealing. The little girl's face shone with delight. My creator's hand, so big around my neck, felt light. His fingers moved with grace and appropriate speed. His musical skill came near to his excellence in crafting and sculpting wood. He'd chosen the finest Englemann spruce from the best trees in the forest of the Medicine Bow range in Wyoming. He'd cut the lumber himself. Then he had carved and shaved and worked and fitted until I came together into this fine form. But then, I supposed I would forever be biased in his favor. He handed me to Estelle.

Estelle took me carefully. I was nearly too big for her small hands. I could feel her fear. She trembled a bit. I knew from that moment she would care for me with a love similar to the adoration her grandfather had shown me. She gathered her courage and scraped the bow across my strings. They trembled. I would have myself if I'd have known how. Both grandfather and granddaughter grimaced at the squeaking sound I made. I thought Estelle would cry, but Grandpa nodded his head and smiled. "Try again," he encouraged her. We suffered through several more squawking noises. Then Grandpa took me again and played the minstrel song once more.

"Oh, Grandpa, I'll never be able to play like you do!"

"Yes, Estelle, Yes, you will. Someday, my dear. You just need to keep trying."

He gave me back to her. Together, we suffered another bout of musical misery. Finally, he laid me carefully on the table where he'd made me. He hugged Estelle. Big tears filled her eyes. "I'm sorry, Grandpa. I can't play."

"Nonsense, child. You just need to practice. Keep trying." He took her tiny chin in his massive thumb and forefinger and raised her face. "We'll practice together. I'll give you lessons every day." With the other hand, he wiped away her tears. "Always remember, Estelle, keep trying."

Grandpa Hampton's words comforted all of us. With him helping her to learn how to bring out my best voice, I felt certain she could eventually master the music. I hoped that the bond he'd mentioned earlier would form. For my fondest dream was to be held by someone who loved me dearly and who would play me as I was meant to be played.

Dreams, I learned that day, don't always take shape as we would expect. None of us realized how short-lived the lessons were to be.

Grandpa Hampton died in his sleep of a heart attack that night. I sensed his passing. His workshop grew cold. The table I lay upon felt icy. I longed for the warmth of hands against my shiny wood again. In the morning, Estelle came with her mother. They bundled me into the flannel-lined case Grandpa Hampton had made. Estelle hugged the case to her as she trudged back to her house. She placed me carefully beneath her bed. She never played me again.

☾

When she became a teacher, Estelle took me with her to a new town on the western Nebraska prairie called Pleasant Dale. One day, a dozen years after her grandfather's demise, she placed me in her classroom at the Meadowlark School near her desk where I could feel some warmth but not too near the wood stove where I would have grown brittle. She wanted to introduce the children to a fine musical instrument, she told me. Estelle had grown accustomed to talking to me. I sorely wished I could talk to her. I would have played out all the hurt her aching heart still held. But it was not to be. She never believed she possessed the talent to learn to play the fiddle. Believing that inaccuracy, she never pursued it. Instead, she turned her attentions to the piano. In this pursuit, she displayed her musical expertise. I ached to be held and played and tried to forgive myself for being jealous of the instrument that gained her attentions.

On this particular day, Estelle Hampton turned her back on the class to write her favorite quote from Thoreau on the blackboard. The students, ranging in age from six to seventeen, were busy reading. The drafty room was quiet. The chalk in her hand whispered across the board. She wrote, *If one advances confidently in the direction of his dreams, and endeavors to live the life which he has imagined, he will meet with a success unexpected in common hours. (Walden).*

Estelle wrote the quotation mainly for the benefit of her eldest student, Pearl Allen, who was reading *Walden*. She hoped the others would take comfort from it as well. As she placed the last period, a noise startled her. Estelle turned round and saw David Lane jump just as the inkwell on Pearl's desk slid from its perch and crashed into a dark pool on the wood floor. Pearl's calico dress revealed a pretty good stain from the splatter as well.

"David Lane," Estelle said as sternly as she could manage, "You will clean that mess up this minute."

"But Ma'am," he began. Despite his rag-tag clothing, the boy was clean. He and his younger brother, John, had only attended school a few days. Undoubtedly they'd be moving along soon. Estelle had grown used to having students for a short time as their parents trailed on west.

"David," she insisted. "Clean up your mess." She kept a faded bandanna in her desk for such emergencies. She took it out and handed it to him. Noticing Pearl's ruined dress, Estelle said, "And you will stay after school. We will discuss your improper behavior then." At fourteen, David was the nearest to Pearl's age. Estelle sighed. Boys often pulled such pranks to catch the eye of a girl they liked, and she could understand why David might be smitten with Pearl, with her long blonde braids and fresh-scrubbed appearance.

No one spoke. I saw what happened but could not intervene. David hadn't spilled the ink. He resented having to clean up Sam Simmons's mess but no one else had seen what happened. Pearl had been so intent on her reading that she hadn't noticed anything until David reached up to try to catch the inkwell. Sam had been steadily pushing it toward the edge of the desk. He had been the one hoping to catch Pearl's attention.

As David knelt down, rag in hand, to mop up the mess, his younger brother, John, the youngest in Miss Hampton's school, caught his eye. He started to speak, but David shook his head. The little boy frowned and remained quiet.

After school, Estelle explained to David that she expected him to stay after school every day and be sure the schoolroom was kept clean. He would also bring in firewood for the stove so that a day's supply was ready when she needed it. He would work until he had paid for a new dress for Pearl. Johnny could read or work math problems while his brother atoned for his inkwell sin.

"Have you anything to say for yourself, young man?" Estelle asked when she finished her rather lengthy list.

David shook his head. Johnny tugged at his sleeve, his eyes wide. David's frown silenced his little brother.

"Then you both may go." She stood, the hem of her brown dress not quite touching the ground. David looked at her for a long moment. I could read his thoughts by the way he looked at her, but Estelle remained oblivious to such frivolity. She was the prettiest woman he'd ever seen except for his mother. She had dark brown hair the color of walnuts and brown eyes to match. Her cheeks held a tinge of red, probably because of her anger with him, but her pale skin was otherwise unblemished. He put on his hat and ushered Johnny outside. Estelle picked me up and held me to her chest as she'd done those many years ago. "No lesson today," she said, half to me and half to herself. "And he's probably the one who needs music the most." I agreed. Once, when David had been handing in a paper, he touched my case. The contact was brief. He didn't want to risk Estelle's ire, but he couldn't resist rubbing his hand against the wooden case. In that one quick touch, his story became clear to me. I don't know how I possessed this extra sense. I had once heard Estelle speak of a deaf person having keener sight because of his loss of hearing. Perhaps I had received the gift of a keener sense of knowing through touch because of all these years I had not been allowed to speak. I knew David as intimately as I knew Estelle. Perhaps more so. She watched the boys walk away. I listened and heard what she could not.

Walking the two miles to their homestead claim, David estimated he'd still have a couple of hours of sunlight left. He'd been working on the dugout they would live in, and as soon as he finished it, they could quit living out of the wagon. With winter approaching, he had to work faster. And now, with this unwarranted punishment, his chore would take longer.

"Davy, why didn't you tell Miss Hampton you didn't spill the ink? I saw who did it. It was Sam Simmons."

David placed a hand on his brother's shoulder. "I know who did it, Johnny."

"Then why didn't you tell her? You shouldn't have to stay after school when you didn't do it. I could have told her but you wouldn't let me. Why?"

"Because then we'd have been figured as tattletales. And worse, I'd be considered a whiner. People don't respect either kind, Johnny." The danger lay in Sam Simmons being seated behind David. Having succeeded in avoiding punishment for one misdeed, David worried Sam would try again. David didn't need the additional work but he didn't know how to stop that if it came to it.

"I don't think you should have to pay for something you didn't do."

"Look, we've got to get along with these people here. Leastways until Ma and Pa come. And I want to have the dugout built for them." He'd prove to his father that he'd been worthy of the trust the older man had placed in him. He'd sent the two boys to claim the land until their mother—whose loss of another child had nearly claimed her own life—felt well enough to travel. "They're countin' on us, Johnny."

Both fell silent for a while as they trudged along through the prairie grasses. David knew it would be difficult to complete all his chores and accept the punishment at school. Had it not been for Johnny, he might have skipped school altogether. He only attended because his folks wanted them to, and Johnny was too young to go alone. He looked at his brother. His curly blond hair caught the waning sunlight and glowed like an angel's halo. The little fellow had such bright blue eyes, always filled with questions about everything. He needed teaching.

☾

By the second week of enforced punishment, David had fallen asleep in school three times. Johnny had progressed through additional reading assignments and looked forward to the afternoons they spent in the schoolroom with Miss Hampton. I remained every day in my place. Estelle had not yet managed the courage to bring me out of my case and show me to her students. She had begun to notice how quiet and careful David was. Exceedingly polite, he didn't bother her with questions or speak out much in class. She noticed he sat near Sam Simmons, whose rambunctious attitude showed in his inattention when she asked questions. David, on the other hand, tried to pay attention until he dozed off.

One afternoon, Estelle followed Johnny outside to get some sunshine herself. "Johnny, tell me something, will you?"

He nodded. She said, "Are your parents expecting David to work after school like I do?"

"No, Ma'am. Our parents aren't here. But Davy sure does work hard on our claim."

She asked him about the claim. The little boy spilled the tale with gusto. He'd only been waiting for such an opening to tell all about what was happening to them.

"Oh my goodness," Estelle said. "I didn't realize." How could she have known that parents would have sent children by themselves to stake a homestead claim. Had she known, she might have altered her punishment slightly.

"Davy's building us a dugout. And it's a fine one, too. You should come see it." As soon as the words came out, Johnny reddened and looked shy. Estelle could tell he liked her. "I'd love to see your dugout, Johnny. But first, maybe you and David could join me for dinner." She knew she could work something out with Pearl's folks. She stayed with the Allens. They had been kind to her, a fact for which she felt deeply grateful. She had heard plenty of stories from other teachers who had been much less fortunate.

(

The next evening, David and Johnny sat at Zack and Cora Allen's dinner table with Pearl and Miss Hampton. The boys ate ravenously. David said, "Mrs. Allen, this is sure good. I don't know how we can repay you though." Having been prompted earlier about the boys' predicament by Estelle, Cora Allen said, "No repayment is necessary, David," and offered more. The others at the table, long since satisfied, conversed congenially while the Lanes took their fill.

When David put down his fork, Estelle said quietly, "David, you didn't spill the ink on Pearl's dress the other day, did you?"

David looked up at her, then blushed furiously and stared at his plate. Before he could formulate an answer, Johnny piped in, saying, "No, Ma'am. It was Sam Simmons."

"Johnny!" David said.

"But he did it, Davy. You didn't. You shouldn't have to—" Johnny looked from David, who glared at him, to Miss Hampton, who looked chagrined. Johnny fell silent.

"I see," she said. "Pearl will get her new dress but at a dearer cost than I realized." She excused herself from the table.

David's cheeks flamed with embarrassment. Now Johnny had done it. Maybe he'd just give up on school altogether and Johnny could try again next year when Ma and Pa returned. He and Johnny picked up their dishes from the table and took them to the sideboard by the hand-pump where Mrs. Allen stacked them. She declined their offer of help. David couldn't help noticing how comfortable the sod house was, with its finery like the pump and isinglass windows. Someday, he vowed, the Lanes would have such a comfortable home.

By that time, Estelle returned, hugging me to her chest. I felt her overwhelming love course through me much as her grandfather's had when he had so painstakingly honed and polished me. Lifting me from the case, she presented me to David.

"David," she said. "I am terribly sorry for punishing you when the inkwell incident was not at all your fault. I would like you to have this to make up for my mistake."

"Oh, Ma'am, I couldn't." He touched my varnished wood. I again saw how rugged a life David had been made to face. Was this then the joy that Grandpa Hampton had hoped to impart through my creation? Sharing music with a scared young soul who needed the happiness so much? "It's mighty fine."

Ah, I was well pleased, and yet very frightened at this unexpected turn of events. In the possession of my mistress, it was true I had played no music but I had suffered no mishaps. She had kept me safely beneath her bed, hugging me to her when she dusted. She regarded me with love and respect. To go now to a young man, temperate though he might be, scared me. Though I felt instinctively David would treat me well, time would have to prove my theory. And another sudden fear overtook me. I'd remained silent for twelve years. Was it possible my voice still existed?

Estelle's voice soothed me. "Yes, it is indeed a most fine instrument," she said to David, "but I do want you to have it. I'll teach you to play after school. It's the least I can do." She laid me carefully in the case. As she tucked me away, my strings trembled. Everyone smiled at the almost inaudible sound. My terror made itself known. Estelle said, "I'll bring it tomorrow. Zack will take you home in his wagon." She closed the lid and my strings vibrated once more. This time, though, I was the only one who heard.

☾

David's days became a haze of building the dugout and trying to keep up with school work and afternoon practicing with Miss Hampton and the town's new parson, Pastor Whitman. While Miss Hampton oversaw the daily lessons, Pastor Whitman showed him how to hold me and how to hold the bow and how to use his wrist and not his arm to draw the bow across my strings. The screeches and squawks David made nearly convinced him to give up music and just sit in the hole in the ground he'd managed to carve out for Johnny and himself. For myself, I could say the same but for the gentle way he held me. I knew he had the music in him. So did Estelle. She saw in the boy a deep love of music, that indescribable quality that defines a musician. She recognized it in small things, like the light that warmed his eyes at the sound of the wind swishing against the logs of the wall and the way he tapped his foot to a rhythm only he heard. I recognized the future of a fine musician by his touch and his determination to continue. We suffered through the inevitable noise and eventually graduated to plaintive notes and erratic scales. But then there were those rare times David strove for—when a beautiful sound emanated from me and it felt as if the music came from

inside his body somewhere and transferred itself through me—and at
those times, Estelle Hampton rewarded us with a smile almost as delight-
ful as the music itself.

Pastor Whitman, bless his heart, played mechanically. He played
hymns. He would not lower his standards to play secular tunes. Under
his guidance, David learned only sacred music. He suggested that David
play for the church services.

At this surprising comment, David shook his head with vigor.

Estelle said, "What a grand idea. David, I think you should. You
should share your talent with everyone." After only a few Sundays it
became clear that the offering plate held more coin when David and I
played than when we didn't. Pastor Whitman was delighted at the
increase. Understanding David's situation, he shared the bounty with
the lonely Lane boys. The young minister knew he could do no more.
He had taught David all the hymns he knew. This might have been the
end of David's musical education but for Estelle. She longed to hear the
tunes her grandfather had played. After lengthy discussion with Pastor
Whitman and a sincere promise not to do so on Sundays, Estelle played
those songs for David on the church organ.

Estelle played tunes that made him want to dance and tunes that
made him miss his folks and tunes to lift his heart. David soon wanted
to play them as well as she did. At first, he'd taken the fiddle lessons just
to help her feel better. She'd done wrong and felt bad about it. So why
make her feel worse? Besides, she was so pretty and kind. David longed
for her approval. So he set his mind to making music and learned.
Through him, I became the beneficiary. After all, Grandpa Hampton
had made me for this.

"This is a listening instrument," Estelle told David, using Grandpa
Hampton's words to her. "You must listen to what it tells you as you
play. Listen for the tones." She clapped her hands and laughed when he
managed to repeat a complete phrase without a misstep. "Oh, David.
You have a definite flair for music."

Estelle taught him three songs, and by the time winter's snow began
to fly, he knew them well enough to perform them in public. They were

"Buffalo Gals," "Oh, Susanna!" and "Oh My Darling Clementine." As the days grew shorter, she soon began to usher the Lane boys home nearly every day with her to the Allens, seeing to it that they had a least one proper meal each day. Estelle had David give a concert for their hosts. Mr. Allen said David's tunes were so enjoyable that he considered the music his payment for the meals and the housing for the boys until their parents arrived. He had helped David build the dugout, and Cora Allen helped them stock their pantry with food, but the Allens continued to let the boys stay with them.

Our musical reveries continued. Had Grandpa Hampton been in the room to hear, he would have clapped his hands with pleasure. David and I formed the special bond that sometimes occurs between a musician and his instrument. He played me with confidence and I responded in kind. I was so appreciative of making music again that I did not see the dangers that lay ahead for David. Had I known, I could have done nothing but what I was already doing—providing a unique sort of happiness through song.

When it came, the letter did not surprise David. Johnny was devastated. David had known for some time that if their parents didn't get a start soon, they would be unable to travel for the winter. But Johnny believed otherwise and he was difficult to convince.

The Allens, doing their best to stand in as the boys' parents, spread the word about their talented young fiddler. On weekends, David played for dances. People paid him to play for them. He hungered to learn more songs and soon learned them on his own, by listening. He listened to people hum the tunes they wished to hear. Soon he became so adept that he could play the song through without a mistake after hearing it only once. He even played for a big shindig at Pleasant Dale's fancy Hotel St. Andrew. On that night, he managed to play "Turkey in the Straw," "Oh Dem Golden Slippers," and "Camptown Races." People were so delighted with his performance that he made the most money ever. This was enough to get him and Johnny through the rest of the winter. And for his teacher, Miss Hampton, he played "Silver Threads Among the Gold." David intended the song to bring her happiness but her eyes filled with tears instead. When he moved to lay me down and stop playing, Estelle touched his arm.

"No, David, I don't mean for you to stop. Your song was so wonderful—" Her voice broke and she paused a moment before continuing. "My grandfather would have been so pleased. He played me that same tune when he gave the fiddle to me."

❨

Things went along well for a while. David played often for the Allens after dinner. The family absorbed the two brothers and nurtured and sustained them. While the Lanes did stay in their dugout a few times, they far more often could be found at the Allens' home.

The Allens knew of hardship—they had come on ahead a few years earlier and wouldn't have let Pearl be on her own for anything. Zack reminded Cora, who continually worried about the Lanes, that things were different with boys. Maybe David's father was trying to teach him responsibility through this and maybe he hoped he'd become a man this way.

"Seems awfully harsh, Zack," she said. "I wonder if the parents will come. If he is ailing and unable as he said in that last letter. Maybe those two kids got to be too big a responsibility and this was an easy way out. They'll survive. But maybe the parents were counting on good folks like us."

Zack conceded the point. "I hate to be so mean-spirited and think the worst of folks. But Cora, aren't we lucky? The boys are trying awfully hard not to be nuisances. David will find his way when the spring comes. We'll help them get in a crop maybe and then they can be on their own."

❨

In the spring, a man named Alexander Burch began courting Estelle Hampton. He was a tall, dark, mustachioed man whom David had seen with Miss Hampton at the Hotel St. Andrew.

"I don't trust him, Johnny," David said one night when he lay in bed next to his brother. Johnny, already half asleep, mumbled something unintelligible. I listened from my vantage point beneath their bed. "I hate to see Miss Hampton involved with the likes of him." I didn't trust Alexander Burch either. I didn't know David's reasoning. I suspected he had fallen in love with Estelle himself. I knew well what caused my own dislike. The man had yawned and looked bored during our rousing musical performance. He did not dance, even when Estelle patted her hands on her knees and tapped her feet to and fro. His naturally stern face took on an expression of intense annoyance at Estelle's heartfelt tears when David played Grandpa Hampton's song. I could not bring myself to trust someone who disliked music so.

☾

David showed me his true character when Estelle asked him to play for her wedding to Alexander Burch. He said yes without flinching, then we proceeded to practice and practice and practice until I no longer felt the yielding pressure of David's fingers against my strings but instead felt the thick calluses on his fingers pressing against my neck. I sometimes, too, felt tears falling against my satiny finish. They stung. Grandpa Hampton's varnish held admirably, however.

I hoped David would work out his disappointment in love through music. For I knew now that he did love Estelle Hampton. He loved her for what she had given him, a chance to enjoy a talent he hadn't even known he possessed. I was merely the instrument of that love.

At the wedding, David and I both surprised ourselves. He never missed a note, and my voice was in fine form that day. I was quite unprepared for what David did next. Following the ceremony, he returned me to my case. He tied a ribbon around the case and placed me on the gift table for the newly married couple. He laid his hand upon the top of the case.

Johnny said, "Davy, what're you doing?"

"I'm giving Miss Hampton back her fiddle."

"But why?"

"Because I will not play the fiddle again."

"But you're good at it."

David smiled at his younger brother. He ruffled Johnny's hair. "Thanks."

Then David removed his hand from my case. No one in the crowded hall heard my strings shaking. I worried that I would never perform again. Worse yet, I worried what would happen to me in the hands of Alexander Burch, a man who clearly disliked music. How could David be so cruel after all the joy I had brought to him?

Estelle's voice drifted to me over the hum of the crowd. "Look at all these gifts. How very kind of everyone," she said. Her voice fell on the last word. She had seen me. She rested her hand on my case. "David," she whispered. She picked me up and hugged me to her. Alexander, her new husband, touched her arm.

"We've not time for that now, darling," he said. He pushed against her arm, willing her to return me to my place on the gift table. "We must go soon or we will miss our train."

But Estelle would not be pushed. "No, Alex. I must find David. I must do it now." She broke free of his grasp. He frowned but did not follow.

Making her way through the crowd, she looked but did not see David. Estelle grew frantic. "David must have this fiddle," she said to herself, although out loud because I heard her words. I agreed.

She searched the wedding-goers in vain. No one at the Hotel St. Andrew had noticed David leaving. At last, she stood on the porch of the hotel. Her eyes naturally came to rest on the schoolhouse. Sitting outside, hair beribboned and bedecked in a blue poplin frock, was Pearl Allen. Estelle smiled. Over the last few weeks, she had noticed that wherever David was, Pearl was not far away. Holding me in one arm, she picked up the black satin skirt of her wedding gown, made of the finest fabric she could buy in Pleasant Dale, and ran to the schoolhouse. She spoke to Pearl. She stopped at the doorway.

Inside, David Lane sat at his desk. Johnny stood beside him, a questioning look in his eyes. He saw her first, and said, "Miss Hampton."

Estelle smiled. "Hello, Johnny. I—I realized I forgot something very important here."

She strode further into the room, her black buttoned boots clicking against the plank floor. David did not look up. When she reached Johnny, she touched his shoulder. "Johnny, I need to talk with David. Would you go outside and play with Pearl for a few minutes, please?"

Johnny did as she asked. She sat down in the desk across from David. She held me in her lap.

"David. What a wonderful gift you gave to us today. Your music was beautiful. I'll carry it in my heart always."

He stared at his hands. He rubbed his thumbs against the calluses on his forefingers.

Estelle's words met with silence. A breeze blew through the schoolroom, making the door creak against its hinges. She hesitated.

"Won't you please keep this fiddle for me? You play it so beautifully. I'd feel so much better knowing you have it."

David bit his lip and shook his head. "No, Ma'am. I can't keep it. You were right kind to me, but the fiddle belongs to you." His pride did not allow him to explain that this was the only wedding gift he and Johnny could afford to give to her.

Estelle smiled. She understood what David was trying to do. "No, David. It belongs to you. You are the one who can play it so well. This fiddle deserves to be played. My grandfather wanted it to be played. If I take it with me, well, I can't play and Alexander—" She let her voice break off at the sound of her husband's name. She cleared her throat. "He doesn't appreciate music like we do."

David still would not look at her. She touched his arm.

He said, "I can't keep the fiddle, Miss Hampton, er um, Mrs. Burch." He coughed to cover his error. "School's over now. I'm going to need to be working from now on. Need to be tending the crops so that we can keep the homestead. Mr. Allen's going to help us." His decision to stop playing music ran deeper within his heart than he could ever allow her to know. She'd been so generous to him, had helped him so much. Keeping me now, especially now, when she pledged herself to a man he didn't like, would only serve as a distasteful reminder.

Estelle bit her lip and squeezed his arm. "Your parents? Aren't they coming soon?"

He shook his head. "Pa's still ailin'. Ma's taking care of him. He doesn't want to let the homestead go. It's up to me to keep it." He looked at her then. His eyes, so clear and brown, held adult worries.

"I'm sure you will, David." She wished things were different. David's education would suffer now. She was determined that his music would not. "But don't you think you'll still have time for the fiddle? You've brought great joy to the people here. They'd still like to hear you play. And—" She paused. "And, it would be like I was still here with you." Her lips trembled. She pressed them together to stay the threatening tears. To Estelle, I had always been a pleasant reminder, a tangible object that kept her close to Grandpa Hampton. In giving me to David in this way, she had to let go of her feelings for her grandfather. The only way she could do that was to pass his words to her student. "Always remember, David, you must keep trying. You must always keep trying."

He stayed silent. Estelle rubbed her hand across the top of my case. She liked David. She knew that part of his reluctance to take me back had to do with her leaving. She ached inside because she couldn't find the right words to help him.

"I see great things in your future, David," she said. "You have a strong character." She lifted me, then stood and placed me on the desk in front of him. "This belonged to my grandfather," she said. "I gave it to you for a reason, David. I cannot accept it as a gift. You must keep it for yourself. The best gift you can give to me is to continue playing, to play often, and to remember me when you do."

She trailed her hand against my case. Then she walked out of the schoolroom and back to the Hotel St. Andrew where her wedding reception continued. David sat silently for a moment. He placed both hands on my case. The bow tickled my strings.

Pearl and Johnny peeked in, having watched the new Mrs. Burch exit the schoolhouse and wipe a tear from her face. David stood and noticed them.

"What're you waiting for? We're missing the party," he said.

The trio made their way back to the reception just before the newly-weds departed. David slid the ribbon from my case. He stood in the background. When the couple came outside a few minutes later, the crowd quieted. The carriage driver urged his horses forward. Amidst the sound of clopping hooves, my voice rose, gentle and sweet. The carriage driver halted. Mr. and Mrs. Alexander Burch stood on the boardwalk, ready to embark on their wedding journey, listening. David played "Silver Threads Among the Gold."

Before she climbed into the carriage next to her new husband, Estelle Hampton Burch rewarded David with a smile.

☾

"I never forgot that picture of her my mind made," David wrote in a diary many years later. "She wore a gray serge traveling dress and a matching hat with a tall, curly black feather. She took the arm of Alexander Burch. I watched them go with heavy heart. Partly for myself, and mostly for her. How she would live without music was beyond me. Once she had taught me how to play, I could never have stopped. She entrusted me with a solemn gift and a large responsibility—to pass on my knowledge to my children and to tell Estelle's story. I don't know what happened to her. I never saw her again. But I kept and played Grandpa Hampton's fiddle often. She remains a part of my life."

David played me at his own wedding—to Pearl Allen. I enjoyed a special place in their home, a log house on the homestead David claimed for his parents. Johnny lived in a house nearby, on the section line. With the Allens' help, David had managed to work a claim for Johnny, too. Their parents had never made it west. Their father had died from his illness. Their mother succumbed weeks later, probably of a broken heart. She never saw her grandchildren, but I welcomed David and Pearl's daughter and granddaughter into the world. I became especially adept at lullabies, but my favorite times were those when David played me for dances and weddings.

Before he died, David gave me to his granddaughter, Anna. In her youth, she loved to play. She had no children of her own. She never married. When arthritis cramped her lovely, delicate fingers, she decided to donate me to the Pleasant Dale Museum.

☾

Standing in the museum that day, Anna hugged me to her as Estelle used to do. Several visitors made their way through the exhibits, enjoying the museum displays as part of the annual Pleasant Dale Pioneer Festival. Anna listened to the curator, Ned Winston, as he explained about his recently acquired temperature-controlled display case. Listening to his smooth spiel, I feared that I will always be on display but never allowed to play music again. He pointed at me. I would never be too warm or feel chilled. I did not appreciate his feeble efforts to make me feel more comfortable. Standing silent in a display case among a cadre of antiques would be a fate worse than being stamped to splinters beneath the hooves of a team of work horses. I worried that I would never feel the warmth of gentle hands against my neck or the swell of a chin against my sound board. What frightened me most was the realization that I would never again feel the music rushing through me from the heart of the player.

Anna hugged me a bit tighter. "I see," she said, having listened to the man's detailed comments about the accommodations here. She herself faced a move into an assisted living facility. I suspected that for her the place would feel not at all unlike a temperature-controlled display case. She cleared her throat. "My grandfather taught me to play on this fiddle." She showed him David Lane's diary. "He kept a diary about the fiddle's heritage. I'm so glad he did. I might not have ever known the story behind this instrument otherwise. I think other people should have a chance to learn about it, too, don't you?"

Ned Winston nodded, pushing a stray lock of thick white hair from his forehead. He wore round eyeglasses and a thick white mustache. He reminded me of an elderly Alexander Burch and I did not like to be reminded of the man who did not like music. Ned said, "My, yes. What a treasure this will be for us. When we spoke on the phone, I was well pleased."

Anna told Ned my story over the telephone one day. Now, she said, "I typed out the diary entries so that people could read it more easily. Grandpa David didn't take to learning fine penmanship."

"You mentioned that you played with your grandfather when you were a child, in the fiddling group here?"

Anna nodded. She stroked my case. David had begun an old-time fiddle players group after she was born. With the advent of radio and automobiles, the old-timers worried that the new generation might forget the importance of fiddles and their music. Anna attended the fiddle group every week throughout her childhood. She continued on into adulthood. By that time, many of the old fiddlers were gone. Few people could now play a riff on a fiddle. Most children were taught the violin and the rigid music of the classical masters like Bach and Beethoven. Not many realized that the only difference between a fiddle and a violin was the music the musician played and not the instrument itself. Anna kept right on playing me all through her life, even when the listeners grew few. These days, she played me often just for her own pleasure.

"And you've kept up with your practicing, haven't you?" The curator's words brought back more pleasant memories for Anna.

She said, "Grandpa David gave me this fiddle when I was three because I stood up and danced to his music and sang Mother's favorite hymn. He kept it for me and gave me lessons until I was old enough to care for it on my own."

Ned smiled at her. "What wonderful memories. What wonderful stories. We will be so glad to have this piece as part of our collection."

They stood silent for a few moments. Anna continued to hold me close. Ned won my affection when he asked, "Would you be willing to play something? Doesn't have to be anything fancy. I'd love to hear you."

Anna smiled and complied with his request. She stretched her aching fingers, removed me from my case, and played "Turkey in the Straw." She missed a few notes because her fingers were stiff.

"Play another," Ned said. People gathered around us. Anna's fingers, limber now, picked out "O Dem Golden Slippers." The crowd lingered. Time stopped for a few precious moments as the tiny woman dressed in black polyester slacks, a cotton shirt, and a gray cardigan sweater played several sweet old-time fiddle tunes for them. When she finished, people in the crowd stated their requests. Anna laughed.

"Oh, please. I'll play one more. Then I need to rest my hands a bit."

She thought for a moment, said, "In honor of my grandfather. This was his fiddle." She lifted me again to her chin. She played "Silver Threads Among the Gold." The crowd stood spellbound by the melancholy notes of the old music. Anna closed her eyes. When she opened them again, she saw a little boy, about four years old, dancing around her to the music. She exchanged a glance with Ned Winston. He smiled at Anna and then beamed at the youngster.

Anna finished the song with a flourish of her bow. She held her position for a moment, not wanting to dispel the enchantment surrounding us. Everyone else stayed quiet. The ticking of the century-old grandfather clock in the corner became evident. The little boy said, "More."

The audience applauded, then fell silent again. Ned asked, "Miss Lane, would you like to come play at the museum every so often? This instrument should be played, not just on display, don't you think? I mean, considering all that it represents."

Anna grinned. "I'd be delighted."

"More," the little tyke insisted.

Anna knelt down to look him in the eyes. "I will play more for you after my hands rest a while."

He reached out and touched me. As his fingers moved against my smooth surface, his eyes grew wide with wonder. He smiled. I felt certain this young man would love me as Anna had. He plucked my D-string. It didn't hurt, but the result was an unpleasant sound. His mother came and took his hand away. "Don't touch that, Billy."

Anna said, "No, it's all right."

"He's always making noise on something. I can't get him to stop."

"He didn't do a bit of harm. He did me good, in fact."

"Thank you," Billy's mother said. "We'll come back in a few minutes." She took Billy away to try to interest him in other museum items. Anna stood, with great effort and welcome help from Ned. The crowd filtered back through the museum.

Anna steadied herself by gripping Ned's arm. She said, "I have a grand idea."

"I thought you might."

Together, they made plans for Anna to play at the museum every week. Anna insisted that Ned encourage Billy's mother to bring him to listen to her. She signed the paperwork to donate me to the museum, adding a line of special instructions of her own. With agreement reached and my future secured, she began to play again. I no longer dreaded my future. Instead, a strange relief flooded through me with Anna's music.

When the crowd gathered around us again, she said, "The fiddle is a listening instrument. You must listen to what it tells you as you play."

Billy stood, rapt, as she ran her fingers over my strings with confidence and drew the bow delicately over them to the tune of "Carry Me Back to Old Virginny." I need not have feared a life without playing. Anna smiled at the little one. He began to dance again.

With the crowd again suitably entertained, Ned read what Anna had written. "When I am no longer able to play the fiddle here on a weekly basis, another is to take my place doing so. When he is old enough, and if he so chooses, this fiddle is to be presented to Billy, who loved it so on this day I played." She had dated it. Ned looked surprised but I wasn't. A hundred years had passed since Grandpa Billy Hampton gave me to his beloved granddaughter, Estelle. This passing on of the instrument was all part of the fiddle-maker's joy. Music is a gift to be shared.

Anna played another tune but her tired fingers slurred my notes. The crowd was gracious with her and did not indicate disappointment. She smiled and shook her head. "Grandpa always told me to keep on trying until I got it right." With that said, she played "O Susanna!" and then ended her performance for the day. She handed me to Ned Winston, who, with extraordinary care, placed me in the display case. My strings did not shiver at all. Billy touched his fingers to the glass. "More," he said.

I felt again the way I had when Estelle had presented me to David Lane. My time without song in this display case was merely to be a pause, like the rest between measures in certain tunes.

☾